ON THE
CARE AND KEEPING OF
ORCS

BY:

KASS O'SHIRE

Book Cover by Phantom Dame

Illustrations by Phantom Dame

Editing by Amethyst Dragon

1st edition 2024

Contents

For anyone who feels like their time might have passed, or is working up the courage for another try.
I see you, you inspire me constantly, and you deserve to get railed anywhere and everywhere you want by a partner who worships you.

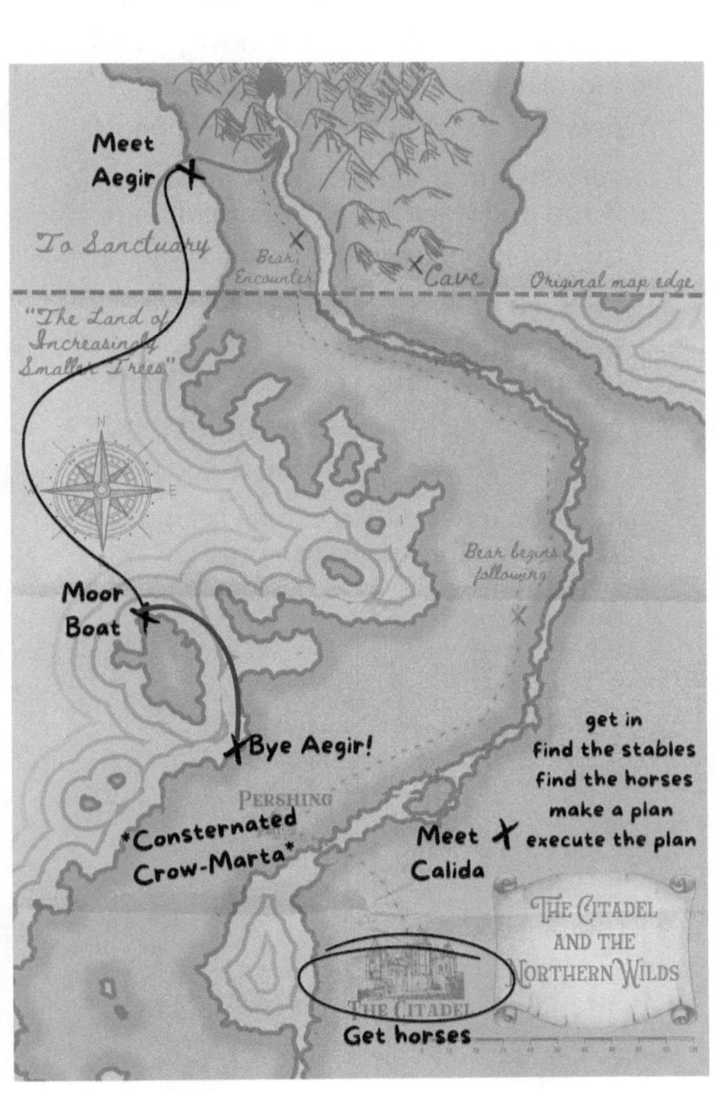

Meet Aegir
To Sanctuary
Bear Encounter
Cave
Original map edge
"The Land of Increasingly Smaller Trees"
Moor Boat
Bear begins following
Bye Aegir!
PERSHING
get in
find the stables
find the horses
make a plan
execute the plan
Consternated Crow-Marta
Meet Calida
THE CITADEL AND THE NORTHERN WILDS
THE CITADEL
Get horses

Piracy is a serious concern for small indie authors like me, who have poured many hours into our books. Piracy prevents us from being able to support

ourselves and continue to write more. If you know someone who might enjoy this book, but cannot obtain a copy legally, please reach out to me at

kassieoshire@gmail.com.
If you are reading a pirated copy of the book right now, please also get in touch with me. I want to work with you to get

my book into readers' hands legally.
Thank you for understanding.

Content Advisory

This work contains: Explicit sexual content, mentions of breeding, mentions of pregnancy, children, parental abandonment, lactation during sex, loss of a sibling (historical), minor violence, and spousal abandonment (historical). If you feel I have missed any content that should be listed here, please reach out to me at kassieoshire@gmail.com, I'd love to update the list if needed.

This book also features a character coming out as transgender, and the beginning of their transition. This does not, obviously, need a warning. However, until that point, the characters and I use their name and gender assigned at birth.

This is a fantasy world, in which magic users can change any part of their body they like and while certain parts of it are deeply flawed, it is intentionally queer friendly. I have imagined a world where there are only positive, supportive responses to someone coming out and believe that someday we will have the same. My hopes for magic are sadly less realistic.

A Note from the Original Author

The events of this work take place prior to the removal of the Lady's Barrier, specifically in the Year Post Slumber 979. My intent is to show the citizens of the Compact of Nations how others live in the rest of the world in a way that feels accessible and amusing. If you would like more concrete facts about the peoples that have long suffered under the regime of the Pathain Empire, or those of the town of Sanctuary, please see my other scholarly works or those cited in footnotes. All of the stories in the "Shades of Sanctuary" are crafted around stories told to me by those that lived them with their express consent, and any deviations from the truth are meant to entertain and have been approved by the involved parties. After my last work, I was contacted by concerned individuals to inquire if my work needed to be *quite* so explicit to illustrate my point, and as such, this book is even more explicit. I will add footnotes to clarify details as needed, but they are not necessary to read for the enjoyment of the narrative. My intent is that these should be treated as one might a work of fiction, because contrary to what one might assume, I did not interrogate anyone about their sex life to this level of exactness, though I hope you can easily imagine us, twenty years later, cackling in my study as we recorded details that simply *must* be included.

–Sirin Agbuya–Broderson YPS 1012

Chapter One
Catrin

IN WHICH OUR HEROINE
WRESTLES WITH POTTERY,
CHILDREN, AND A FIGURE
FROM HER PAST

CATRIN SLAMMED HER CLAY down onto the wheel and stretched her neck to the side. *Fifty mugs to go. Only fifty and then I'm free,* she reassured herself.

Yes Cat, just fifty. *Those, then the fifty greenware that need trimming and sanding, the probably sixty that need firing, and the nearly one hundred that need glazing. Oh and don't forget, your reward for completing all that is the joy of spending the week before solstice trapped with your mother, perfecting her yearly recipe so she can win a prize and show everyone how close you are.*

Holding a deep breath, she stopped herself from crying. Her sister-in-law was constantly telling her it was important that she "feel her shit" but Catrin wasn't certain Sirin knew what she was talking about. She was undoubtedly the smartest person Cat knew, but she also had the wildest ideas.

Two mugs later, she heard her daughters' giggles and her brother's resonant laughter. She glanced at the sun, only early afternoon, *barely* afternoon-they weren't due back for hours.

"Don't worry Cat," he laughed, "we're just back for a change. I think you sent me with two little otters instead of sweet little half-orc-girls; the way they were swimming!"[1] Berne bent over at her front window, waving through the display of her finished wares to indicate the children on his back.

"I'm not a little girl, I'm an otter!" Ingrid giggled."Hi, Mama!"

"Hi baby, all right, you're an otter if you want to be an otter."

"We were building a moat for our burrow!" chirped Ursule. When Berne let them down, a laugh burst from Cat. Both girls were glowing. Cat

---

1. Readers of my first work may note a lack of accent here. My husband has an accent when speaking my tongue, as do the rest of the people of Sanctuary. For the majority of this text however, all parties are speaking Gailage. I do have a small accent when speaking it, though I'm too proud to transcribe it when I write my own dialogue.

could barely see the green of their skin under the thick layer of bioluminescent algae that covered their bodies.[2] Slowing her wheel, Catrin rose to help Berne get the girls cleaned off.

"You stay right where you are!" he called. "I'm just gonna hose 'em off, get 'em some clean clothes and we'll be off again. I can't guarantee they won't need another bath when I bring 'em back tonight, we do still have a burrow to finish, after all."

Catrin smiled gratefully. Being a single mother to twins had never been the plan, and while she wouldn't trade her girls for anything, she couldn't deny how hard it was most days.

Cat blew them a kiss before turning back to her work. She heard the girls squeal as Berne pumped water out of the canal and she smiled at the sound. A few seconds later, she could hear the three of them tromping upstairs for dry clothes. Yes, she was a single mom, but she was luckier than she had any right to be.

From upstairs, she could hear the girls yelling and bickering between little giggles in their room. A few moments later, Berne returned downstairs with a little girl under each arm. In his mouth he

---

2. While *lunula pyrocystis* serves as a conduit for magic wherever it is found, there is a degradation of potency that happens over time. Because of the extreme proximity to the source in Sanctuary, the lunula found there glows extra brightly and is extremely powerful.

carried the roll of string that they used to tie off their braids.

"I don't suppose you could help me with these two hooligans for a moment." The two girls kicked and tittered under his arms. Cat nodded and they sat together, a girl between each of their knees, as they braided hair. In many ways, Berne had stepped in as if he was the girls' father, and she was grateful for his help. She looked at her brother out of the corner of her eye and saw his mouth working even though he wasn't speaking.

"All right, out with it. What are you working up to say?" Cat asked. Her brother sometimes had difficulty getting his words out, especially when he wasn't sure how the other person would respond. Berne growled at her and she chuckled.

"It's not that I don't think you deserve to know, I just didn't know if this was the right place or the right time," he said, motioning with his eyes to the girls' heads between them. "But, well, you know those negotiations coming up?"[3]

"Obviously, it's all anyone is talking about." she said, assuming a high pitched voice she used when mocking Gunna, their lead councilor. "'Oh, they'll be

---

3. Edrigu's outburst was not the only event that caused the breakdown in negotiations, but it also incited division among the emissaries separately. The dwarves and dragons sided with Catrin's interpretation, whereas the orcs remained baffled.

here for solstice, better make sure everything is perfect."'

Her brother chuckled, and Catrin grimaced before continuing."Anyhow, it's hard to forget when my own ex-husband was the reason the first attempt blew up in our faces." Cat's blood drained from her face."The orcs aren't sending him again, are they?"

Sending Edrigu back would be a disaster. He had leave to return to Sanctuary to see his children, but only just. He'd ended the first talks between their peoples by throwing a tantrum about "deceitful mating customs" and "unreasonable expectations."

"No!" Berne said, throwing his hands up to placate her."No, nothing like that... but Torsten is."

He spoke slowly and held her eyes, his fingers deftly assembling a braid.

"I see," Cat said. And she did. Torsten had been Berne's best friend growing up, still was, she supposed. He'd also left Sanctuary with the broken pieces of twelve year-old Catrin's heart in his hands.

In some ways, seeing him again might be worse than seeing Edrigu. At least with the girls' father she'd securely have the moral high ground in any argument. With Torsten, she'd just feel pitiful.

"Girls," Berne interrupted her thoughts, "why don't you go get your coats and your wellies? We'll see if we can't find any berries to make a pie."

Once the girls left the room, he turned to Catrin.

"Are you going to be alright?" he asked. "You know, seeing him again?"

Catrin slapped on a smile and laughed. "I think you think it's all much more dramatic than it actually is, Berne. I was a girl. I've married and borne my girls since then. The man broke my heart when I was twelve, for Lady's sake. I'm not going to treat him like shit for the rest of my life because of it. We've both lived our lives and become different people since then. I have my own friends. I don't need to hang around you two all the time anymore. I'm sure it won't be an issue."

Catrin would ensure it wouldn't be an issue. Sure, Sanctuary was small, but she would have no reason to interact with Torsten regularly during the time he was in town. Even more importantly, long years had passed and she doubted that she'd even recognize him now. She didn't know him as a person any longer, and she certainly wasn't still in love with some version of him she'd made up as a teenager.

T HAT EVENING, AFTER PUTTING the girls to bed, Cat sat near the fire trying to clear her mind of thoughts of Torsten. She'd trimmed and filed three pieces of greenware when a shriek made her bolt from the couch toward the girls' room. When she opened the door, Ursule was howling at Ingrid, who was gnawing on their bookcase.

"Ingrid!" Ursule scolded, "That's the nice bookcase uncle Berne made us! You stop it right now!" Ursule stamped her little green foot on their bedroom floor, her white brows drawn low in anger.

Tears streamed from Ingrid's eyes and she sniffled, reluctantly pulling her mouth off the bookcase and shoving her fingers in. "It huuuuurts!" she wailed around them, shoving her other hand to the opposite side.

Cat rushed across the room and sat down next to Ingrid, pulling her into her lap and stroking her hair. "Ssssh, what hurts baby? Mama's here. What hurts?" Cat asked.

"My moouwfth," Ingrid moaned, looking up at her mother with watery eyes. Catrin kissed her head and wiped sweaty hair off of her daughter's brow.

"Alright love, I need you to show me, ok?" Cat coaxed, gently easing her daughter's hands from her mouth. "Ursule, could you go grab sissy a washcloth?"

"Not sissyyyyyyyy!" Ingrid wailed. Of late, she'd taken a disliking to the term and in the tumult Catrin had forgotten.

"Of course, darling, I'm sorry," Catrin said.

Ursule nodded and ran into the kitchen, her tiny feet slapping on the floorboards.

Catrin focused back on Ingrid's mouth, squinting inside to see the problem. Everything looked entirely normal, as far as she could tell. It was *possible* that her six year molars were coming in, she supposed, but it would be early. Or at least, that would be early for a human child. For her little half-orcs, who knew?

"Can you show me, honey? Point to where it hurts," Catrin said. Ingrid raised her small hand and pointed to her lower canines. Cat frowned. There didn't seem to be anything visibly wrong.

"There? Are you sure, lovie?" she asked. Ingrid nodded and pressed her finger on an offending tooth, wailing anew.

Catrin stood, scooping her daughter up with her. The girls were arguably too heavy for her at five, but her little girl was hurting, so Catrin carried her anyhow.

As they left the bedroom, Ursule came running from the kitchen, where she'd dumped nearly the entire towel drawer on the floor. She clutched a washcloth in her hand and presented it gravely to Catrin. Catrin smiled and thanked her before sitting the sobbing Ingrid at the table.

Hand resting on the icebox door, Catrin sighed. She'd forgotten to refill it, so she said a silent prayer to the Lady that there was at least a tiny chunk that hadn't melted.

The heavy insulated door opened with a creak and she let out a sob. Inside was a great block of ice, much larger and heavier than she could have lugged.

Thank you, Berne, she thought gratefully. He must have refilled it when he brought the girls home. Grabbing her ice pick from its hook, she hacked off a few chunks. She tucked them into the washcloth and held it to Ingrid's lower gum. Ingrid grabbed it, whispering her thanks between sniffles. Poor thing was obviously still in great pain, but Catrin's girls were nothing if not tough.

Behind her, Catrin heard grunts and turned to see Ursule attempting to shove the rest of the towels back into the drawer.

"Oh it's alright Suley, I-" Cat started, but her daughter's pushing took the drawer straight off its pulls and sent it crashing down on her foot.

Ursule's mouth opened in a silent wail as she turned toward her mother, her face scrunched in pain. The moment seemed to stretch as Catrin rushed over to her. Ursule drew a breath deep into her lungs and began shrieking as Catrin arrived to toss the drawer aside.

Ursule's tiny green foot was already beginning to deepen to purple."Oh sweetheart!" Catrin gasped, gently clutching Ursule's foot and peppering it with light kisses."We can get you some ice too, okay?"

Ingrid hopped down off of the table and held out her own ice washcloth."Here, Ursule, you can have mine." Ursule pressed the washcloth to her foot and Catrin made another for Ingrid. For a few moments, they sat together, a huddle of sniffling, miserable females. Catrin stroked their hair, kissing each girl's head in turn before rallying to see to their injuries. She had a few pain tablets in the bathroom but worried that Ursule's foot really ought to be looked at by a healer, never mind the fact that the girls couldn't swallow pain tablets just yet. A furtive glance at the wall told her that there was no way Arndis was still awake, and she felt terrible waking her. It couldn't be helped, she supposed.

Catrin wiped her hands on her long nightgown."Girls, we need to go see Arndis now. So Ingrid, can you go get your shoes and one toy for each of you?" Perhaps it was silly to bring toys, but Catrin knew that this late at night, the girls would be on the thinnest ice when it came to their ability to self-regulate. Before they left, Cat refreshed Ingrid's ice poultice and tied Ursule's to her foot. She carried Ursule, while Ingrid chewed on her ice rag and dragged a sack containing a small wooden sword, a drum, and two picture books. Cat hadn't mentioned bringing anything to read, but she couldn't deny that it was a good idea.

Downstairs she shut the door to the shop, locking it behind her. While she'd never worried that anyone would steal from her, the heat of the kiln always made her nervous to ever leave it unlocked and unattended.

Ingrid sprinted down to the water, the light from the lunula in the water illuminating her face in the dark. Ingrid leaned over their small rowboat and placed her bag inside. Cat stepped in, cradling a sniffling Ursule to her as she stabilized the boat. She settled Ursule down and held a hand out to help Ingrid in. Her daughter furrowed her little brows and gave what Catrin assumed was meant to be a stern look.

The rag dangling from her mouth and her messy hair spoiled the effect but Cat nodded seriously anyhow. Ingrid sat at the rowing station and picked up their oars.

"I'm gonna row, Mama, auntie Sirin says I do real good," she said proudly.

Might as well let her give it a go, Cat thought. At least that way she could get Ursule settled. She sat down lightly, ready to begin rowing as soon as Ingrid gave up.

Instead, the boat lurched underneath her, launching them forward with a force Cat likely could not have mustered herself. Ingrid had a wild smile on her face, her painful teeth forgotten as she beamed at her mother around her rag, barely exerting herself. Cat's mind was a raucous jumble of surprise and disbelief. There was *no way* that Ingrid should be that strong, *Berne* probably couldn't even row at such a speed!

Their rowboat cut through the water so quickly that they nearly missed their turn toward Arndis's house. Cat flung her arm wide at the last moment and Ingrid dug in an oar to turn them. Ursule didn't seem the least bit surprised, as if this sort of extraordinary event happened every day. She sat cradling her foot in her lap as the boat sped through the water.

"I told you Mama! Auntie Sirin says it is *so* fast," Ingrid said, Cat blinked widely at her and nodded.

"It *is* so fast! Can you slow us down a little bit? Ursule is hurting but this feels a wee bit reckless," she asked. Ingrid nodded and the little boat settled back into the water when they slowed. She eyed

Ingrid, shocked that she had apparently missed her daughters' first forays into lunology[4].

It was more common for children to start subconsciously modifying themselves at around seven or eight, but she supposed it was *possible* that Ingrid was early—though this was *quite* early.

When Cat looked around, they were nearly at Arndis's house. Ingrid had moved them through the canals of Sanctuary with exceptional speed, speed which would have been terribly dangerous in the daytime when the canals were riddled with boats large and small. The light of the lunula in the water and the moon above made it so that they didn't need a flashlight, especially with Catrin's modifications and the girls' orc blood. They often saw better in the dark than she did, despite her lunula fueled enhancements.

Catrin twitched her nose and tried to swivel her ears, a nervous habit from her shifted form. It didn't matter that she knew her ears didn't swivel as a human, her body still kept some of its instincts.

---

4. Despite recent increased knowledge about lunology and *lunula pyrocistis* in general, I find many people are still unfamiliar with the use of the algae and it's limitations. In short, after consuming lunula, lunologists are able to take complete control of their body, at a cellular level. In Sanctuary, their proximity to the Lady has amplified the magic so greatly that most residents don't even think in order to use it. While I learned intense anatomy and physiology in order to control my lunology, Residents of Sanctuary do it instinctively.

She was exhausted and worried, the night's string of disasters piling up in her mind in a way that put her hare on edge. Those parts of her brain dedicated to a snow hare's instincts told her to gather her young and run and *hide.*

They bumped up against Arndis's dock and Cat hopped out to tie them down. Her girls were silent and Ursule was beginning to yawn, despite her foot. "Ingrid, go knock on the door and see if Arndis is awake," she said.

Ingrid shot off, scurrying toward the house. A moment later, Cat heard *banging* and the distinct splinter of wood. She whipped around to see Ingrid looking at her with a panicked face, so pale that her skin almost matched Cat's. The door behind her was buckled inward, split down the middle and the hinges were twisted. Ingrid's mouth rag began quivering and Cat could see that she was about to start crying again. Grabbing Ursule, she rushed toward Ingrid, where she sat cradling both girls until Arndis opened what remained of her door.

"Sorry," Cat said over the girls. "We have had a rough night, and I think Ingrid has accidentally made herself much too strong for anyone's good. Ursule's foot is hurt, and Ingrid's teeth are paining her. We will pay for the door, of course. I am so, so sorry." Cat could feel tears pricking at her own eyes. They had come to Arndis for help and had instead managed to destroy her front door.

"Oh hush yourself," Arndis said, waving her hands to Cat. "It's been years since I had an orc bang down my door in a panic, and I can't tell you how it warms my heart to have it happen again.[5] Now," she continued, scooping Ingrid up off the ground, "Let's have a gander at those teeth and that foot. If yer half as sturdy as other orcs I've treated, you'll be right in a moment or five." The healer walked inside her house and flipped on the light.

Unlike Cat who liked a good separation between her work areas and her living space, Arndis had always seemed to like the cozy atmosphere offered by mingling the two. Arndis led them through her living room, which had always served as a waiting room, and into one of her three small examination rooms. Arndis was tall and rangy with warm brown skin that made the white hair of someone born in Sanctuary stand out strikingly.[6] She was clearly in her pajamas, a robe thrown overtop

---

5. The prior time she's referencing is when Torsten broke down her door because his sister had gotten her menses. Their parents were at work for the day and she'd been napping. He was much younger and though he knew about menarche, he'd been convinced it was too much blood.

6. Studies have shown that while the first filial generation born in Sanctuary already has white hair, their hair will deepen if and when they leave. F2 and beyond however, have white hair even if they leave, though of course lunologists are able to alter it if they wish.

that somehow still managed to look clinical. From the pocket of the robe she withdrew a ribbon and quickly tied her curly hair back, all business.

"Now," she said, indicating that Cat should put Ursule on the exam table as she settled Ingrid next to her. "Let's look at this foot first." Arndis squatted down, pursing her lips as she unwrapped Ursule's foot. Ursule hadn't made even the slightest noise of discomfort, and Cat knew if she had unwrapped her daughter's foot, there would have been no shortage of whimpers. *It's true what they say,* Cat mused, *kids* are *better for other people.*

Arndis hummed when she finally saw Ursule's foot, which looked shockingly less bruised than it had been when Catrin had wrapped it. Arndis prodded it a few places and Ursule hissed in pain. Eventually, Arndis nodded. "Well, that's shaping up nicely. She'll be running around by tomorrow afternoon. Now, let's see these tusks-" Arndis said, swiveling to face Ingrid as Catrin sputtered.

"Tomorrow? I was pretty sure she *broke* some of those bones! Is she healing with lunula already? I mean, Ingrid *is* really strong already, but since their dad was... I mean, I just worried they might not be able to practice at *all!*"

"Yes, Cat," Arndis said in a voice entirely too gentle. "Their father was an orc. They are half-orc. They might be a bit delayed for their tusks coming in, but it seems that their strength and healing are right on schedule."

Of course. Of *course*, there would be differences. Until that point, the girls had progressed on par with their human peers, or at least the humans who lived in Sanctuary. Cat didn't really have any frame of reference about humans who lived elsewhere. She was shocked that she hadn't thought of it earlier in the night.

Since Edrigu left, she'd constantly worried that she might not be enough for the girls, that she would fail as their mother because she couldn't connect them to their culture, and that she wouldn't be able to care for their needs in the ways that an orc would. When she'd confessed her fears when she was pregnant, Edrigu had laughed and said, "Well, it's a good thing that their father is an orc then! Don't worry about it, it's not that different."

It turned out it was different enough that her kids had to get *hurt* for her to know about it, and their father wasn't involved enough to be of any help.

Perhaps, she thought wryly, *I'll write him and six months from now he'll explain the problem.*

Every fear about failing as a mother came rushing to the forefront of her mind. She tried so hard, working insane hours to make sure that the girls spent their days doing engaging things with people that loved them. But it felt like it didn't matter. She could be the perfect human mother but still couldn't give them everything their orc halves needed.

She sighed and rubbed her eyes. *There is nothing I can do but what I am able to do right now, and that's figure out what's going on.*

"So, tusks come in after the rest of their teeth?" Cat asked. "And healing and strength? Please tell me you know more about this than I seem to." She was pleading. Arndis paused where she was gathering some pain medication for the girls and smiled.

"Yes, yes, lass," she said. "All this is very normal. Seems we all left you in the lurch to raise these two after Edrigu left." She took a deep breath and her smile turned bitter. "Seems *I* left you in the lurch, especially. Now," she turned to her bookcase, "let's see what we have in here about orc-rearing."'

Chapter Two
Torsten

IN WHICH OUR HERO IS LOST,
IN MORE WAYS THAN ONE

T ORSTEN RAN HIS MITTENED hands over the rock before running them down his face. He'd been searching for the entrance to Sanctuary for what felt like hours, and it was looking like he would have to wait until someone left the village to get inside. The good news, he supposed, was that Sanctuary was extremely secure. He'd been through the entrance more times than he could count before moving to Caihalaith, and he knew, in theory, how to find it.[1] No one with less knowledge would ever have a chance.

Fifteen years it had been, and he was only *now* returning home. It was shameful. He should have returned years ago. He'd been within a day's travel of the village almost quarterly since, but he'd never been able to bring himself to make the last leg of the trip, to face the life he'd left there. In the end, he hadn't been able to face the emptiness he was sure he'd find.

Drawing in a slow breath, he tried to calm his nerves. Maybe he couldn't find the entrance because some part of him didn't want to take this final step. Sanctuary had always felt like home for him, even after all this time. Once he went through that passage, something might be different. He might not *have* a home any longer.

He turned from the rock face to retrace his steps. He must have missed a sign somewhere, a marker, and had gotten turned around. He could have sworn that the crevice had been under the outcropping that looked like a man's face in profile, which should have been across from the gnarled tree. Hands on hips, he stared down the wall, as if a stern look would force the rock to open up

---

1. Though the continent of Caihalaith was ruled almost exclusively by the Pathian Empire, I will refer to both depending on whether I am referring to the continent or the ruling body.

and admit him. His ear quirked to the side, and he sniffed the air. Distantly, but approaching at high speed, he could hear something galloping through the snow.

Shit! He began sprinting in the opposite direction. That sound, and scent, meant only one thing: he was being hunted.

By a huge polar bear that would surely tackle him to the ground and gloat about it for days.

He pumped his legs with all he had, swinging his arms back and forth as the wind whipped through his long, black hair.[2] A few strands lashed across his face, but he wasn't about to slow. Behind him, snow sprayed from under great paws. Hoping he could use his agility to evade the bear for longer, he dodged between trees. Adrenaline pumped through him, the familiarity sending jolts of joy throughout his body.

Torsten grinned maniacally as he heard the crunch of snow at his back. He took a quick breath in before he felt those massive paws land on his back and tackle him to the ground. The second he was on the ground though, the *real* fight began. He wrapped his arm around the bear's massive head and bit his ear. Once they were engaged like this,

---

2. As Torsten's parents were born on Caihalaith, the Continent where the Empire ruled, Torsten is F1 generation. As such he had white hair as a child, that darkened during his years away.

they were on an even playing field, and the real
battle could begin.

When they'd been boys, their fights had always
ended decidedly in Torsten's favor. Since Berne
had gained his polar bear form, however, things
had gotten significantly more interesting on their
quarterly visits.

Torsten was no longer larger or stronger.
Instead, he was evenly matched with Berne, but
years living amongst his own people had taught
him a few new fighting techniques. Berne on the
other hand, had little opportunity to fight while
shifted, so he took any chance he could to wrestle
his best friend.

They rolled and grunted, the balance of who
was winning constantly shifting. It ended, as it
almost always did, with them laughing on the
ground. Neither had roundly defeated the other,
and Torsten wasn't certain who had won. What he
was certain of, however, was that being with Berne
had settled something in his soul.

Next to him, Berne shook his head, his great
muzzle transforming into something slightly more
humanoid. "Trouble finding the entrance?" Berne
asked now that he was capable of speech.

"A bit." Torsten said, looking away from his
friend. Berne clapped him on the shoulder with his
massive paw.

"Well, it doesn't help that they cut down the tree we used to use as a marker, and the face on the mountain fell off a few years back.[3] It's probably my fault you couldn't find it, on account of the fact that I didn't tell you. Now get your arse out of the snow and let me show you the new markers," Berne said, grinning. There was something about his half shifted form that made the grin seem slightly feral. But as most of the humans of Sanctuary, and now that he considered it, the orcs as well, could be described as partly feral, he decided it was comforting.

Berne walked him over to a nearby area, which, except for the missing face, looked familiar. Berne depressed an area of the rock, and he heard the grinding sound that heralded the cave's entrance opening.

Berne reminded Torsten to duck as they went through the entrance, smirking and patting Tor on the head.

They crept sideways through the cave systems that led to Sanctuary. The quiet, twisting caverns pressed in on Torsten in a familiar, comforting way. Distantly, he heard the drips off of the

---

3. Known affectionately as the "old man of the mountain" this face had served as the marker for nearly a thousand years. After an earthquake, they'd reinforced it, but eventually allowed the old man to fall, though the outline of his face was often used in symbols throughout Sanctuary.

stalactites from the ceiling, and the dim blue light brought him back to their days of sneaking back late into the hidden village.

Once inside, he was happy to realize he remembered the path easily. During his meetups with Berne to pass off reports or letters, he'd never made the entire journey back to the village of his birth. When he was young, it'd seemed silly to go to a place he'd just left, and he'd been certain Catrin wouldn't want to see him. He'd always figured that he would visit Sanctuary again on another trip, in the way that time always felt infinite to the young. Eventually, it felt like it had been too long. He could never stay, and had always been in a rush to get back to the Empire, since the messages he carried were of great import.

"So," Torsten began, feeling out of sorts. "How're things? With your mate? With, you know, everything?"

Great Torsten, you sound like the biggest idiot ever, like you don't even know your own fucking best friend.

Luckily, Berne only chuckled. "It's going well. I got lucky finding Sirin. She's happy getting her research in. She's got a new project, watching for movement of the Lady, and she's real fired up about it. We're uh—" he coughed and looked away. "We're considering cubs soon, but I need to finish the loft."

Torsten raised his brows in surprise. "Cubs! Berne! That's wonderful!"[4]

Wow. Kids. Were they really old enough to have children?

Torsten and Berne were both over thirty, so logically he knew it was a perfectly normal time to have kids. He was over here about to lose his life's purpose, and Berne was mated and thinking about kids.

"How about these people you've brought? Think it's going to work this time?" Berne asked.

"I think so. I hope so," Torsten replied. He'd left the emissaries from the rebellion several hours' hike away. They knew Sanctuary existed, but the council didn't want them to know the exact location until it officially approved them for entry.

The whole endeavor was a big risk for both parties, but an alliance could be the key to liberating not only his people for good, but countless others. He was grateful that *his* only job had been getting them here. Now, it was up to them to see if the two governments could forge something lasting.

Nearly fifty years of quiet, careful negotiations via letter and one spectacular failure of a summit

---

4. As shifted forms are chosen, not inherited, it should be noted that the word cub here is used as a colloquialism rather than an implication of the forms our offspring might have.

had led to this. Hopefully, his two peoples were going to sign a treaty, an alliance for the protection and preservation of both.

"Everything seems to point to yes. My Dadjo seems to think so, and this is a good group I've brought. If anyone can do it, they can," Torsten continued.

They were quiet as they made their way through the caverns. It had often been this way between the two of them. They'd always felt comfortable and content with silence in each other's presence, though this time, there was an underlying tension rooted in the importance of the negotiations.

Torsten had waited most of his life for this task. He'd organized his life around it. When his family had arrived in the Empire, they'd set up a late apprenticeship with a blacksmith so he could avoid being drafted. Blacksmiths were valued by the Empire, and because they didn't travel with the army, it'd been easier for him to slip away to deliver the mail between Sanctuary and the rebel factions in the Empire.

He'd worked the last fifteen years, and potentially earlier, to escort the emissaries of the orcish armies to Sanctuary. His father had attended the first disastrous conference because the Empire cared little for the movements of old men. Torsten's master, however, wouldn't have been able to conceal his absence from the Pathian officers for long.

He and Berne would enter the town, he'd inform the Council that the emissaries had arrived, he'd lead the envoy back here to Sanctuary... and then he'd be done.

Torsten would finish the goal of his life within the week, and he didn't know where to go or what he would do after.

He had no obligation to return to the Empire. It was made clear to him he could stay in Sanctuary, should he wish. His buru, the leader of his village and regiment, had even subtly hinted that it might be for the best if he stayed in Sanctuary. The job he'd done for the last fifteen years, carrying messages between the settlements, would now be done by a dragon, his spindly orc legs not required.

As they stepped out of the cave and into the bright sunlight, Torsten squinted down at the village of his birth.[5] How many times had he and Berne tumbled down the side of this hill, wrestling and laughing as they returned after a long day aimlessly roaming outside the Barrier?

---

5. As it was nearly winter, the sun had mid-autumn, and other than lanterns or fire, Torsten had spent the last week in darkness. The Lady's Barrier simulates an artificial day–night cycle and more temperate climate for the settlement of Sanctuary.

It was late autumn, and the valley was all reds and golds and oranges. The brown of thatched roofs blended in with the turning leaves and grass, making the quaint settlement fade to highlight the Lady's river. On the far side of the village, the river left the mountain under which their goddess slept, before splitting into the many canals that provided the primary method of transportation through the city. Closer to the mountains, they reformed into a river and plunged underground to resurface miles south of the pole.

Torsten's breath caught at the sight of the river again. Its waters brought the magic that made up the Lady's being to the isolated continent that housed the humans of the world. They enjoyed the blessing of their Lady's waters, entirely oblivious to the peoples that populated the rest of the world, or the severity of the outcomes at stake.

Berne shook Torsten from his contemplation by clearing his throat. He'd paused, staring down at the valley. Berne nudged his shoulder, but didn't ask him what he was doing or goad him to share his thoughts. Berne was a good friend that way. He'd never pressed when Torsten needed a moment to think.

"Are you sure you're ready?" Berne asked.

"No, but it doesn't matter, does it?" Berne clapped him on the shoulder, and Torsten walked down into the valley to put the capstone on the culmination of

his life's work, and set himself adrift from purpose
entirely.

WALKING THROUGH SANCTUARY WAS like being
in a dream. Everything was the same, yet
nothing was. He saw people he knew, who seemed
excited to see him, but he didn't know them at all
anymore. In his mind, Sanctuary had been frozen,
timeless, but things had moved on without him.

The meeting with the council was done quickly,
full of people who'd already been old when he was
a child remarking at how old *he* was. They'd given
him leave to escort the emissaries back, it was
only a formality after all. The whole affair had
been negotiated through letters over the last several
years.

Afterward, Berne invited Torsten back for
dinner, but he opted to return to camp. He wanted
to meet Sirin, but this close to the end of his
mission, he also wanted to get it over with so he
could see what the rest of his life would look like.

He arrived back at camp well after dinner was
done. The contingent wasn't exclusively orcs, but
since the Wayfinder rebellion had been started by
orcs, they made up much of the party. Vibrant

melodies greeted him before he could even see the light of the fire. Balendin's flute and kick drum floated over the snow, the familiar sounds leading him to camp easily in the dark. As he neared, the light of the camp slowly peeked through the forest. The sound of Kemen's lute strumming a familiar melody.

He associated the songs with his childhood, with his parents playing them for him and his sister in the evenings. In Sanctuary, all non-humans worked hard to keep their culture alive, so it hadn't been out of the ordinary to hear strains of conflicting songs on the night air. Now though, the songs he'd loved had accumulated new memories, new associations.

The specific song they were playing reminded him of a night during his first year in the Empire. He'd sat alone by the fire, looking longingly at a group of orcs about his age. When he'd first spoken to one girl, Osane, she'd giggled at his accent. The night in question was the first time he'd realized that their giggling had been at his expense. She'd stood on the other side of the fire, swaying to the music. He'd watched her, entranced by her movements. She looked in his direction and caught his eye. Seconds later, her future mate, Mitxel had caught her eye, laughed, and dragged her off to dance. As one, the rest of the group had followed his gaze, their faces scrunched with repressed laughter.

It hadn't stopped either Osane or Mitxel from joining him for the night in the following year, but they'd always disappeared, like every one of his partners, before the sun rose.

He'd probably always associate the song with that night, and the chill he'd felt at the dawning realization. He would always be different in their eyes. Perhaps he'd be a fascination to them, amusing to poke fun at, or even to sleep with if they were adventurous, but he'd never be one of them. Any happiness or satisfaction he'd felt coming back to camp drained away as they took up the chorus.

Inigo, the leader of the delegation, hailed him as he neared."Well come, Tomax!"[6]

"I see you, Inigo," he called back.

As he neared, Inigo clapped him on the back."Everything set?"

"Yes, the council has cleared me to bring you all tomorrow, though they were clear that we shouldn't come in on Calida's back," he said with a chuckle."I guess they don't have a proper, designated dragon landing area yet. Gunna, the

---

6. Though we use his Sanctuary name in this book, it should be noted that Torsten's own people call him by his Orksaran name, both when they speak their own Orksara and ours.

current council lead, is still as particular as I remember, it seems."

"Well, I can't judge based on our own leadership," Inigo said. "What of the rest of the council then? What should I expect?"

Torsten summarized, as best he could, the current state of the council. He explained what he knew of their present dynamics, but reminded Inigo that it had been years since he'd been home properly.

Inigo nodded, leading Torsten back to camp. They walked through the space left between Calida's head and tail as they entered. The large dragon had wrapped herself around their camp, insulating them from the frigid northern autumn weather. This far north, snow had coated the ground for weeks, and though generally non-humans were heartier than humans, her care of them was more than welcome.

She chuffed a blast of warm air toward them as they passed through, and he turned to pat her on the nose. Calida was a good friend and he appreciated the gesture.

When he neared the fire, he was ambushed by several others with similar queries. The other orcs were, as always, cordial to him, though as soon as they had their answers they backed off, leaving him sitting by the fire alone with the non-orcs.

Late into the evening, Inigo settled down next to him.

"You know Tomax, you don't need to come back with us, should you wish to stay. Truthfully, once we enter Sanctuary, your role here is complete."

"I know. I've not yet decided what I want to do, but I appreciate it." Torsten was grateful that Inigo hadn't grown up with shifters as Torsten had. It was difficult to lie to a shifter when they were so in tune with body language and scents. The reminder grated. He didn't need Inigo's words to underscore his lack of direction; he was acutely, painfully, aware.

Chapter Three
Catrin

IN WHICH CATRIN LAMENTS
BAD THINGS HAPPENING TO
GOOD PEOPLE, ATTENDS A
DINNER, AND RUINS A PLAN

PUTTING THE LAST OF the greenware into the kiln, Catrin's ears perked up, trying to swivel like her hare's when she heard her daughters' squeals outside. Moments later, the girls came tumbling in the door, shrieking with excitement.

"Mama! Mama! You'll never believe what we saw!" Ursule shouted.

Over her, Ingrid squealed, "He's the biggest, greenest thing I ever saw!"[1]

---

1. The twins did meet their father when they were around two years old, but neither has any memory of that visit.

Ursule shot her twin a glare, sticking her tongue out. Behind them, Sirin and her assistant Sigfinn walked in, carrying the girls' waders. Sirin laughed and waved him in. Catrin smiled, happy that the young man was working out so well. He'd had difficulty fitting in, being the only fishkin of his age. In such a small community, it was painfully obvious when that was the case.

"So, now what is going on?" Catrin asked, kneeling down between her daughters.

"Well, we were *going* to have you guess, but Ingrid ruined it," Ursule pouted.

"I did not! Do you know what we're talking about Mama?"

Catrin laughed, shaking her head. "I haven't the foggiest idea, my love."

Sirin smiled, placing a hand on each of the girls' heads. "On the way here we ran into their uncle, and his friend Torsten, who is in town now." Sirin paused, eyeing Catrin in a way that made her feel like squirming.

It's not like she expected her brother to keep secrets from his wife, but Sirin was never the most subtle about such things.[2]

"The twins were very excited to see an orc! I told them that in a few days the entire contingent should be here and they will see a whole plethora

---

2. I cannot argue with this assessment, subtlety is not my forte.

of orcs, just like them." Sirin bounced on her feet, practically vibrating with excitement. Catrin wasn't quite sure how she felt about her daughters being excited to see Torsten. It made sense though. The last time their father had bothered to visit, they had been only two, and they barely remembered him. He claimed to have plans to come out within the next year but an orc today was more exciting than a theoretical future father. Until today, they'd been the only orcs in the entire village. Catrin only wished that they had literally any other orc to be excited about.

"Oh! How lovely!" she murmured, trying to hide her discomfort."And did you speak to him?"

"Only briefly," Sirin replied."As you can imagine, he was eager to speak to the council. The delegation needs permission to enter the city, and I think he'd like to get back to them as quickly as possible."

Looking down at her daughters, Catrin thought that if their crossed arms and pouty lips were any indication, the girls felt they'd not received their due time with the fascinating new orc.

Considering the events of last night, she wouldn't mind asking Torsten for advice on young orcs. There had to be some way of helping them rein in their strength. Surely there were teething strategies. Though, she could probably just as easily speak to the other folks in the envoy instead, surely there were even some that had their own children, rather than speaking from memory as Torsten would have to.

That is, if Torsten didn't have children. She didn't actually know one way or the other. It was something she imagined Berne would have mentioned to her if he knew Torsten was mated or had children, but it was also entirely possible he might try to spare her feelings.

The thought of Torsten mated sat uneasily with her, twisting in her stomach. Yes, it would be much better to ask one of the other folks who were part of the envoy. They'd arrive in only a day or so, and surely she could last until then.

"I was thinking," Sirin said, looking at some of Cat's work."Tomorrow, Berne's got the girls during the day, and I know you've been really busy getting things done for the festival. Do you want to come over for dinner? I recently got some new spices in, so I was going to try a few more of my auntie's recipes."

"Please," Catrin said."I know it's only a matter of time before my mother stops buying my excuse that I need to make mugs and insists that I help her with her entry for the competition."

Sirin picked up a small bowl, inspecting it."If you don't like helping with the recipe, why do you? I'm sure she'd understand if you just told her you'd rather not."

"Ach, see that is where you're wrong." Catrin said, a sad smile creeping onto her face."She absolutely would not. Cooking was one of the things she did with Annika, so of course that means that now it's something *I* need to do with her."

When Catrin's older sister had disappeared at fourteen, she'd effectively become her sister's stand in. She didn't like doing all of the things that her sister had, but her mother was extremely effective at guilting her into doing them regardless.

"Cat... that's-" Sirin started.

"It's fine," Catrin said, waving away her thoughts and Sirin's skeptical look."I'll help her eventually, it's just... difficult. I can only stand in for Annika for so long, you know? She's been gone for thirteen years. I miss her too, but eventually, my parents will have to give up and realize I'm a different person, right?"

Sirin squeezed her tight, a steady embrace that reassured Catrin that she didn't need to have all the answers.

T HE FOLLOWING EVENING, CATRIN was helping Sirin in the kitchen when the sounds of her children's laughter drew her attention. She looked out the window to see what had them so excited, and there *he* was.

Torsten.

He looked like the young man she'd known, while somehow every inch a different person. He was taller than even Berne, and her two girls were already climbing all over him as he snarled playfully at them.

Her throat constricted. This wasn't fair. What was she even meant to *do* with this? Fifteen years should have blunted her feelings for him. She thought they had, but suddenly she felt like a girl again, weeping into her pillow over his rejection.

His long hair was black now, which was startling, as was the stubble that covered his chin. He was tall and solid rather than lanky. He'd added piercings to his ears and brow, which only increased the feeling that while he was her Torsten, she didn't *know* this man he had become.

The look of mirth in his eyes or the scar he'd gotten on his cheek while rescuing Annika and Catrin from a high tree limb were at least familiar sights. Catrin scanned his form, looking for any indicators that he might be mated. A bite, a ring, maybe. How did orcs even show such things?

It's not like I'd know, she thought bitterly.[3]

Catrin's heart squeezed in her chest. She was a kind person; she lived a good life. Why was the Lady doing this to her? What had she possibly done to deserve this? Torsten, *here,* playing with her children, somehow looking even more devastatingly handsome than she remembered.

As often happened in times of stress, she felt her body start to shift. A fundamental part of her wanted to run, to hide, to be as small and as quiet as possible. Catrin had learned to suppress those urges. Her hare's instincts had rarely served her in her everyday life. Still, she needed to resist harder than she had in a long time, could feel her ears attempting to tuck down and her body longing to scrunch in on itself.

Stop it, she scolded herself. *He's just a man, like any other. A boy you have known for half your life. He probably can scarcely remember your pathetic little confession.*

Catrin took a deep breath, squared her shoulders and set her expression. She could face him, face this. She could be happy to see her friend again and let it be.

---

3. Catrin and the twins' father were never officially mated. Mated orcs have caps on their tusks.

Sirin touched her shoulder, causing Catrin to about jump out of her skin. "Cat, are you alright?" she asked, rubbing Catrin's back.

Sirin's face was pinched in concern, her brow furrowed.

"Why would you ask? Of course I'm fine," Catrin said.

"I see. Well, if I look like I am about to turn tail and run the next time I am 'fine,' call me a liar. So really, what's wrong? You look like that orc outside is the most dangerous thing you have ever seen. I thought you'd be thrilled to see him. Berne said you were all great friends growing up," Sirin said.

"We were," Cat said, "and I am just being silly. I made a cake of myself before he left and we haven't really spoken since. It's just nerves and shock. I didn't expect to see him here outside my home, playing with my girls."

Sirin hugged her and Cat was struck, not for the first time, by how caring Sirin was, how her hugs were always the perfect balm when Cat was overwhelmed. Perhaps it was partly that she always smelled of Berne, but Sirin never expected her to change how she was feeling. Sirin never hugged her to get her to stop crying. She just hugged her while she cried, with no expectations.

At that moment, she didn't need to cry. She'd die of mortification if Torsten saw her with reddened eyes. She straightened her spine. She could do this.

She didn't need to make this a big deal. It was *not* a big deal.

"I am so sorry," Sirin whispered."I didn't know. I thought you'd be happy to see him. I thought you'd be so surprised—which I suppose is the case—but I didn't mean for this to happen! Do you want me to ask him to leave? Or—"

"No!" Catrin interrupted."No, it's fine. I'll be fine. Please, don't worry about me. I'm serious, it was fifteen years ago. I'll be shocked if he even remembers! Actually, I am just going to go outside and say hello. Just get it over with. There is nothing to worry about!" Catrin repeated as she straightened her shoulders, and prepared to face her past.

For as long as she could remember, Catrin had been convinced that she would marry Torsten someday.[4] It had never occurred to her, at least before he left, to even consider that she might grow up and marry someone else. When his family had been suddenly called back to the orcish armies, she confessed her feelings out of desperation. The look of horror on his face when she was done speaking, was one that had echoed through her nightmares for years afterward.

---

4. When clearing out their parent's house years later, Catrin and
  I found her old journals, complete with their names in hearts.

If that had been all, it probably wouldn't have been so mortifying. But before her confession, he had promised to write to her.

He hadn't written, even once. He hadn't even bothered to visit, which she'd always assumed was to avoid seeing her. So now, she had to face him, fifteen years later, when their last conversation had been potentially the most mortifying conversation she'd had in her life.

Catrin inhaled through her nostrils, and out slowly through her mouth before cracking the door. She stepped outside in a hurry, and all four sets of eyes turned to her. Catrin plastered a smile on her face and looked over Torsten's shoulder rather than right at him. Perhaps if she didn't look at his face she could hold it together.

To make matters worse, she had no idea what to say. She'd gotten outside and had somehow failed to plan how she'd even say hello.

Luckily, bless the Lady and small children, the second her girls saw her, they started asking if she could see how tall he was, how green he was, how handsome he was? They pointed out how his hair was dark like auntie Sirin's, instead of white like everybody else.

Catrin tried to avoid blushing as best she could as they pointed out how muscular he was, how he had scars on different places on his body. He was dressed after the fashion of most masculine folk in

Sanctuary, in a light linen shirt and pants, both of which he'd rolled up. Peeking out from under the sleeves and pant legs, she could see that he now had tattoos. In the orcish fashion, he had an array of piercings in his ears and another in his nose and a pair of distinctive bumps under his shirt hinted that his piercings might not stop there.

Overall, the general effect was that his virility seemed to be barely contained by his clothing. His shirt seemed too tight across the chest, drawing Cat's attention to twin protrusions where his nipples must be. His form seemed more exaggerated, somehow, than she remembered, his skin straining to contain his mass.

It was astonishing to her that he was the same man. Still, the second he smiled, it was obvious that he was, and she was instantly pulled back to being a girl.

"I do see. He is quite strong!" she replied as her girls climbed all over her.

"Hello kitten," he rumbled, smiling in the sheepish way that had always made her go weak for him.

How was she supposed to not blush when he called her kitten? She didn't see why he wouldn't, considering she couldn't remember him ever calling her anything but kitten, but she'd never felt the instant feminine warmth from hearing it on his lips before. That was something entirely new.

"Hello," she replied.

Hello? Hello was all she could muster? After fifteen years, and countless hours of practicing what she would say to him if she ever had the chance again, "hello," seemed entirely insufficient.

"It's good to see you. You look well," she tried again. At least it was longer than a single word.

"So do you," Torsten said, smirking in the way that had always made her weak in the knees when she was younger. Like everything else today, it was worse. Her insides flipped like a fish and she suppressed the urge to giggle like an idiot.

They stood awkwardly for a moment, while the kids danced and chattered around them. She and Torsten seemed unable to look away from one another. She could feel his eyes studying her, and she was desperate to know what he thought.

Truthfully, this was worse than she'd anticipated. She could handle the boy she'd known. She knew what to expect from that youth. This man though? With his lazy smile and purposeful movements? She'd no idea. Her children danced around him, demanding his attention, calling for him to look at this or that, peppering him with questions about himself, but between his answers, his eyes strayed back to Catrin with an assessing look she thought might hold appreciation.

Fuck. If she'd thought pity was the worst possible outcome, she'd been wrong. Surely desire was the worst case scenario. She was in no place to enter into any sort of affair, and didn't have the time or energy for anything further in her life. She fell into bed at the end of each day exhausted and certainly didn't have the emotional capacity to navigate even her own feelings on the matter. No, whatever light his eyes held, she needed to stop it before it kindled into anything more.

Though admittedly, with her relatively limited experience, she had no idea how one went about such a thing.

Did she come out and say it?

Did she tell him she didn't appreciate his gaze, even though that surely was a lie?

Because a small, quiet part of her was... flattered. And, she had to admit, for once it was nice to have someone look at her like this, as if she was new and interesting, instead of like they knew exactly who she was and everything about her.

The only time she'd ever had anyone look at her like that ended with her pregnant and alone. Bile rose in her throat as she thought about it. The misunderstandings, followed by her fear and loneliness afterward. No, she'd learned her lesson well. Her ideas of relationships had no compatibility with orcish ideas.

That thought sobered her quickly. Yes, she needed to stop whatever this was before it had the chance to get her in another rough spot, though she still had no inkling of how to broach the subject or send that message.

But thankfully, dear Berne saved her with an interruption.

"Lovelies, would you mind going and helping your auntie set the table? I need to speak with mommy about something," he said.

So only a partial save, then. The girls acquiesced and went inside the cabin. When they were gone, Berne waved both Catrin and Torsten away from the cottage."Come here." He led them a fair bit farther than Catrin would have thought necessary, then pitched his voice so low that both she and Torsten needed to lean in to hear him.

"I need your help. I'm panicking. The solstice is coming up, and I know what I want to get Sirin, but I don't know how to get it to her."

"What do you mean?" Catrin asked, intrigued, grateful for both the interruption and the distraction.

"Well, you know she had to leave her horses behind at the Citadel when she left," he said."Generally speaking, she seems happy, but I know she misses them. She couldn't bring them with her, on account of the weather. I'd really love to see if there was some way we could get them up here. I'm uncertain how we'd manage it, and so I wanted to know if you had any ideas."

"I see. That *does* seem complicated," Torsten said, sounding not quite as surprised as he should have been.

Catrin was immediately reminded of her youth, the three of them with their heads together planning some scheme. It had often been this way, the two boys would come up with an idea, and pull her in to refine it, pretending all the while that they'd only just thought of it. She smiled, the familiarity a balm to her prior worries.

Torsten rubbed his hand behind his neck and Catrin looked away. She would *not* focus on how his muscles flexed under his shirt. It seemed scheming wasn't the only familiar thing. Apparently her brain was also intent on mooning after Torsten still, too. No, that might be familiar but that was one well-worn path she'd not follow again.

"As luck would have it, though, one diplomat I brought with me *happens* to be a dragon," Torsten continued, picking up speed now that he was getting into the thick of their plotting. "When she's shifted, she'd be big enough to carry a horse, and I think her internal fire could help regulate the temperature. She carried us a good portion of the way and heats the camp at night. So, if we could get to the horses, she could rendezvous there and fly us all back."

Sirin really would be overjoyed to see her horses again, she talked about them constantly. Catrin didn't particularly understand the appeal, never having seen a horse. They seemed kind of like antlerless moose and everyone knew that moose were grumpy bastards you didn't want to cross.

"So is she going to fly you down ?" Catrin asked. It only made sense, Torsten made it sound like the dragon could fly them quickly.

Berne sadly shook his head."She's going to be needed for at least the first week and a half of the conference, and we've only got two weeks or so until we're dealing with a hard freeze, and weather that's too harsh for even Torsten. We were thinking that we could travel by boat to the coast near Pershing, then cut across to the Citadel. Then, once Calida is freed up, she could meet us and get us back quickly."

Catrin blinked rapidly, looking back and forth between the two men."And what were you planning on telling your wife about why you were gone for a week or so? Don't you think she's going to be a little curious ?"

Rolling her eyes, she shook her head. It just didn't make any sense. Sirin was probably the most curious person Catrin had ever met. She'd want to follow them the second they left, or she'd pepper

Catrin incessantly with more questions than her girls until Catrin finally broke.

"Your plan needs work, boys."

"Well, that's sort of where we were hoping you would come in." Torsten said."I remember you had a devious mind for pranks and elaborate ruses when we were younger."[5]

Catrin didn't like the way her traitorous heart flipped when he complimented her. It was true though, among the three of them she was the one that could always be counted on to smooth out the wrinkles in their plans, regardless of the fact that she was five years their junior.

Behind Berne, Sirin was already pulling aside the curtains to call them to dinner.

"We'll have to find another time to talk about this, she's already getting nosy,"

---

5. I had no knowledge of this aspect of their childhood until after this whole affair. Catrin had lost this part of herself, and I'm happy to report that she's well and truly back to masterminding schemes with these two.

Chapter Four

Torsten

IN WHICH A DELECTABLE
MEAL, A WALK AT TWILIGHT,
AND A SOLUTION IS FOUND

THROUGHOUT SUPPER, TORSTEN FELT as if
someone was holding him by the throat and
by the balls. Somehow, he'd expected Cat to be as
she had been in his head, a gangly thing, entirely too
young, constantly nipping at his heels and getting
into scrapes that required him to save her. Instead,
he was confronted with a highly capable and
stunning woman, both self-possessed and beloved
by everyone she interacted with. Her girls were
adorable and charming, and they were a credit to
her. The passing of time was never more evident
than when they all sat at the supper table.

Catrin arranged her daughters' plates, helped them with cutting their food, and made them giggle when Ingrid's strength accidentally bent the metal spoon she was holding. Little movements kept catching Torsten's eyes: the grace of her fingers as she dished up their meal, the rise and fall of her breast as she laughed, the color that rose in her face and how breathless she looked after.

No, Catrin was not gangly any longer. She was vibrant and voluptuous, curved in ways that made him long to dimple her thighs with his fingertips.

Normally, Torsten was food focused to the point of absurdity. But he had trouble keeping his attention on his meal. Distantly, he knew that Sirin's food was amazing, some sort of rich oxtail soup and fried rolls, but he barely tasted it because he was so fixated on Cat.[1]

He missed his mouth more times than he'd like to admit, since he spent most of the time worried about Catrin's. Her lips had grown to thick, plush pillows that he wanted to kiss. He wasn't sure what it was about her. Why did each swipe of her napkin against her mouth make his own mouth water?

---

1. He now frequently requests both. Recipes can be found in the cookbook I wrote with my daughter "Reclaiming Our Mother's Islands, a Pangasinan's Journey Home.

As she recounted a story of her daughters' silliness to Sirin and Berne, he felt like he was home for the first time in as long as he could remember. Her voice called to him, echoed in his soul, and settled him. Her lips and laughter caressed the sounds, and he felt silly for being jealous of words.

He shifted, realizing that her voice and her lips didn't just settle him. He grew uncomfortably aware that his hardness was only hidden by the table. He'd not anticipated getting aroused at the dinner table, so he hadn't positioned his cock to not be so goddamned obvious. Instead, it hung down the leg of his pants and was now surely tenting them, like he was some sort of boy. He set his spoon down and tried discreetly to reach under the table and adjust himself so that he'd be less obvious.

Sirin, who was sitting next to him, met his eyes after he did so. Her eyebrow quirked upward in barely suppressed mirth. She turned back toward the group and patted his shoulder when he was finished.

"It will be so nice for the girls to have an orc around. Won't it, girls?" she asked.

The question riled the twins up so much it took both Berne and Catrin to redirect their focus back to their food.

Sirin smiled at him, all innocence, until Berne and Catrin turned to help the girls. Then, her smile morphed, her eyebrows waggling in a way that reminded him of Berne. What the hell was she playing at? She winked at him, and he knew. She'd caught him staring at Cat and had decided she liked the idea.

Sirin seemed like she could be a valuable ally in… whatever it was he'd decided to do with Catrin. He admittedly only had experience with short liaisons—one night stands, really- but that didn't feel *right* with Catrin.

When paired with his lack of direction it was a decidedly confusing stew of emotions.

T HROUGHOUT THE REST OF supper, Sirin made sure to subtly ask him questions and remark on how interesting his life was, and he was honestly impressed. She was selling him to Cat, in the most subtle way, like some sort of prize cow.[2] He was grateful, especially since he didn't really yet have a direction, only the simple desire, immediate

---

2. Sir, I see no hump on your back, you'd win no prizes in my home village. Though those tusks might fetch me a nice price if I sold you as a boar…

and instinctual, to spend as much time with Catrin as possible.

After supper, Berne pulled him aside, all nervous energy. He grabbed Torsten in a hug and whispered, barely audibly, in his ear.

"I'll meet you both at Cat's as soon as I can. Leave something behind so I can realize that you did and bring it to you. Then we can plan, all right?"

Torsten nodded against Berne's shoulder and clapped him on the back. "I'll see you soon.

"Why don't you let me walk you home, kitten?" he asked.

Cat opened and closed her mouth, looking like the most fucking adorable fish he had ever seen.

"We don't need an escort. The girls and I know the way well enough," she said as the twins began jumping up and down screaming that they'd love it if he accompanied them. Torsten tilted his head toward the girls and smirked, so Catrin threw up her arms with an adorable growl of frustration and agreed.

After waving goodbye to Sirin and Berne, Torsten stuck his hands in his pockets so that he wouldn't try to hold Catrin's hand or throw an arm around her shoulder. He couldn't count the number of times when they were young that he'd held her hand while taking her places, or guided her with an arm, or the countless treks that ended with him carrying her.

He'd never once thought of her how he was thinking of her now, and suddenly carrying her sounded like a much more tempting idea. As a boy, he'd always been extremely frustrated when he had to tote the wiggly little thing that was Catrin, but now the idea of holding her while she wiggled set fire to his veins.

"I assume you wanted to have a moment to speak with me about your ridiculous plan?" she asked.

"What about it is ridiculous? I think it's a pretty good idea. Your brother wants to get his wife something that she desperately wants. We can make that happen." He tried not to be offended that she didn't like his idea; he thought his solution had been pretty tidy.

"Of course I want to help Berne surprise her, she deserves so much happiness. The thing is, though, she's terribly smart Tor, shockingly so. What were you planning on telling her about why you were leaving?"

"A guy's trip, we figured we haven't had much time together recently, and we wanted to have a chance to catch up."

"There's one glaring problem with that. Me." Catrin said, as if it should be obvious. "I'll know where you are and she knows I'm a terrible liar. She'll hone in on my discomfort and seize hold of it. She'll question me relentlessly until I break and then I'll have ruined the whole surprise."

Torsten grimaced as memories of young Catrin flooded his mind. Catrin running her mouth about their plans to Annika in hopes her sister would think she was clever. Catrin coming to them, sheepish, after spoiling their plans in front of Torsten's little sister. Catrin's face red with tears after one of her classmates had tattled on them.[3]

Ah yes, now he remembered. Catrin was amazing at making plans, and absolutely horrible at keeping secrets.

"I see what you mean," he said. "I remember why we always used to bring you in at the last minute now..."

Catrin sighed. "Exactly, I'm sorry to say I haven't gotten better about it. But another issue is that Berne has been glued to her side for the last year and a half. He's changed his entire work schedule, so he doesn't have to be away from her. I'm telling you, she'll know that the *only* thing that would keep him away from her for that long would be if he was doing something for her."

"And I obviously can't go alone," he said. Really, *he* was the weakest link in this plan. If he hadn't been so conspicuous, he'd have been able to execute the whole thing himself.

---

3. Perhaps their exclusion of her was unkind, but when one is young, a five year age gap can feel cavernous and Catrin was desperate for approval.

"I want to help you figure this out," Catrin said, her voice soft and sincere."I think it would be a wonderful surprise. I just don't know how to accomplish it."

"Oh, come on kitten," he said, bumping her shoulder."You were always the devious brain in this trio. Maybe that sneaky part of your brain might be rusty, but give it enough time, and I think you'll find a solution. You always did before."

"You've really got to stop calling me kitten," she said with a blush."I'm not a little girl anymore. I don't know if you've noticed—"

"Oh, I've noticed."

His words hung in the air between them. He was honestly surprised he'd said them, but couldn't bring himself to regret it. Catrin caught his eyes and blushed, the color exceedingly attractive on her. Tearing her focus away, Catrin cleared her throat and rushed ahead to the children. It didn't appear they had an actual need of her, but Catrin allowed him to step into line with her once they ran ahead.

They walked silently for a moment, the twins laughing and giggling once more. Catrin led him across the bridge and into the area of town where most of the craftspeople lived.

"What do you do, Catrin? I've realized I don't even know. Berne never mentioned it." They wound their way among the paths, trailing the children who skipped and teased each other.

"I'm a potter," she said."It's not glamorous, but I enjoy it."

Torsten chuckled."Is any job in Sanctuary glamorous? Perhaps one might consider guarding the Lady's Sepulcher as glamorous, but I think most jobs here are quiet and practical.[4] It's something I've missed."

"And you?" she asked, looking up at him out of the corner of her eye.

"Me?" he asked, surprised and unsure how to make his life sound less pathetic."Oh you know, I'm a blacksmith when I'm not traveling, but I spend quite a bit of time on the road. It's hurt my smithing, but I do well enough to blend in and it lets me travel between settlements without much fuss."

"So you've traveled a lot?" she asked, seeming interested.

"Sure!" he said, picking up speed."The Empire's huge, and the orcs are pretty spread out, seeing as the Pathians use them as a peacekeeping force. They've got all kinds of different places, jungles and mountains-you should see the place where the dwarves live."

He motioned with his hands, painting a picture for her as he spoke."They live deep underground,

---

4. You can read about how "glamourous" it is to guard the Lady in my work "The Great Cookie Snackcident of 979."

in cities beneath the mountains, so secret that the Empire doesn't know of them. Dragons populate the mountains above, keeping watch and alerting the dwarves to come up to their surface city whenever the Pathians come for taxes."

"Wow, it sounds fascinating!" Catrin said, her face alight with interest.

"It is! I couldn't believe it the first time I saw it! And the dragons? You're going to flip when you meet Calida." He smiled thinking of how impressed Catrin would be with his friend."I'll make sure she gives you a ride sometime."

"A ride? On a dragon?!" Catrin exclaimed, practically squealing.

"Sure, you'll love it," he said. Tension eased from his shoulders. It seemed like he'd done a good job of making his sad, lonely life sound interesting. Next to him, she smiled, a faraway look on her face until she led him to a wide, three-story structure, one that he recalled being the potter's house.[5]

Catrin pressed her lips together and nodded."Why don't you come in for some coffee or tea while we wait for Berne?"

Torsten's breath caught. She was inviting him inside. He knew having grown up with humans

---

5. In Sanctuary, housing was most often assigned to individuals by the housing bureau based on family size and in certain cases, like Catrin's, profession.

that it wasn't of any significance, but for the past fifteen years, he'd lived among the orcs, where inviting someone into your dwelling implied interest when both parties were un-mated. His stupid heart seemed to be ping-ponging around in his chest.

The first floor had wide windows that housed displays of utilitarian pottery and delicate, intricately painted, almost sculptural works. Catrin blushed as she opened the door.

"It isn't much, but it's ours," she said flippantly.

"Are you kidding me?" he asked."I still live with my parents, though that's an orcish thing, not a 'Torsten still lives with his mommy and daddy' thing, I swear. This is great."

Catrin's house was charming. He'd forgotten that many of the shops in Sanctuary had housing over top. He'd never actually gotten to go into the housing portion of one as a child, so he couldn't wait to see what it was like. Catrin's pottery lined shelves along the walls, and in the center of the room, there was a work section that housed several potter's wheels, implements for working clay, and in a storage area there appeared to be various glazes and sanding supplies.

Catrin didn't let him linger downstairs, turning him to the right and unlocking an interior door.

Catrin led them upstairs and through a door on the first landing. The stairs continued up to the third floor, but it seemed their destination was the second.

The girls tugged him through the door and immediately began chattering about their room. They dragged him into a chamber which housed two small canopy beds, a bookshelf, and a multitude of toys.

"This is our room," Ursule said, dropping his hand to give him a tour."You can tell which is my bed because it's pink. That's the best color."

"It's not the best, you just like it the best," Ingrid said before indicating to the other bed."Mine's green."

"That's what I said," Ursule said.

"No, you didn't, you said-"

"Wow, that bookshelf is great!" Torsten cut in, pointing to a bookshelf that looked like a tree.

"Uncle Berne made it." Ingrid said, seeming pleased he'd noticed."When I'm big, I'm going to be just like Uncle Berne and make fancy things, too."

"Well, I'm going to make fancy clothes, because I like to look pretty!"

It was fascinating to see how different their personalities were, especially when compared to his sister's son.

"All right you two, teeth and jammies, it's already past your bedtime. Then you can have quiet-time until Uncle Berne gets here if you're good."

"Uncle Berne's coming to say goodnight?" Ingrid squealed.

"Yes, but only if you're ready in time, so get moving." Catrin shooed her children into their room and shut the door, leaning back on it and smiling.

"Sorry," she mouthed. She waved him behind her down a hall lined with art and books that opened into the main living space. It housed a cozy little kitchen, a snug sitting room with a large fireplace, a piano, a desk, and yet more bookshelves. Toys littered the place, and he decided immediately that he loved it.

"Take a seat," Catrin said, pulling a chair out from the table. Across from him, a drawer had been pulled free and was sitting on the ground. Catrin bustled about grabbing a kettle and mugs. She turned with a mug in each hand and opened her mouth to speak, but blushed when she saw where he was looking.

"Oh, we had a bit of an incident last night. Ingrid was having trouble with teething, and Ursule was trying to help put some washcloths away. She pulled so hard that the drawer fell off and broke a few small bones in her foot. She seems fine today, which Arndis suggested was an orc thing."

Torsten pursed his lips. "I think you're spot on there. The drawer incident was probably just an orc thing, too," he said.

Next to him, Catrin stopped dead in her tracks."Of course it's an orc thing. Why hadn't I thought of that? I suppose I should just assume everything is an orc thing first and save myself the trouble."

"I take it this isn't the first 'orc thing'?" he asked.

Catrin deflated, her shoulders slumped, and her face crumpled."Not even remotely. I'm trying, but I don't know about all the different things I should."

Torsten had grown up around humans, so he felt he could probably raise a human or half–human child, but as he considered it, he could think of at least six different things that would likely confuse a human raising an orc.

Gritting his teeth, Torsten tried not to look angry. Catrin shouldn't have to be dealing with this alone, but he wasn't surprised. As a result of restrictions by the Empire, almost all orcish children were raised by their mothers and grandparents. He didn't know the whole story of her previous relationship, but he was beginning to see the groundwork for how she'd ended up a single parent. The girls were five according to Berne which meant they'd be going through their first puberty.

"If I remember correctly, " he told Cat, "the girls are five? So they'll be starting their first puberty I'd bet. I imagine they're getting significantly stronger, and they're probably teething, and I'd say you can reasonably expect them to have increased energy for the next little bit here. That should settle down once they are through it. We often like to take kids their age on long hikes, or have them play in ways that stretch their physical limits. You could try that. I'm sure Berne could help with it, too."

"Oh, thank you," Catrin said, sitting down across from him."I feel so silly."

"Don't," he said, grasping his cup tight so he wouldn't reach for her hand."You'd have no way of knowing if no one told you. Now you know."

"Now I know..." she said, trailing off as she looked out the window.

Around them, the village of Sanctuary was settling in for a peaceful night. The canals were lit low with lunula, windows shone with the cheery yellow light of gas lamps, and across the valley, chimneys pumped out smoke.

"Now, about this scheme of yours. It strikes me that a pair of horses is probably not going to respond well to a dragon. Obviously they've never seen one, but I imagine they'd know a predator when confronted with one, regardless." She pursed her lips, and Torsten shook his head to keep his focus on the mission.

"That is an issue, aye. Perhaps the healer could give us some sort of sedative? I'll bet they've had to sedate a centaur or two in their time..."

"Oh she has, for sure. Last year, Elijah got stuck on the far side of the river and Elliot, his dad, broke his leg—"

"Wait, Elliot Creekseeker? He's a dad?" he asked. Elliot was several years younger than he was and Torsten could scarcely believe he was a father. Time had always moved slowly in Sanctuary, especially in hindsight after he'd moved to the Empire, but it certainly hadn't stopped. The place he'd mentally frozen in time had progressed, without him. It... hurt.

"Yes, for several years now," Cat continued, oblivious to Torsten's pain. "Anyhow, Elijah was stuck and Elliot slipped on some ice while fetching him. He broke his leg and Arndis had to operate. He kept moving so she sedated him. She's got experience."

Torsten sat back, sipping his tea and shaking his head. "Arndis is the healer now? I really have missed so much..."

Something in what he said must have made Cat uncomfortable, because she bristled. "Yes, well, time does have a tendency to pass when we aren't looking."

"Mmm," he agreed, marveling at how incredibly kind time had been to Cat. "People grow up, mature and then you turn your head and find they are someone new. Someone you almost know, but don't."

"Indeed." Catrin sipped at her own tea. Sitting across from him at the table, cheeks red from the walk, she was the most beautiful woman he'd ever seen. He wanted to know everything about her, every intricacy. What did her days look like? How did she like her eggs cooked? What did she look like when she came? He fixated on that last question and chewed on his lip.

"Well, that's the trip back dealt with," Catrin said. Torsten sat forward abruptly. Hopefully she'd not seen any indication of his thoughts, she didn't seem like it.

Footsteps on the stairs heralded Berne's reappearance and Torsten blushed.

He needed to get his brain under control before he had such wandering thoughts in front of Catrin's older brother. Berne had never indicated that he'd have a problem though.

Berne opened the door, snarling, quickly followed by the sounds of the twins' shrieking laughter. Perhaps letting her brother come right at bedtime wasn't Catrin's best idea ever. He briefly waved hello to Catrin and Torsten, and burst into the girls room.

"Excuse me one moment," Catrin said, holding up a finger and rising from the table. Torsten turned to see her stand and lean against the doorframe to her daughters' room.

"They've finally figured out they can team up on you, have they?" she asked.

"Oh they have for a while, it's just this is the first time they've been successful," Berne said, slightly muffled.

"All right, you two, if you aren't in your beds in three seconds, uncle Berne isn't gonna be able to give you a kiss good night."

Minutes later, Berne exited the room, placing his hands on his hips and shaking his head, leaving Catrin to finish their bedtime routine."They're getting stronger by the second."

He crossed to the desk and grabbed a sheet of paper and a pencil, clearly familiar with Catrin's home. Setting those on the table, he began fixing himself a cup of tea. A quick rummage through some cabinets yielded a tin of cookies which he deposited on the table with a gleeful grin. He sat down, and seconds later, Catrin sank into her own seat with a huff.

"All tucked in," Catrin said."Now, to business." She wrapped her hands around her mug and leaned toward Berne.

Sipping his tea, Torsten decided to let the Brodersons take the lead. It was Berne's quest, after all, and they needed Catrin's mind to bring the plan to fruition. Once again, he fulfilled the role of "warm body that can do things." He was admittedly, well versed for his role.

"So, I was thinking," Berne began."If Catrin has found some problems with the plan, we should document those and any others we can think of. Then we can work through them, methodically." He titled the page Berne's Ridiculous Plan.

"Well, so far, Cat's identified three problems," Torsten said."First, I'm a big green guy, and it would cause a great deal of problems if I was seen. Next, according to Cat, it would be very out of the ordinary for you to leave for that long, and from what I hear, Sirin's astute enough to realize that means somethings up." Berne nodded his head, transcribing Torsten's identified issues on the page.

"Further," Catrin said, tapping her finger on the table."I think you're forgetting that I would be alone with her, and I can't keep a secret to save my life. Especially not when someone like Sirin is interrogating me!"

"So, we've got to keep Sirin away from Catrin," Torsten said."Next, I thought of another reason that Berne probably shouldn't go. To us, Berne, just smells like Berne, but to two horses, he smells like a bear. I'm sure, given time they will warm up to him eventually, but as the only person in the room who has actually worked with horses, if he walks into that stable, they're going to spook... bad."

Catrin's eyes went wide."That's a very good point. No prey animal is going to willingly go with a predator."

Berne tapped his face with his fingers. "Well damn, I know we're still documenting problems, but I was starting to think that Åsmund might be able to go, since he's the one that runs my old route now. But I doubt they would respond better to a wolf shifter than a polar bear shifter. OK, we're focusing on questions, not solutions yet. Next problem. How do we get the horses out of there? I think it's a reasonable assumption that they are still there, considering Sirin paid for boarding upfront for a couple of years. The real worry is that they might be readying them to be sold. We're nearing the end of the time she paid for."

Torsten nodded, and squeezed his eyes shut; the plan was looking more complicated by the second.

"Well, if we're tallying up problems with this scheme, the fact that nobody in Sanctuary but Torsten knows a damn thing about horses should probably be on the list too." Catrin was chewing her lip. "In books, they always have all of that tack and gear that you have to deal with… " she trailed off waving her hands about.

"And for that matter, you're the only one that really knows anything about interacting with their culture. How do you disseminate years worth of information in a short time? Not everyone's gonna know that they need to talk to Marta at the Consternated Crow if they want to know the local gossip." Berne's eyebrows rose.

"You remembered the name of the Inn?" He asked.

Catrin shrugged."Of course I did. I've had to listen to your stories about going there for years, but we need to figure out how to get that information into somebody else's brain." Berne sat back in his chair, stroking his beard, a twinkle in his eye.

"Yes, and we do need someone that's shifted form is a prey animal, so the horses wouldn't be scared," Berne said, head bobbing with a faraway look.

"Right," Torsten agreed, a smile tickling the edges of his mouth, the flicker of an idea flaring to life."Someone who could have an excuse for going off with an orc for a couple of weeks."

Catrin nodded her head."It would be helpful if they spoke the language too, most people don't these days. I only learned so I could read their books."

Across the table, Berne seemed to be coming to a similar conclusion. He nodded to Torsten. *Catrin* was their solution.

Chapter Five
Catrin

IN WHICH MEN ARE SUSPICIOUS, PERSUASIVE, AND INFURIATING

THE TWO MEN LOOKED... suspicious. Catrin squinted between them, trying to figure out what she was missing.

"What is it?" she asked. A growing worry built in her stomach.

"Well," Berne started, in the careful voice he used when he knew she wouldn't like something. "I know someone that fits all of those requirements quite well."

Torsten raised his brows and tilted his head.

Wait. No, they couldn't mean... her?

"Absolutely not," she said, shaking her head. "Not me, I can't. Find someone else."

"You've got to admit, Cat," Torsten said."You do fill those needs pretty neatly... "

Hands shaking, Catrin ran through their mental list of problems, trying to think of how she couldn't possibly be qualified.

Prey? Check.

Knowledge of the Compact? Arguably more than most people.

Someone who knew the language? Fluently.

And... someone who'd have an excuse...

"Well what reason could I possibly have for going off with Torsten so close to the solstice?" she blurted.

"Even I know that one, Cat," Berne said, shaking his head."You have a convenient ex-husband who might have sent word with Tor that he needs to speak with you."[1]

Well, damn. That made sense. She'd even mentioned to Sirin how they needed to stop communicating through letters because the delay was so bad and things kept getting confused.

Catrin looked to Torsten, hoping he'd save her. Surely he wouldn't want to spend two weeks with her, the awkward girl that had blurted out her love

---

1. It was good enough that I bought it, I was genuinely worried for her meeting with Edrigu. By the end of the time they'd been gone, Berne was fed up with my fretting and I'd had it with his reassurances that there was no reason to worry.

for him at twelve. Instead, he sat there, nodding along with every word Berne said.

"And," Berne continued, "You wouldn't have to develop recipes with mom..."

What a dirty, low blow.

Before their middle sister Annika disappeared, her parents had been nothing but exemplary. Growing up, they were never short on hugs or kisses. There was always an ear to listen to woes, a snuggle during a dark time, or an encouraging word when she was frustrated.

After Annika vanished, it was like they were entirely new people—if they were even around. Her parents spent months of the year away in the Compact of Nations, convinced that Annika was still out there somewhere. When they were home, they spent hours poring over the research they'd brought back.

They'd been so consumed in their own grief they'd ignored the fact that their other two children were grieving, too. Catrin and Berne had clung together out of desperation, and Cat had never been able to heal the rift it had created in her heart.

They were arguably even worse grandparents to her girls than they'd been parents to her. At least she'd been a teenager at the time they began ignoring her. The single time they'd tried to watch the girls had ended in tears for all parties. In their hurtful words, the twins were "too loud, too wild, too disruptive."

In hindsight, she understood how she'd latched onto Edrigu in a futile attempt to make a new family to replace the one she'd lost. In a way, she'd succeeded. Berne had been ever-steady, the rock that provided her life a foundation of stability and support. She had Berne, her girls, and now Sirin. She'd likely never really have parents again, but she couldn't fault them for how losing a child broke them. She had a family she loved, and whatever semblance of a relationship she could scrounge together with her parents, and that was enough.

Regardless, his words soured her stomach. The preparation for the solstice cook-off was the only thing she and her mother did together anymore. They'd spend the first morning bickering and debating options and the afternoon amassing ingredients. Over the course of a week, they'd make and re-make the recipe for nearly every meal, exhausting their family's palates until her mother deemed it "just right." By the time the cook-off arrived each year, Catrin was ecstatic to visit other booths to taste literally anything else. Each year, the cook-off prep was more of a slog and each year she'd debate delaying her pottery so she "couldn't spare the time."

Torsten looked between them, confused. "Is recipe development... bad?"

"It's probably not shocking news that she wasn't the best parent after Annika disappeared. If you remember, the solstice cook off was their thing, except now she ropes me into it and makes me feel bad for not being her other daughter the whole time. He knows I'd do damn near anything to get out of it." She turned to Berne. "Regardless, Torsten doesn't want me to go with him, it would be like when we were kids but worse."

So much worse. The thought came unbidden, because really *he* was the biggest problem. The man was fucking dangerous, temptation incarnate in a tidy package. If she went-which she wouldn't-it would be the most tortuous two weeks of her life.

"I think it would be fun," he said, shrugging a shoulder. "I'd rather go with you than someone else."

"What? Why?" she asked. There was no way he actually meant that.

"...Because it would be fun?" he said, shrugging. "You were always the brains behind our schemes, so it makes sense, and I remember you used to love camping..."

Catrin looked around her house. She *liked* her life. She liked the quiet, mundane nature of it all. She loved her girls, wouldn't trade them or her job for anything-so why did Torsten's words make her feel like something was *missing*. A week ago, she'd been so confident that her life was going exactly the way it needed to. She was settled, content. And now?

Now she had no idea.

Suddenly, her life seemed bland and milquetoast. Like she was a washed-up widow who lived with her gaggle of children and shook her fist at the young people being too loud. None of which, she knew, was true. She wasn't widowed, just intentionally divorced. Two children didn't constitute a gaggle, and she'd laugh at anyone else who thought they were old at twenty seven. Besides, Torsten was even older than she was. But somehow, his life, which she knew next to nothing about, seemed more vibrant and exciting than her own. He was virile while she felt drained, dynamic compared to her lethargy.

"I think we could have a lot of fun together," He smirked in a way that had her face heating. Was he *flirting* with her? In front of her brother? "I know you have the girls, but maybe they could stay with Sirin and Berne?"

She turned to Berne, surely he wasn't going to let his baby sister go off with such a virile specimen of manhood. He *had* to know what a bad idea that was. But when she looked at him, the dirty traitor was *nodding*.

"Of course they could. It'd be good for you, Cat," he said nonchalantly, as if he wasn't throwing her to the wolves, or rather *the* wolf. "You could use some time away, a break. And anyway, think about how happy Sirin would be."

He fucking pouted. That big bear of a brother batted his eyes at her and stuck out his bottom lip. "Please? For me? We'll take such good care of the girls..."

She was cornered. They'd teamed up on her and now she was trapped. How could she say no to him? She groaned and turned away from him, facing Torsten so her brother's big sad eyes weren't in her line of vision.

"I can't believe I am saying this... persuade me. Sell me on this stupid trip. Convince me that you think I should go."

"Really?" Torsten asked, perking up.

"Don't ask me again, Torsten. Tell me why I should upend my life for this trip, or you two can find another way."

"Well, first, it sounds like you don't really want to do this solstice stuff with your mother," he said, looking at Berne who nodded. "So, that right there is a huge win. Second, even though Berne has helped you with the girls, I doubt you've had much time to yourself in the last five years. It could be good for you. I know my sister went through this whole thing where she felt like she didn't know who she was anymore without her kiddo. She said her whole self was wrapped up in motherhood, which is also partially an issue with orcish society... but, that's neither here nor there."

Across the table, Berne was waving that he should hurry up.

"The point is," he said, getting back to the crux of his argument."The girls will get some great one-on-one time with their aunt and uncle, and you will get a break. When we were kids, you used to *love* camping, so this would really just be a week-long camping trip. You'd get to spend some time on Aegir's boat, which I think you'll like. I love it. And Cat, you could see a bit of the rest of the world. I have *so* many memories of you talking about how you wanted to travel and see how other humans lived. You could see the things that you've always read about in books."

Catrin pursed her lips, she had always wanted to go to the compact of nations. To see the places that her books described.[2]

"Furthermore, it seems like you and Sirin are really close. This would be a huge favor to her and Berne. Sirin will be so very happy to have her horses back, and you know bringing her joy is Berne's main goal in life. You said he's taken fantastic care of you and the girls. Helping him

---

2. Catrin's library of books is impressive. Almost all are in Norsk or related languages and neither Berne nor Catrin speak more than a few words in any other tongue spoken in the Compact.

with this would be a really sweet gesture that I know he'd appreciate. Having the horses around would be good for the girls, since they are so important to orcish culture. They could learn to ride so that if they want to spend time in the Empire, they wouldn't have to show up and learn from scratch like I did."

Catrin closed her eyes, and he stopped to let her contemplate. She breathed in, thinking about how grand and exciting his life had seemed in comparison to her quiet, tidy one. She had no desire to leave it entirely behind, but she couldn't deny that a brief time away could be invigorating. Avoiding her mother and recipe development was compelling, though spending time with Torsten felt extremely dangerous. She'd always been putty in his hands, but they were adults now, surely that changed things.

Adults who knew the pleasures of sexual congress, to be sure, but also had much firmer control of their emotions. Of course, he was gorgeous, and she would have had to be blind to not want him. But, if she refused to go on this trip, because she was scared of him, what would that say about her? Was she just admitting that he still held sway over her? Perhaps, she could use this trip to prove to herself how far she had come, and how capable she was of controlling her emotions.

The more she thought about it, the more it made sense. So much of her initial resistance to going, had been for fear of spending time with Torsten. Refusing, for that reason, started to feel like failure.

"And it would be just a week and a half?" she asked, squeezing her eyes shut.

"At most. I could have Calida come a few days early if you like, in case we make better time than I expect."

Catrin groaned and looked up at the ceiling. "I can't believe I'm actually considering this. Are you doing some sort of orcish mind magic on me?"

Torsten chuckled. "You know I'm not. And I wouldn't even if I could. What do you say, Cat? Would you like a little camping getaway? Help your brother?"

"This is *entirely* about avoiding my mother and helping my brother. Everything else about this is a horrible idea." Catrin knocked her head down on the table and shook it.

"But that's a yes?"

"Sure. Fine. Grand," she said into the table.

"Don't worry, Cat, it's going to be a great time. It will be a little holiday and you'll be so happy you went!" Torsten bounced a little in his seat, shaking the table.

Across the table, Berne beamed at him and mouthed "Thank you."

"It's not a holiday! Do I need to help with anything?" she asked.

"No, I've got it. Give me a few days to get it arranged with Calida and Arndis, Aegir too, and we can be off! I'll get us some gear ready. I've spent a lot of time on the road, so I should have everything we need. You just get it arranged with Sirin and Berne about the girls, aye?"

"Of course. Obviously I can arrange things for the girls. I *am* their mother. I'll get them sorted, and get my mugs ready for the festival. I shouldn't need longer than a few days," she said, eyes closed and mouth pinched.

"And then we can go!" he said, joy bubbling inside of him.

"And then we can go."

I N JUST TWENTY–FOUR HOURS, Catrin was strapping Sirin's old pack onto her back, and suiting up to leave. The girls were extremely excited for their weeks with their aunt and uncle, and they ran around Berne and Sirin's yard hooting and hollering. Over the last year, Berne had finished the second story of their house, and the kids seemed extremely excited about being the first to sleep up there.

"Mama, did you know that here we get to have our own rooms ?" Ursule asked, coming to a stop next to Catrin and tugging on her hand.

"I do," she said."Though, remember, that's only for a little while, once auntie Sirin, and uncle Berne, have kids, you'll need to share."

"Or..." Ingrid said from her other side."We could just share with the baby, if it's a girl she can share, and if it's a boy I can share."

Catrin smiled, taking some of Ingrid's curls behind her ear."Of course, darling, though babies can be very loud, so you might prefer to just share with your sister."

Torsten stepped out of their house, buckling on his own pack, which was noticeably larger than Cat's. Berne and Sirin followed, Sirin loudly reminding him of all of the things he needed to look out for.

Torsten chuckled, a smile lighting up his face, and his thick biceps flexing as he gripped his back straps."Thank you for the advice, though, I will remind you that I have made this trip four times a year, for the last fifteen years. I think it will be OK."

"I have too, but Catrin hasn't," Sirin said, shaking a finger at him."So I'm not reminding you about things I know you know, I'm reminding you about things that she might not know."

Berne followed blithely along, picking up Ursule when he came close. He placed a hand on Sirin's lower back."I wouldn't be sending my sister with him if I didn't trust him implicitly."

"I know," Sirin said, ringing her hands."Something just feels off about this. Did Edrigu say what he needed to speak about so urgently?"

Catrin snapped her mouth shut and looked anywhere but at Sirin. Thankfully, Torsten spoke up."Not especially, but considering what's going on with the girls, I think it might have to do with that."

"I'm not a little girl, I'm a fierce orc warrior!" Ingrid piped up, squinting up at him.

Catrin scooped her up and nuzzled her."You are the fiercest orc warrior. There are plenty of little girls who grow up to be fierce orc warriors. You can be anything you want to be."

"*I'm* a beautiful orc princess," Ursule said from Berne's arms.

Berne set her down on the floor, so Catrin could kneel and look at them both. They were so different, but they always seemed to just look right next to each other."Well, I expect you two to be the best behaved warrior and princess to ever stay at their aunt and uncle's house. I want you to make sure you are listening to your aunt and uncle, and I will rush back home as soon as I am able."

She pulled them to her, eyes stinging. They were so small, and yet so capable. Her throat burned with how much she loved them, and how much she missed them, they nodded and promised to behave.

"I'll draw you lots of pictures while you're away, mama," Ingrid said, holding Catrin's face between her tiny hands.

"And auntie Sirin and I will make sure you have lots of yummy food for when you come home!" Ursule added.

"That sounds perfect," Catrin said, trying to keep the tears from her voice.

With a deep breath, she stood up, patting her hands on her thick winter skirts. Berne had just finished hugging Torsten goodbye, an affair that involved both whispers and stern looks.

"Be safe," Sirin sent, pulling her into a hug. "It's a lot colder out there than you think right now."

Catrin smiled at her. "I am an arctic hare, I'm built for this. I'll be fine. And safe, I promise."[3]

Passed next to Berne, Catrin found herself between her brother's arms, her safe space where she'd cried so many tears. He quickly squeezed her

---

3. Honestly, with how terrible Cat is at lying, I am shocked I didn't notice here, but I was truly so concerned for her meeting with Edrigu.

tight before holding her at arm's length and looking her in the eyes.

"You can do this, I believe in you," he said."And try to enjoy yourself. I know it's not all going to be fun, but I'm sure you and Torsten will have lots to catch up on. And, remember the plan, you scout and then you go back and make a plan, no haring off and doing your own thing alright?"

Catrin smiled and rolled her eyes."Yes, of course, I'm not twelve."

In what felt like the blink of an eye, she'd given her children extra hugs and kisses, waved goodbye to her family, and was hiking toward the mouth of the cave with tears streaming down her face. She'd never been away from the girls like this, and she felt like she was leaving a part of herself behind.

They were quiet for the first little while, and Catrin was grateful. The passage out of the valley always felt like a sacred place that inspired silence. She could feel the second they left the bubble that surrounded the sanctuary. The cold hit her like a wall, and the fall's daylight disappeared, plunging them into darkness. Torsten unhooded his lantern, and the cool blue light of the lunula shone out.

Catrin had been outside of the bubble plenty of times, but usually in the summer, or for short times. Once they left the cave system, it was actually brighter than Catrin anticipated. Instead of the complete darkness of the cave, the moon reflected brightly on the snow. It was absolutely freezing, but her gear, their activity, and a few tricks from Sirin kept her safe from dangerous temperatures.

Torsten set a brisk but manageable pace. Catrin would have preferred to go a bit slower, but she was not about to show any weakness in front of him. Several hours of hard walking saw them to their first stopping point, a cave in the mountain range that stretched to the coast. The exertion made any attempts at chat near impossible, and the air felt like it damn near froze her lungs any time she tried.

She still wasn't entirely certain how she'd ended up on this trip. It'd seemed like one moment she was going to dinner at Sirin and Berne's and then the next she'd blinked and was laying in a cave with the boy-no-*man* she'd pined after for years, listening to him sleep. Logically, of course, she remembered a conversation at her kitchen table, and thoughts of avoiding her mother. But trapped in a cave, she wasn't sure how it had progressed so far.

Each of his breaths echoed through the small cave-each shift he made against his blankets skittered across her skin, heating her through to her core. She couldn't seem to get comfortable, couldn't get her brain to quiet. Her mind raced with questions she couldn't ask him.

Why did you never write? Why didn't you visit? What have you been doing for the last fifteen years?

Then, in the confines of the damned cave, he somehow made *sleeping* sexy, which was patently unfair. Instead, she measured his even breaths, counted them like coins thrown into a well. Each sliced through the air and tore a new hole into her heart. Honestly, it wasn't *fair*. She'd mourned her feelings for him; she'd moved on. And now, he had the audacity to waltz back into her life, upend it, stir up old feelings, enchant her kids, and whisk her off on some exciting adventure.

He had no *right* to make her feel this way. It made her want to smack him.

Worse, he'd likely feel horrible to know he made her feel that way. He'd always been so considerate, so thoughtful. Torsten had always been the one to make sure she found all of her toys at the end of the day, to make sure all the stains were scrubbed out of her dresses, and to always include her-even when Berne had wanted to ditch her.

On any other night, if she were wound up like this, she'd masturbate her brain into submission and get to sleep in a timely fashion. But with Torsten sleeping not even a foot away, she was doomed to writhe in the torture of his scent filling the cave, his sounds muddling her senses.

She'd lay there all night, and be exhausted in the morning. She'd slow them down to the point that she'd likely need to take Torsten up on his offer to carry her he'd made earlier as a joke. She wouldn't weigh much in her snow-hare form, but the indignity of needing to be carried might just kill her on the spot.

No, she *had* to find some way to get to sleep, get past this tension, and get some rest.

Torsten rolled, so that he was facing her, confronting her with his painfully handsome face. She'd avoided looking at him too closely during the walk. It was bad enough that they shared the mortifying memories of her confession. If he somehow figured out that she was attracted to him now, the shame would swallow her whole.

But in the quiet dark of the cave, she let herself study him. Her eyes caressed the long line of his nose from his heavy brow to where it ended over his pert cupid's bow. She marveled at his thick black brows and the way his lashes fanned across the mossy green of his cheeks.

How was it possible that he was so aggressively strong and masculine during the day, the perfect image of all an orc was supposed to be, while looking so *soft* in his sleep?

In some ways, his appearance was jarring. His huge form and muscles matched nothing of the personality she remembered. As soon as he was in motion, though, she could see his easy nature, and his geniality shone through in the fluidity of his movements. At rest, his ferocity and grace bled away, leaving a painful vulnerability that resonated with her own.

His mouth hung open, his bottom jaw pulling toward the ground under the weight of his tusks. Or perhaps their adornments. In the corner of his mouth, a single bead of saliva clung to his lip and threatened to roll down his cheek onto his pillow.

Catrin's attention focused on that single drop, her mind racing with thoughts of tasting him, of him painting her with his tongue, and most insidious, of being the pillow upon which he slept-the recipient of a tiny spot of wetness that signaled his trust. The image left her breathless as it burrowed its way into her brain, settling in as if it was the most wonderful, natural idea she'd ever had, instead of just another round of the torture she'd spent years getting over.

Throat constricting, Catrin felt the sting of tears at the edge of her eyes. How *dare* he do this to her again? She'd known, somehow, that this would happen. She should have fought harder to avoid going on the stupid trip.

It didn't have to be her. There were plenty of people in Sanctuary that could have helped. If only she hadn't been so keen on missing solstice prep, she might have had the strength to resist.

Anyone would have been better than her, because anyone else wouldn't go through this pain. Or perhaps, someone else would share her attraction and they would fall madly in love, solving the problem forever. Yes, that was exactly what she needed. He could fall in love, get married, have babies and she would-continue her life as it was. She'd be peaceful and... and she'd have to watch as he did so, if he fell in love with someone from Sanctuary. Wouldn't that be worse?

Surely, the solution was for him to just go back to the orcish armies. She'd already experienced one orc who couldn't be happy among her people, it would be terrible to submit anyone else to the same. She'd just have to spend the week convincing him that going home was for the best.

Catrin nodded her head, decided. She'd convince him to go home and her life could return to its peaceful rhythm.

None of it solved the problem she was having tonight specifically, but she felt marginally better with a plan. She stared at the ceiling of the cave and began counting backward from one hundred.

Around eighty-nine, the bastard had the audacity to *moan* in his sleep.

Whipping her head to the side, she glanced over at him aghast; his face had flushed deeper and his breaths were uneven.

He had the *gall* to have an erotic dream when she was *right here?* She scoffed. The *nerve* of this man was astounding.

Well, she certainly would not sit there *counting* if he was going to be so audacious as to fuck someone in his dreams.

Her anger boiled inside of her, a rage that built and shot straight down to her clit. When she snaked her hand under the covers, she was slick with arousal. She bit her lip to keep from moaning as she pressed, but a little whimper snuck out of her throat.

Catrin froze, waiting for any indication that Torsten had heard her, but neither his breathing, nor his movements changed. Releasing a shuddering breath, she began to work her clit. She gave into the fantasy that Torsten was imagining *her* in his dreams.

Pressing her lips together tightly, she circled her hood, each movement sending courses of pleasure through her.

She could imagine it incredibly vividly, what it would be like to be with Torsten, and in her mind, it was so *easy*. He'd surround her with that beautiful mossy body of his, and hem her in from the sides until he was all she could see. He'd smile down at her, the low light of the room flickering, his eyes and the adornments on his tusks glinting. She imagined his eyes would dilate, almost to enclose his entire iris when he was in the throes of passion.

Catrin focused on his quick breathing, the sound of him as he rutted against the ground. He'd bucked off his blankets, and in the cave's dark she could just see the outline of his round arse moving with each thrust. Swirling two fingers from her other hand in her wetness, and she plunged them inside. She worked herself on her fingers, and quickly matched his pace. Her two fingers were not enough. He would stretch her. She'd feel stuffed full of him. The exquisite sting as he breached her would be an apt metaphor for what he'd done to her over the last few days.

With each thrust of her fingers, every pound into the ground he made, he shattered another part of the wall she'd built, dismantling her progress bit by bit. Behind it, she was not that young girl any longer. Instead, she was far more vulnerable. A tear slipped out of the corner of her eye. He had *no* right to do this to her-she was infuriated with the both of them. Because she couldn't believe that she'd allowed herself to be in this position again. She was an idiot for allowing him even the remotest access to her heart.

Torsten's pace picked up, and she slammed her fingers home, brutal in her movements to match him. In her mind, she fucked him mercilessly, wringing out moans for every year, every month she'd spent miserable because of him. He could pay her back in pleasure.

The thought of that, of him groveling, worshiping her, writhing underneath her, made her breath hitch. The tension in her body heightened, and she closed her eyes, squeezing them shut.

Torsten's movements turned erratic, and he growled. The sound shot through Catrin's body, rumbling its way along her spine and settling into her cunt, her orgasm shattering through her. She didn't know if she was successful in staying quiet, because it was so violent in its pleasure. Calm, she pumped her fingers a few more times and circled her clit, drawing out the orgasm. As she came down, she pursed her lips and blew out a labored breath.

As a wave, shame and regret washed over her. Why did she always do this to herself? Why did she insist on indulging in wanting things she couldn't have? She knew well that this wouldn't go anywhere, couldn't go anywhere. But apparently she hadn't grown as much as she'd like to think—she'd still dangle an unrealistic relationship before herself at the earliest opportunity.

A chuckle rolled across Catrin from Torsten's side of the cave.

"Next time, kitten, we should do that together. Though this *was* a good deal of fun."

Catrin's brain refused to process the words. She understood enough for her shame to whip itself into a tempest, a deluge of regret that immediately doused any remaining embers of arousal she felt. While before her regret was a well-worn path in her soul, this shame far surpassed anything she'd ever felt.

She needed to run, to hide. This wasn't safe, her brain shouted. Her hare's instincts were overriding whatever semblance of control she still had. Quite unintentionally, she felt the shift overtake her.

Berne had described how his shift felt like taking a deep breath and expanding. To Cat, her shift had always felt like folding. Her body shrank, the lunula converting her mass to energy and storing it. Though most of her shrunk, her ears seemed to unfurl. Within moments, she was, once again, a snowshoe hare.

The form was as familiar and comforting as a pair of favorite slippers. She burrowed deep into her covers, tucking her ears back along her body and squeezing in tight. Her brother had also said that he had no real trouble maintaining more human thought processes as he became his bear, but Catrin had never gotten the knack.

Instead, she and her hare always seemed in disagreement about how best to handle things, and when she was the hare, it was the hare's instincts that ruled. Because her mind had framed the current emergency as a dangerous storm, the only appropriate action was to seek shelter immediately. She needed to hide; she needed protection, and her small body shook with the regret of it.

Chapter Six
Torsten

IN WHICH A GRAVE MISTAKE IS
REVEALED, A SHIFTY HARE IS
STUBBORN, AND CONFESSIONS
ARE MADE

"FUCK."

That was not at all how Torsten had imagined that going in his head.

Waking to Cat's arousal permeating the cave, and the sounds of her pleasuring herself, was probably the best wake up Torsten had ever experienced.[1]

---

1. Many of the peoples of Caihalaith have heightened senses, a trait they share with shifters and lunologists who opt for those modifications.

Hell, he couldn't really remember a time in recent memory when he hadn't immediately wondered where he was upon waking. The armies were nomadic, and he spent a good deal of time traveling to meet Berne to pass the mail. He often had a moment of disorientation until he established where he was, even when he woke up in his own bed at his parents' house.

It didn't occur to his sleep-addled mind that she might not know he'd woken up. He'd simply had the idea that next time they should do that together and voiced it. For a moment, he'd been witness to one of the most sensual sights he's ever seen. He could have sworn that she said "Tor" at some point, and as soon as she'd orgasmed, he'd followed.

Now he lay there, sticky with his own seed, laying next to a rabbit rather than the woman he was trying to woo.

Torsten cleared his throat. "Kitten—I mean Cat, I'm sorry, I thought you meant to wake me up. Seems that was not the case. I'm sorry to have startled you. I just thought you were trying to tell me something, and I was trying to tell you the same thing back." He ran his hand through his hair and pushed a breath out between his lips toward the ceiling.

"I'm really sorry. I don't want you to think—well, I don't even know what you would think. I don't want you to feel whatever you felt to make you shift. You're safe with me, Cat. I'd never hurt you. I *thought* we were both enjoying ourselves."

Laying there silently, he listened to the faint sounds of her panicked breathing. A human wouldn't have been able to hear it, but if he focused, he could hear her tiny heart beating a tattoo. He noted that when he spoke, her heartbeat seemed to slow just the tiniest bit. Perhaps, if he kept talking to her, she'd feel better.

It was surprising how much sway her sounds held over him. Mere moments ago, they had brought him over the edge with their sweetness, and now every labored breath dug into him like a thorn.

Either way, he was still a sticky mess, so that likely needed to be dealt with first.

"I'm going to get a handkerchief from my bag, so I can clean up," he said. "I've never been one to insist on hashing something out the second it happens, not very orcish of me, I know, but a lot of times what we say in anger is not what we mean. Not that I'm angry, mind, but I'm certainly experiencing a lot of emotions right now. So I'm going to clean up and get some rest." He moved out of his blanket to grab his handkerchief, dabbing the sticky wetness from his chest.

"If you decide you want to talk or anything, I'm here."

THE FOLLOWING MORNING, CAT remained in her snow hare form, so he packed up their camp, folding the clothes she'd shifted out of neatly and stacked them close at the top. He grabbed her cloak and draped it over the top of his pack.

Catrin stormed around among the lichen and scrub, indicating her impatience to be gone with kicks at pebbles. It was always remarkable to him how his friends' personalities persisted when they shifted. Catrin still seemed entirely herself in this form, her movements somehow echoing when she was in her human form.

They progressed slower with her shifted, but Torsten tried not to let it bother him. He was used to keeping his own company when traveling and was no stranger to silence. His instincts told him that Catrin needed time to get used to hearing his voice, too.

So, he spoke.

He spoke about the weather and the scenery, mundane things that would hopefully make her feel more at ease. He avoided their interaction the previous night, or even anything about how he felt about her, instead describing what his life had been like in the years he'd been gone. He described what it was like to live and travel with the orcish armies. It was possible that some bitterness crept into his voice. He'd so looked forward to when he would go to live among his people, an eventuality that his parents had never concealed from him or his sister.

"I thought I would show up and there would be people like me, and they would understand me in ways that the people of Sanctuary couldn't. And to an extent that was true, but I grew up in the culture of Sanctuary and so being with orcs was foreign to everything I knew." He followed behind her as she hopped slowly along, easily shouldering both of their packs.

"Suddenly I'd arrived in my ancestral homeland, and I didn't have any of the correct instincts. I didn't say the right things, react in the correct ways or draw the correct conclusions. Orcs have a much more violent culture, but I made the mistake of assuming that violence meant hostility, when often it really just meant that someone cared enough to fight. Sure, Berne and I tussled growing up, but the way they go about it made little sense to me."[2] He shook his head, remembering how many times he'd

---

2. Isolation from one's own culture is a frequent topic of conversation in our family. We hold connecting the children to their culture as a priority even though it is something both Torsten and I struggle with to this day.

gone too hard or too far because he hadn't realized it was a friendly match.

"Anyway, the point is, I never quite fit. There was eventually a blacksmith who let me apprentice with him, so at least I gained some skills. But to be entirely frank, I don't know that I want to go back. I don't want to get into fights over every little thing. I don't want to make weapons for the rest of my life. And more than anything, I don't want to move around all the time, leaving my family trapped at home."

Torsten grimaced, images of his ancestral village flickering through his mind. He was running his mouth and not making himself sound particularly appealing as a partner, but his talking *did* seem to help her, so he kept at it.

By noon, they hadn't even made it to the first marker that he would have expected for the day. Normally, he would've hemmed and hawed over bringing it up. He knew it would vex Catrin. But, by that point, he was so used to maintaining a stream of consciousness chatter that his frustration just popped out.

"Blast!" he called out as they finally reached their first landmark of the day, five hours late. "Well shit, Cat, this could be a problem. We should've come across this hours ago, and I'm not sure we're going to make it on time."

Consulting their map, Torsten did some estimations based on the speed they were currently traveling. At their pace, they wouldn't even get halfway to their original destination for the night. If that continued, they would be over a week late for their rendezvous with Calida.

He cursed quietly, thinking how much faster he could travel if he could move at his own at normal pace. There was no way that Catrin could match that, even in her human form, she was much too short. He paused, and looked down to see her standing by his feet.

He'd have to carry her. She wouldn't like it, but if they wanted to arrive on time, it was the only way they'd make up for the lost time.

"Now Cat," he said. "I don't think that you're going to like this idea, but I think it might be our best bet if we want to make that shelter for the night. I need to pick you up. I can make it easily, but you'll struggle to keep up. And-" he continued, eyeing the sky. "Those clouds are looking angry. Berne marked a cave I don't usually use on the map. It would be a much better place to weather a storm than the tent."

Catrin stopped hopping and slowly rotated her head back to look at him. He'd never known rabbits could glare like that, but Catrin's little rabbit face looked ridiculously angry. He pressed his lips together, smashing them down so that he didn't crack a smile.

"We never have to mention this happened. I just think we will get there faster and we'll be able to be dry tonight," he said.

Catrin set her tiny rabbit brow and continued hopping. Anytime he approached her, she hopped away from him. There was something about her furrowed little forehead, and the huffy way she had of hopping that was adorable.

After an hour, the clouds loomed threateningly over the horizon, and Cat's breaths became ragged. He opened his mouth to urge her to let him carry her. Instead, her large ears swiveled, and she dashed toward him, leaping into his arms.

As an orc, his hearing was better than an average human's, but it was nowhere near as good as hers when shifted. She burrowed her head into his armpit, and he could feel her shaking.

He didn't know what had scared her, but he set off at a lope regardless, their two packs, stacked atop one another, bouncing along behind him.

After twenty minutes of moving along at a quick clip, they seemed to outpace whatever had worried her, as she relaxed in his arms. After another ten, her breathing had steadied to where he thought she might be asleep. She was soft and warm in his arms, and it wasn't long before he found himself stroking her fur.

The next several hours passed in a blur as he settled into the quick rolling movements. By late afternoon, he was confident that they would make the ranger cave, just not before the storm hit in force. Worse, the storm advanced faster than he thought it would and in minutes the snow was caked onto him.

Catrin was clearly no longer asleep, shivering against him. He re-doubled his efforts, running as fast as he could maintain while he began searching for the shelter. The snow was slowly melting into this clothing and with them soaked as they were, it could get dangerous quickly. When he was younger, he'd assumed that as long as someone had an arctic animal form, they should be fine in all sorts of weather. The problem was, if Catrin were a real snowshoe hare, she'd have a den which she would likely never be far from. It wasn't normal or natural for her to be out in inclement weather for extended periods of time.

Torsten extricated one lapel of his jacket from under the strap of his pack and tucked her inside. Her shaking slowed, and he thought he might have bought them a bit more time.

The storm fought him every step of the way. The wind lashed driving snow into his face, and he frequently found himself disoriented. His feet were cold and wet in his boots, the waterproofing on them no match for the myriad of times he stepped into a marshy hole that looked like more lichen.

It was, to say the absolute very least, miserable.

It wasn't long before he was flagging. While his years with the orcish armies had acclimated him to running long distances, they avoided running in harsh weather, didn't carry nearly as much as he was currently carrying, and they rotated who was riding on horseback. The chill seeped through his clothes and settled into his bones.

His one consolation was that after a few moments, Catrin seemed to fall asleep once more. She'd been one of his biggest concerns, so if she was comfortable enough to fall asleep, at least he'd done *that* right.

Really, this entire situation was his fault. Making the journey with just the two of them had been his idea. Opening his fat mouth, and trying to be witty instead of pretending like nothing happened, was also his fault. He should have insisted he carry her hours ago. Who could blame her for her embarrassment? His mood soured progressively as he marched them toward the canyon they were meant to traverse. After what felt like ages, he finally arrived, sighing in relief.

The canyon provided some shelter from the driving rain, and it wasn't long until Catrin woke up and wiggled so that she could poke her head out of his jacket. She looked up at him quizzically, though he had no idea what questions she might be asking.

"We made it to the canyon, at least. I'm keeping an eye out for shelter," he said.

After nearly an hour of painstaking travel through the canyon, he spied the entrance to the cave.

He'd nearly walked past it. The hole was set back along a wall and he needed to duck to get in. It was atrociously small, and he'd need to block the door with the tent to give them any break from the wind, but at least it was mostly dry.

When they got inside, he set Catrin and their bags down near the back before digging out their tent and staking it into the wall around the opening with a few pitons. It was messy and wouldn't hold up against extremely strong winds, but it would keep the worst of it out. Next, he scooped the existing snow out to clear the ground. Catrin hopped to sit atop their bags and watched him, her small eyes wary.

Torsten scrubbed a hand through his hair, wringing out what water he could before setting up their tent stove near the entrance where it could vent. It was small, contained, and would cook whatever food they needed for the night.

Once he had a fire going, he began stripping off his layers, draping them next to the fire, laying out to dry. He smiled awkwardly at Cat, reminding himself that shifters tended to be extremely nonchalant about nudity. His cock hung heavy between his thighs as he squatted near the fire, but he could feel it thickening as he thought about Catrin's eyes on him. What did she think? Was she intrigued? He hoped so.

When it came to Catrin, he could feel *something*. A beginning, perhaps, or hope. Cat would never treat him like a quick fuck, so if he could get through to her, he thought it might be his first chance at something *real.*

He wouldn't get *anything* real though if he didn't show her he was worth it. So, he resolved to get her fed and resumed his small talk strategy.

"I am not sure if you are going to eat human food or rabbit food tonight, so if you could just hop to my pack if you want me to make enough for you, or stay there if you want to eat whatever you've brought for yourself. For that matter, did you bring rabbit food? I saw you nibble on some stuff on your way here, but I don't know if you have any rabbit food, or if you ate enough while we walked."

Luckily, Catrin immediately hopped decisively onto her own pack. When he opened it for her, she immediately burrowed inside, pulling out a small bag between her teeth. She pulled the bag over next to the fire and sat down. He tried to open the bag for her, but she nipped on his finger and closed her eyes for a moment.

He realized that while she'd slept in his jacket for the past several hours, she'd also probably expended far more energy earlier in the day than any natural rabbit was meant to. He threw together some ingredients, cooking something significantly simpler than he had the night before when he'd been feeding them both. More than a thousand years of travel had led the orcs to a diet heavily featuring foods that were easy to prepare on the go. He pulled out one such item then, a powdered stew that would reconstitute quickly and easily with water.

As he often did, Torsten wondered how much of his culture was an adaptation to the obligations imposed by the Pathians, and how much was what they would be like without the Empire's interference.[3] Even something as small as the powdered stew he held resulted from the Empire's enforced organization.

Enrollment in the army was compulsory for all childless adults. When a female fell pregnant,

---

3. To wit, the Lady's journals provide some small context. While she initially created the orcs to be the foot soldiers of the evil empire, subsequent revisions of the world include documentation of cultures she was inspired by, notably "Bask." While I have no further information on this culture (it is presumably off-world), this has only led to additional confusion. As the Lady modeled many cultures on other, established cultures elsewhere, we are all left wondering what we actually have a right to call our own.

she returned home to raise a family. Grandfathers were allowed to retire and take up a trade only upon the birth of their first grandchild. Soldiers were allowed brief visits home, with the express purpose of breeding, but the result was that most orcish villages were populated by women, children and older men for the majority of the year. The Empire railed at their low birth rates but didn't allow couples regular time to breed. First babies often came easily between soldiers, but seconds or thirds were rare except in the cases of people who weren't exclusively coupled.

After growing up with both parents in Sanctuary, his ancestral village had felt... empty much of the time. He could understand how, perhaps, during a large war such measures might be needed, but his people had been living that way for over a thousand years. It wasn't *right.* He could feel that his people were supposed to be extremely tied to their homes, and instead, their young men lived most of the year isolated from their people and their culture. The stew was just the surface of it all.

Once it was done, he opened her bag of food and shook some onto a plate, waking her up with some scratches behind her long ears. She opened her eyes, clearly bleary. Once she was awake, he talked his way through the meal, explaining about the stew and what it contained.

"I'll make it for you tomorrow night if you'd like to try it. I'm not sure if humans will like it or not, but don't worry if you don't. My mom made this batch, and since she knew I'd be around humans, she tried to make it to their taste, but it's been a while," he said. Hopefully, all the mindless babbling he was doing was soothing her. He was incredibly attracted to her-well, when she was a human, at least-but he'd settle for her not hating him anymore.

After he cleaned up from supper and positioned the stove closer to the door, he looked at the space available to him. It wasn't much. Between the bags and his size, he had just enough room to lie down on his back. He wasn't used to being cramped for space, and he knew he liked to flop back-and-forth between sleeping on his stomach and his back. He slipped on his pants, warmed and dry from the fire, and laid out his bedroll.

Catrin hopped first onto her pack and wiggled around, trying to get comfortable. Then she tried nestling between his feet, but when he twitched his legs, her ears shot up an alarm and she jumped onto his chest. There, she circled several times before curling up. Maybe they really were making progress. She felt right as she settled down on his chest, a warm, soft lump that belonged there. She yawned and rubbed her face with her paws, refusing to meet his eyes.

"I really am sorry, kitten," he said as she stopped fidgeting."I'd never want you to feel uncomfortable because of something I did. Especially not like that."

He paused, his stomach tightening as he considered making her feel that way. She cracked an eye, her tiny eye assessing.

"We don't even have to talk about it, if you don't want to. We could wake up tomorrow, and it could be like nothing ever happened. I hope you can forgive me, and forgive me for saying one more thing..."

His stomach roiled, his very body rebelling against showing vulnerability, but he knew he'd regret it if he didn't say it.

"I think maybe you were embarrassed, but honestly, waking up like that? It was one of the most erotic things I've ever experienced and you didn't even touch me. I just keep thinking... how explosive could it be if we did?"

Chapter Seven
Catrin

IN WHICH CATRIN'S BODY BETRAYS HER IN THE MOST DELECTABLE FASHION

CATRIN WOKE WITH A start. She was cold, and her bed wasn't very comfortable. She blinked her eyes until she realized that her bed wasn't comfortable because it was an orc.

Torsten's eyes snapped awake, a look of sheer terror registering almost immediately, before he squeezed his eyes shut and he blushed a deeper shade of green. She could feel goosebumps all over her own pale skin and heat rising in her core. She was splayed over Torsten, her breasts squished into his warm chest. Her pulse beat through her, fast and insistent.

Curse my fucking body!

It had been years since she'd shifted unintentionally, even longer since doing so in her sleep. If she shifted in her sleep, it was usually because she felt safe. She realized though she felt uncomfortably aroused at the moment, she still felt entirely safe. She remembered Torsten talking to her all day, taking care of her. She hadn't had anyone look after her since she'd moved out of her brother's house.

Torsten's hands flew into the air in a gesture of surrender. "Now Cat, I-" he started in a strained voice, eyes still squeezed tight.

Panic rose within her again. She could feel a storm brewing inside her. She didn't want to talk about it; she didn't want to let it out. She breathed in, attempting to calm her tension when, nestled between her thighs and pressed against her sex, the hard bar of Torsten's cock twitched.

He let out an embarrassed groan at the same time she involuntarily whimpered, earning her a second twitch. He opened his mouth to say something, but she decided that she'd really rather not discuss any of it.

How many nights had she spent dreaming of this-of him? She didn't want to— couldn't—think about the future, or what any of this might mean. Instead, she pushed herself up, so she was even with his face, and slammed her mouth down on his. There was no grace in it. It had been years since she'd kissed anyone like this, and the smoothness of his lips against hers was everything she needed. Catrin was sheer desperation as she thrust her hands into his sleep-mussed braid.

Torsten only delayed a second, letting out a surprised sound where they were joined before dropping his thick arms around her. The slide of his arms across her back was decadent. Strength and calluses, healed scars and tickles of hair teased her as he enveloped her. She slipped into his mouth, learning his taste and the feel of him as she snaked her tongue around his, twining with him in ways that echoed what she wanted from him. He shifted, and the fabric of his pants rasped between her legs, damp from her arousal. He hummed against her, like he was enjoying a fine meal as he took control of the kiss, caressing her tongue.

Breaking the kiss, Torsten moved to caress her neck, the drag of his tusks an exquisite counterpoint to the slip of his slick mouth. He nipped his way up to her ear, suckling on her earlobe and swirling his tongue inside. Catrin moaned and bucked into him, grinding her pussy onto the tip of his hardness, desperate for friction.

"Seems like you don't want to talk, kitten," he growled into her ear. "But I'm no good at stayin' quiet. I need to tell you how good you taste, how fucking lucky I am to wake up with the most gorgeous woman I've ever seen spread out and dripping all over me. You don't have to say a word if you don't want. I'm happy to do all the talking."

Cat wasn't sure if she *could* speak. His words seeped into her, enthralling and seductive. She still couldn't believe this was happening, that he was here, and that he *wanted* her. It felt fleeting, and she was suddenly terrified that they were in some surreal pocket of time. This was the only moment during which such a thing was possible. If any small detail had been different, any things they had said, or done, like anything she did, could ruin the moment.

Torsten was whispering dirty, filthy praise in her ear, and she was terrified to even breathe. And instead, she ground her pussy against him, luxuriating in the feel of his arousal against her.

As she bucked against him, he groaned in her ear, "Do you like that gorgeous? Feeling how fucking hard I get for you? Using me to grind that sopping pussy on?"

Cat whimpered again, letting out an "ah" that only seemed to spur him on.

"Are you gonna come on me, precious? You going to use that thick cock to take what you need? You are such a needy girl, but I'm happy to help you take care of that."

With his words echoing in her head, Catrin sat up to ride him in earnest, his thick hands grasped her around the waist and exaggerated the rock of her hips.

Again, she was hit by the sorrowful realization that she was living out years of fantasies in this one possibly fleeting moment. As she settled back on him, she forgot to move. She stared at him lying underneath her, hair mussed from her hands, lips swollen from her desperate kisses, and the look he had on his face broke her.

He *looked* like he believed everything he'd just said. And she couldn't take it. How was she supposed to live with the memory of him like this? Of the memory of how he looked yesterday, holding his cock and smiling over at her?

When he left, he'd leave her a mess, but she was used to it. Catrin was painfully familiar with picking up the pieces. She squeezed her eyes shut, unable to look at him any longer without crying, and let herself sink in to the feeling of him beneath her, of his hands snaking their way up to her breasts.

She gasped as he cupped and teased her nipples. She knew she had great tits and was happy he seemed to appreciate them. He hefted them, relieving some of their ever-present weight, which was its own kind of delicious seduction.

She smiled hazily down at him, the prick of tears teasing the edges of her vision, but she was determined to enjoy this time. She'd distill it, bottle the experience to take out and torture herself with later.

Lady knew she had precious few such memories to savor as it was. Her memories of Edrigu were tainted by how quickly everything turned. Their time of happiness had been so brief and was overshadowed by all the times they'd struggled.

"Where'd you go precious?" Torsten asked, tweaking her nipples."You looked so sad all of a sudden. Do you want to stop? We don't have to do this." His brow furrowed in concern.

"Either talk dirty or shut the fuck up, Tor," she snapped, annoyed that he'd switched to being sweet. She couldn't handle sweet from him. She wanted to experience this, but she couldn't bear to have it tainted by him being emotional and sweet. Catrin felt the rumble of his laugh travel up through her thighs and settle into her cunt.

That was more like what she was looking for.

"You're thinking too much," he admonished playfully."You want to stop thinking, kitten? Say the word and I'll make sure you can't think at all."

Cat nodded, ashamed at how pitiful she must look, but she wanted this and she was too in her head when she was left to her own devices.

In one fluid motion, Torsten lifted her off of him, and gently rolled to swap their positions. Suddenly she was laying in the bedroll, warm and comfortable, surrounded by his scent and caged in by his arms. Torsten leveled his gaze with hers, the dim firelight casting half of his strong features in shadow.

"You don't have to talk, but if you don't like something, I need you to say so or to pinch me, all right?" Cat nodded, desperate for whatever he wanted to give her.

Sitting back on his heels, Torsten smirked and licked his lips obscenely, "Oh kitten," he rumbled, "you are a fucking feast. I've been imagining you naked since the moment I saw you again." He grasped her breasts, pressing them together and nestling his face between them."But these beauties make my mouth water."

He snaked his tongue out, wrapping it around her straining nipple and sucking it into his mouth with an obscene slurp. He moaned as he pulled on it, his tusks dimpling into either side of her nipple. Catrin rubbed her legs together. She could feel her slickness gathering without his pants to soak it up.

"Lady preserve me Cat, these fucking tits are driving me wild, but I can hear how needy that pussy is." He pushed up so his face was level with hers, stealing her lips in a searing kiss."I am going to devour your needy little cunt. I want to hear your noises. I want to hear you scream my name, and I don't want you holding back." He sucked her bottom lip into his mouth and she let out a whimper. If he didn't touch her soon, surely she would die.

She cried out when she felt one if his thick blunt fingers slip through her folds and gather her wetness. "Open for me, precious?" he asked, the finger wetly hovering near her mouth. She opened, fascinated as he smeared her arousal on her lips before slipping it inside and onto her tongue.

"Taste how fucking much you want me. Do you see how good you taste? Why my mouth started watering when you pleasured yourself last night and hasn't stopped? You know I can smell you. I know the second you are wet, and your scent is so thick I can taste it on my tongue, but I want more. I am *always* going to want more."

His words muddled her senses, the tang of her mixed with his own deep musk on his finger made her eyes roll back in her head as she lapped it up. She wasn't nearly done with him when he removed his finger with a pop. She whined, but he replaced it with his mouth, chasing the taste of her with his tongue, scouring it from inside. He nibbled her lip and broke the kiss, leaving Catrin panting as he kissed his way down to her sex.

He groaned and buried his nose in her curly pubic hair so that when he spoke, his whispers and growls teased her. "Goddess Cat, you smell so fucking amazing, I just—" He stopped and immediately set upon her like he was ravenous.

His tongue dipped and pressed into her, sucking on her labia and humming his pleasure. He teased her, avoiding where she really wanted him, lavishing attention on every other part of her.

His hands couldn't seem to find where they wanted to stay. They toyed with her breasts, skimmed over and massaged her stretch marked tummy, grasped her full ass, and kneaded at her sides. She understood, if this was her one chance, she wanted to experience everything. She wanted to feel every inch of him pressed against her until there wasn't a single part of her body that hadn't been graced by his skin.

"I don't know what the fuck I did to deserve this," he said. "But I must have been a very, *very* good boy. You taste just as good as I imagined. Better, because I know that this is all for me. I know that this needy little cunt is dripping, because she wants what I can give her."

When Cat whimpered, he chuckled darkly. "Oh, don't worry kitten, I'm going to give her everything she needs."

Catrin moaned through her closed mouth, and a moment later, she felt Torsten's thick thumb on her bottom lip, asking her to open her mouth. "Don't hide those noises from me," he whispered, each word flicking against her clit. "I've earned those, and I don't think I've ever heard a better sound."

He returned to his work, alternating between gentle, insistent presses, fast flicks, and every so often, he would give her the shortest suction.

Outside it was freezing, the rain had been threatening to switch to snow all day, and it was short moments from doing so, but Catrin was boiling. He'd stoked her desire to where she was flush and overwhelmed, a needy, desperate puddle, begging for his attention. She fucked her hips into his mouth, reveling in the dangerous, tempting feeling of his tusks.

At the edge of her hearing, as if he'd not meant her to hear it at all, she heard him whisper "fucking perfect" against her.

He moved lower, the bristle of his facial hair and his nose now teasing her clit. He eased his long tongue inside of her. Her eyes widened, and she let out a surprised scream, moving to press herself down on him, wanting more of that writhing tongue inside of her. She'd felt nothing like it. He lapped at her inside walls, caressed along her g–spot, and in moments, she was grinding on his face, screaming that she was so close. She could feel the tension in her body wind until she was tight enough to break. Just before she did so, he pressed into her with the two blunt fingers and returned to suck on her clit.

She shattered. Her body shuddered, breaking and rebuilding itself, her awareness focused on only the points they were connected. He nursed on her clit, gently fucking his fingers inside of her to prolong her orgasm.

She floated in a sea of euphoria, rocked on the rhythm of his thrusts, lulled by the soft encouragements he whispered to her.

As she came down, he eased off, switching to gentle kisses on her thighs. He ruffled her pubic hair with his fingers and settled with his chin resting on her pubic bone, smiling like a fool. Catrin looked down at him, suddenly cognizant enough of the situation to feel the beginnings of embarrassment creep in.

Her eyes widened in mortification, ashamed at how wantonly she'd used him, how casually she'd succumbed to her desire. Still, she didn't regret it. She was grateful she'd always have this memory, but she wasn't sure how they'd get through the rest of the journey together.

His brow furrowed, his lips pursing in disappointment.

There it was.

She'd known this was inevitable. So much for "perfect." So much for "always wanting more." He hadn't even fucked her and already he was done with her.

"I don't know what that brain of yours is telling you right now, kitten. But I am going to need you to tell it to shut the fuck up. These are not the faces I ever want to see you make after you come chanting my name."

Chanting his name?

She had no memory of saying his name, but she hadn't been fully in charge of her faculties either. Torsten sat back, smiling wryly at whatever he saw on her face."Did you think I was done with you, precious?" His eyebrows rose."I see. Well, if you want to be done, that's just fine. I can step out and take care of myself, but I'd really rather keep playing with you." He raised an eyebrow, waiting for her answer.

Cat felt like she couldn't get her footing. She was vacillating wildly between emotions. She nodded, overwhelmed with her confusion, but wanting whatever crumbs of affection he was willing to give her. At her nod, his hands dropped to unlace his breeches.

"Play with yourself for me, precious?" he asked. His voice was softer, more timid.

Catrin's hands flew to her breast and pussy, surprised at how quickly she obeyed. She craved that look in his eyes and wanted to do whatever it took to keep it there. She played tentatively at first, but after he made his first sound of pleasure, she teased herself in earnest. He stood, towering over her to remove his pants. He was so tall, or the cave was so small, she was unsure. He couldn't even stand entirely upright.

Catrin couldn't stop the gasp that burst out of her when he lowered his pants, his thick, hard shaft springing free with a bounce. It had been a while since she's seen a cock, but from what she remembered, this was... exceptional.

The deep green of his body faded into a purple head that peeked at her from his foreskin. It was long and thick, and she could tell just by looking that it would be a stretch. Her only other experience of a penis had been with her ex. Like Edrigu, Torsten's cock was pierced, but apparently there was variation in how it could be done. Where Edrigu had a ring through the tip, Torsten had bars in an X pattern. They glinted at her through the tip, and nestled in the thick patch of hair at his base she could see another piercing.

Whimpering, she imagined grinding her pussy on that. Torsten smiled, clearly pleased by her reaction.

"Well, I'm glad to see you're not disappointed, kitten," he said, lowering himself over her, returning immediately to kiss her, deep and slow.

Torsten tucked his face into her neck, sucking and laving at her. His sounds and smell flooded her senses, so she heard the catch in his breath when he ground his glorious cock against her.

"Oh, kitten," he whispered in a growl. "This sweet, hot little pussy is so wet for me, does she want me to fill her up? Do you want my cock inside of you?"

He pulled back, wiping a few hairs off of Catrin's brow. He smiled down at her.

It was too tender, too intimate. She could feel the panic rising in her chest as he leaned down to capture her lips in a sweet, sensual kiss. It was too much. She didn't have weeks to recover from this, she didn't —

"None of that," he said, smoothing her furrowed brow with his thumb. "We'll return to this, but right now, I need you to tell me how you like to be fucked."

Catrin opened her mouth as if to speak up, but only whimpers came out. If she forced sound out now, she didn't know what would come out. Would she beg and plead and embarrass herself? Would she rail at him and tell him to leave her alone to protect her heart?

No, it was better to stay silent. She nodded her head wildly and pushed out a single syllable, "Please." Her eyes searched his beautiful face, begging him to show mercy on her, pleading with him to give her what she needed and not make it too complicated.

Torsten smirked and shook his head, leaning down to kiss her. He rolled them, so that she was instead laying on top once more. He sat her up so that her clit ground on the underside of his shaft. She moaned as she sat up, pressing her hands into his chest to keep upright.

It had been years since she'd had sex at all, let alone taken an orc cock. Though she knew from experience there was always a transition period, an uncomfortable time of stretching, it always worked out. She'd manage just fine in the end. Catrin grimaced, raising herself up and notching Torsten's cock at her entrance. She took in a deep breath, preparing for the uncomfortable sensation.

"Kitten, what the fuck are you doing?" he asked, frowning up at her.

Cat recoiled, offended. "I was trying to get this log of a thing in there, forgive me if it's not super comfortable the first time. I don't know if you remember, but you are an orc, so while I can stretch, it will not be particularly pleasant at first."

"Not like that, you're not," he said. "Gods, more faces like that and I'll go limp."

He raised his hand to her face, caressing the side of her cheek.

"Don't misunderstand me. I want you more than I can possibly express right now, but not if I hurt you. I don't want this to be something that you get through."

Dear Lady, everything until that point had felt so good, and Catrin wasn't sure *anything* had ever felt as good, but she certainly didn't want to talk about it. She set her jaw and furrowed her brow open. "Too much talking," she bit out, grabbing his length and setting it against her opening once more. His hands flew to her hips, holding them securely.

"You can try, if you're determined," he chuckled, "but I'm stopping you the second it seems like you're actually in pain." Catrin nodded her head. The feeling of him brushing against her entrance was almost more than she could bear.

She lowered herself, the metal of his piercing, providing a shocking counterpoint to the plush head of his penis. Torsten could say that he didn't want to stretch her all he wanted, but the fact was, he was still huge.

Somehow, though, between how wet she was from wanting him and potential subconscious help from her magic, he slipped inside. As one, they let out surprised grunts, as if they've both been punched in the stomach.

"Oh fuck, kitten, if that isn't the sweetest thing I've ever felt," he groaned, eyes flicking over Catrin's face. "Gods, I don't know if I'm going to last very long. You're taking me so well. Is that greedy cunt nice and full now?"

Catrin nodded her head. She was more than all right. The stretch of him was just enough that it rode the perfect edge of pleasure and pain. On her hip, Torsten's hand shifted so that his thumb could work her clit. He applied a gentle steady pressure that made her roll her hips. With each roll, she sank deeper onto him, the length of him slipping inside and stretching her.

"Oh, I didn't know if you—guh—I, Torsten..." Catrin said, stumbling over her words until she was reduced to wordless noises of pleasure.

The rumble of Torsten's laughter transmitted through him, so that she swore she could feel it all the way to her stomach.

"Oh, does my sweet little kitten like being stuffed? Do you like being so full of me that you can't think of anything else?"

Catrin nodded her head frantically, and Torsten smiled wickedly."Well, I think we could handle that."

Torsten pulled almost all the way out, the thick head of his cock dragging along her inside walls, before sliding inside and seating himself to the hilt.

The piercing at the base of his shaft rubbed her clit, sending shocks of pleasure through her.

"Fuck precious, this pussy was made for me. You take me so perfectly."

Catrin's inner walls clenched. Now that she'd started, her orgasms would come quickly. Torsten grunted as she tightened around him. Inside her, she could feel his knot begin to swell at the base of his cock. She expected that he'd pull back then, Edrigu always had. Instead, he thrust into her, grinding his piercing against her to prolong her shocks of pleasure.

"Oh kitten, I'm going to—"

"Give it to me," she whispered."I want it."

Catrin's eyes and mouth opened wide as he pressed into her, the round firmness of his knot entering her with a satisfying pop. The stretch was almost more than she could take. It was tempered by the profound pleasure of the pressure placed on her G spot. He thrust a few times more, though much gentler.

Like this, he was overwhelming. His piercing teased her clit, his cock stretched the length of her, and his knot stimulated her front wall. In seconds, she was screaming, and grasping him, her pussy clutching and milking him as he came with a roar.

THE CAVE ECHOED WITH the sound of their labored breaths. Torsten trailed his fingers down Catrin's spine, smiling as she shivered. And she was still sleepy, she had no idea what time it was, but she was more than content to float in the aftermath of their meeting. On Torsten's chest, Catrin whimpered as his cock twitched inside of her.

He rumbled a laugh."Sorry about the knot, precious, I didn't think we were going to go that far.

Don't get me wrong, I'm not sad to be locked with you, but I do feel bad that you're stuck for a bit now."

"It's my own damn fault, I told you to," she whispered. She wiggled atop him, likely trying to find a more comfortable position. Torsten's hands shot up to her waist to steady her.

"If you want off of this anytime soon, you're going to need to stop that." He said, lip quirking as he teased her."Or have you forgotten that part?"

"Oh, I didn't realize, I guess," Catrin whispered. Torsten trailed his hand up her spine until he found a lock of her hair to play with, twisting it around his fingers.

"You didn't realize? Isn't this how you ended up with twins? It's not an uncommon occurrence for an orc."

Catrin buried her face in his chest, face red as she mumbled a confession.

"If you want me to actually respond to that, princess, you're going to have to say it in a way that I can understand."

"I've never been knotted before. I ended up with twins through desperation," she whispered.

"I see," he said, a smug smile spreading across his face."You never — with your husband?"

"He said he didn't like it, that it was unnecessary since I could control so much of my conception, that we would just be stuck and he much preferred being able to just roll over and go to sleep."

"I see," Torsten said, his brow furrowed. "Well since orcs can go several times in a row, it plugs it, so that none of my cum spurts out on subsequent rounds." He rubbed his forehead, shaking his head, "I'm honestly just confused that you never did in all the time you were married."

"Then you have a *very* different impression of my marriage than I did," she said. "I think it should probably speak volumes that we were only ever married, and not officially mated in the orcish custom. It also really wasn't all that long, a couple of months really. I don't think we *ever* had the same definition for our relationship. When we were talking about conceiving, I was talking about right then, and later, I found out that he had been speaking in theoreticals."

Torsten nodded his head, "Speaking both languages, I can see how that could happen pretty easily. They have a special tense for theoretical things, but shit, remind me when we get back to tell the council and the ambassadors, we don't want that to happen during negotiations." Cat lifted her head to look up at him with wide eyes.

"That could be terrible. And don't get me wrong, while Edrigu and I weren't a forever thing, I don't want you thinking he was some kind of bad guy. We just had different ideas of what we wanted in life, and different ideas about what we were to one another. Once we figured it out, we were on very different pages. It was really just a matter of finding a way to disentangle our lives. Which was honestly easier than you might think, considering he'd been planning on returning home the whole time."

She buried her face into his chest, shaking her head."Oh, Lady, that makes me sound like such an idiot. Oh yes, my husband was planning on it being a short-term marriage the whole time. We talked about having kids but I didn't realize he was talking about me raising them alone. After he found that wasn't my intent, he told me he'd be fine with it if I terminated the pregnancy. When I talked to Berne and some of my friends, I decided that I'd rather keep the girls."

"He wasn't gone very long. Did he leave before you'd even given birth? It's normal for an orc to be granted leave to stay through the birth," Torsten said.

"He did." Catrin said."We decided it might be easier for all of us, since I'd only get more attached while, according to him, it was fairly normal and expected that he'd leave."

"Sadly, that's true." Torsten said."I knew it, before I returned, but it was still... distasteful to me."

"Regardless, it's not really safe for the girls in the Empire, considering they're so obviously half human. If they get to the point where they can use their lunula enough to pass for full orcs, I'd love for us to spend some time with his family and him. But until then, he sends letters, and I've been teaching the girls what I can of Orcish, so they try to write back."

"You're so much more level headed about it than I would be," he said, rubbing her back."I'd be furious and bitter about the situation."

"Oh I was," she said."but I've had years to deal with it, and realize that it wasn't the right fit." She quieted, taking time to just drink in the feeling of being draped across him, sated and happy.

"Eventually, you just have to accept people how they are and for what they are willing to do," she said, refusing to meet his eyes. It wasn't an ideal situation but she didn't need him judging her for it."When I thought about it, I realized I wanted the kids, regardless. Berne helped, of course. He's been very involved and the girls know about their dad. They just haven't seen him recently."

"And your parents? They've helped too?" he asked, squeezing her arm.

"Yes and no? When we lost Annika, it broke them, and I understand why. I'd be lost too. But because of that, they just haven't ever really been the same. Honestly, Berne finished raising me more than they did. But he's been great with the girls, and with me. I've been very lucky."

"I should say so," he grumbled."I had no idea about any of this. I'm so sorry. I would have—"

"You would have what? Left your life to help your best friend's kid sister raise some babies? What would you do, Tor? You don't have any responsibility to them, or to me," she said, eyes trained on the flickering of the fire on the wall of the cave. She had her insecurities about parenting the girls, but she'd done damn well with them and didn't need to see his disappointment, or worse, his pity.

"I'd have come." Torsten's voice was stern."I'm serious, Cat. Just because I turned you down when we were kids doesn't mean I wouldn't have come. You were a child, so of course I wasn't *in love* with you, but I still loved you. I still cared. You should have said something."

For the briefest moment, something like hope flared in Catrin's chest.

No. She'd had more than her fair share of disappointment and heartbreak, this was a one time thing. It *needed* to be a one time thing. She could recover from where she was now. Her heart was intact and she'd have a lovely memory. The last thing she needed was for him to build up some sort of expectation that he'd only betray.

Repeated misery welled up inside her. Her loneliness after Edrigu left. Confronting that she'd not been enough for him to stay. Her parent's abandonment after Annika. Her heartbreak after Torsten had left. She'd cried for days, which

had only been worse after her letters went
unanswered.

"Torsten, you can only expect me to write to you
with no response for so many years before I stop. I
wasn't about to reach out again."

She must've hit a nerve because he stilled
beneath her. He drew in several deep breaths.

"Kitten, that's not funny," he said, his voice hard.
His hands clasped her ass, probably harder than
he'd meant."I wrote you for months and you never
once-"

The blood drained from her face. He couldn't
possibly be saying what she thought.

"That's not possible," she said, voice wavering."I
checked, I waited..."

"I gave them directly to Berne with all of the other
mail. If he-" Torsten said, a growl creeping into his
voice.

"No!" Catrin interrupted, placing her hands on
his chest to calm him."He always delivered the
whole package sealed to the council and then
my parents would have fetched ours. I asked my
mother every time and there was always nothing."

"There were letters, Cat. Not in the very first one,
because I was trying to give you time, but after
that, there were... gods at least three letters in each
package for a year or so..." He ran a hand down his
face, groaning.

"And you," he continued."You wrote to me?"

"Yes," Catrin had to push the word out."I gave them to my mother to deliver with the rest-"

Stomach rolling, Catrin put a hand over her mouth. Her eyes stung and she blinked back unshed tears. Whatever comfort she found from knowing Torsten *had* written to her was shattered by the anguish she felt. Her parents must have intervened. They'd seen how unhappy she was, and let her believe that he hadn't cared enough to write. After a while, she'd questioned their entire relationship. Had he ever cared for her at all? Not romantically, to him, she'd been a child, but the rest of it. Had he hated having her tag along? Had he pretended to listen to her when she spoke? Worst of all, had he made fun of her when she wasn't around?

Her parents *knew* how much she'd missed him, and they'd let her believe that he hadn't cared enough to write.

"My—my parents," she whispered. Torsten stroked her hair as her tears splashed onto his chest tattoo."They lied to me."

She felt like an old rag, twisted up and discarded.

After Annika at least, she could somewhat understand, but she'd sent letters for a year and a half before her sister had disappeared. Torsten didn't shush her, like Berne might, he just held her and let her mourn yet another time her parents had let her down. He twined a curl around his finger, letting her sob until she was dry.

Once she was done, Torsten wrapped his arms around her, squeezing. His knot loosened, spilling his seed out of her onto him, though he ignored it. "So, you sent letters, and I never got them. And I did the same. How many years did they rob us of?"

"What do you mean?" Cat asked, still sniffling.

"How many years could we have been together if they hadn't kept your letters?"

Together.

What is he talking about? We aren't together. He's going home and I have two kids.

A shaky, panicked feeling fluttered in her chest. Her breathing sped and she wanted nothing more than to *run.*

"Torsten, you were on a different continent. Nothing would have changed."

He recoiled from her, looking down at her, brow furrowed and lip in a snarl. "What are you talking about? I'd have come when you had the girls to help, if I wasn't back already. How are you going to raise two orcs on your own, even with Berne's help, knowing nothing about being an orc?"

Catrin blinked rapidly. "Excuse me? How fucking *dare* you! I think I have done a damn fine job raising them, I'll thank you. I don't know much about being an orc, but I know *plenty* about being their mother. And if you think that I need to be an orc to be damn good at that, you are dead wrong."

"Kitten, that's not what I meant," he said, running his hands through his hair. "I just know there are some things that you might not know about and it angers me that you're out here doing it on your own, when I would have come to help. The *point* is, I would have come when Edrigu left. Or, honestly, I'd have come earlier if I'd have known you'd welcome me. I thought you never wanted to see me again--"

"I didn't." She interjected. "After the way you left and then ignored me?"

"I don't blame you, kitten," he said, stroking her hair. "We didn't know. You didn't know. So, do you think this is going to be a long-term problem? Do we need to work on it?" he asked, his voice soft once more.

"Work on what? What do you mean?" Catrin asked.

"On us, on how we clearly hurt each other, perhaps me more than you," he said, voice flat as if it should be obvious.

"I don't see why. There isn't an 'us,' Tor. This was fun, but it's not like it's forever. This is... I don't know, a fling, I suppose?"

"A fling?" he spat. "Are you fucking joking, Cat? If you've had sex casually in the past, that's great for you, but that isn't what I want with you. I'm... I'm not interested in that with you. I care too much."

"Well, I suppose it's none of your business if I do or don't sleep with people casually, since, as I said, there isn't an us." Catrin looked away, unable to move as more of his seed gushed from her. Her cheeks heated, what a horrid situation.

"Why?"

"Why what?" she countered.

"Why isn't there an us, Cat? Why can't there be?" Torsten's voice softened.

"Because…" she trailed off. What was she supposed to say? Because you'll leave? Because I don't know that I can get hurt like that again? Because I'm scared? "It's just not something I can have in my life right now. I need to focus on the girls, and my career. I can't be splitting my focus. This was…" she trailed off. Life changing, magical, more than she'd ever dreamed? "Great. This was great. But this isn't a forever thing, and it just can't be."

Torsten growled. "That's the biggest pile of horse shit I have ever heard. I've thought about it. If everything worked out, I could help you with the gi—"

"Stop." she pushed off of him, crawling away so she could sit on her bag. "Stop right there. You don't get to do that."

"Do what?"

"Promise things and take them away." The words burst from her unbidden. The shame of them rolled in her belly, making her sick with it. Did he really not understand?

"Cat I'm not going—" he said, shaking his head."I don't want to—"

"No." She shook her head sadly."It's just what happens. It's just a fact of my life, Tor. I've accepted it, you should too."

Outside, the storm seemed to have let up. It felt closer to early morning than late night, so she figured they had better make progress when they could."It stopped raining, I'm good to move on if you are. We might even be able to make up more ground if we push it."

Chapter Eight
Torsten

IN WHICH AN OFFER IS MADE,
A GLIMPSE AT AN ACCORD, AND
ITS IMMEDIATE DISSOLUTION

"YOU MIGHT BE RIGHT about the rain, but we're not done talking about this, Cat. In the most respectful manner possible, that's a crock of horseshit. We need to move before we miss Aegir. So I'll let you be done, for now, but we're going to circle back to this because I don't think either of us are done talking about it."

A fling. He was still reeling with it and as much as they needed to talk about this, he could already tell he was too raw. She'd flayed him open, perhaps without even realizing it. Was that really all he was to her? Torsten sat up, resting his arms on his knees, shaking his head as he studied her. She refused to look at him as she dressed in her layers.

They packed up the cave in silence, the air inside thick with tension. Catrin jerked about, shoving items into bags. Torsten discreetly rubbed his chest. A tightness there had started during her speech, and was building to pain. Did she really regard him as a toy? A quick fuck to pass the time?

Honestly, it was pathetic how many times he'd been in this exact scenario, awkwardly dressing while his emotions roiled within him. Cat didn't move like it had been a quick fuck, though. If she didn't care, she'd act like it hadn't mattered, right?

Instead, she avoided his gaze and was ready to go in record time. No, she cared, maybe even as much as he was realizing he did.

Starting early let them make up for some lost time. Their route took them across to the ocean. He'd sent a message for Aegir to wait for them, but hadn't *exactly* heard back by the time they left. Even if he hadn't gotten the message, Aegir should be just waiting at the coast to take anyone who needed to go back to the Empire for at least another day or so.

There was a small section of the barrier along the northern land bridge that allowed for passage between the continents, though the crossing was treacherously close to the shore. This gap had allowed Aegir's duties of late to include small bits of espionage and subterfuge. There were places along the coast that the orcs didn't have any reasonable excuse for going. Aegir had learned to shift into a form that looked remarkably like a Pathian, allowing him to blend in and gather intelligence that no one else in the rebellion had been able to.

As they walked, the dark winter sky cleared, allowing them to see the stars. It was nearing the solstice and soon there wouldn't even be a few minutes of light. He'd grown used to the strange day-night cycles of the pole, though he wondered if it was odd to Catrin, who'd spent most of her life in the Lady's Bubble. He wanted to ask her what she thought of it, if it was strange for her. Instead, he held his tongue and wrestled with the damage she'd done.

She couldn't know of his years of loneliness, of how as a blacksmith, he should have been a sought after partner. Instead, he'd been alone, and the few times he'd slept with female orcs, they'd made him pull out when he came, clear evidence that they wanted nothing of him. He'd always dreamt of a family, but over the years, he'd started to worry it wouldn't be possible. Cat though, Cat made him wonder again. The attraction he felt for anyone else paled in comparison to what he felt when he looked at her.

Here she was, his little kitten, all grown and tempting. More, she seemed to *need* him. He could almost see it, the outline of a life they could have if they took a chance. Instead, she insisted she didn't want it, that it wasn't possible. As deep as she'd cut him, he didn't buy it, and he wasn't ready to give up on the best chance he'd ever had at a relationship. Perhaps... that was the key. Maybe if he showed her how he could help, what an asset he could be in her life, she'd reconsider.

A warmth swelled in his chest as he thought about it. He could offer her what no one in Sanctuary could. He was the one person that could truly understand both sides of her children. If he could get Cat to see that, maybe she'd give him a chance.

"So," he started, "I was thinking about the girls' teeth." Catrin's eyes widened in surprise before she looked pointedly away.

"Their teeth?" Her voice and mouth were tight as she answered, but she at least answered him. He'd meant it when he said they weren't done, but perhaps it was better to explore other avenues first.

Torsten furrowed his brow and toyed with one of his tusk bands with his tongue, a habit his mother had always scolded him for, but one he couldn't seem to break, regardless.

"We usually give young orcs a small willow branch to chew on. It has some anti-inflammatory properties and I think it helps with pain, too. If nothing else, it gives them something to focus on."

"Oh. I hadn't really thought of that. I didn't realize that was a thing people did. But, I suppose it makes sense." Catrin scrunched up her nose in the way that she'd always done when thinking."When Edrigu left, I just assumed parenting the girls would be like parenting anyone."

"In many ways, I'm sure it is. They seem happy and well-loved and that's really the most important part."

"Thanks," she said, barely audible.

"I was thinking, if you'd like, and you'd be all right with it, I'd be happy to tutor the girls in orcish language and customs. I'd hate for them to struggle when they visit."

"Actually, I suppose that might be helpful." Catrin nodded."You said you struggled when you first went to the Empire? Among the other orcs, I mean?" she asked when she spoke again.

"I did," Torsten said, crunching his way over frozen moss."I spoke orcish with an accent, and I didn't understand some of the unspoken rules that hadn't applied with just my family. I wouldn't want your girls to have to go through what I did. I suppose, before I moved there, I hadn't realized how odd my parents are in our society. They are loved and respected, but most people see them as eccentric at best."

And me as even worse.

Several hours of trudging through the mountains later, the coast line burst into view as they crested a hill. Next to him, Catrin gasped and Torsten turned to her, raising an eyebrow.

"Is this your first time seeing the ocean?" he asked.

"No, I've seen the ocean, but never at night like this," she said, her voice hushed and eyes wide. "We only come in the summer."

In the sky above, the aurora borealis painted the heavens, reflecting vibrant colors onto the water. Each wave that crested glowed with the purple algae that lived there. Nearly every major body of water housed its own variety, and different species often inhabited different areas of the same ocean. This purple variety wasn't magical, as it wasn't infused with the Lady's magic like their own was. Only the Spine, the river that flowed south from Sanctuary and into the Compact of Nations imparted her magic.[1]

If she'd never seen the ocean at night, nor the northern lights as they shone off of it, Torsten could see how the tableau would be especially transfixing. He'd grown so used to it on his

---

1. This lack of magic is the largest part of the Pathian Empire's motivation. When the Lady entered her slumber, she took magic away from the high elves, her ultimate enemy, and they've spent the last thousand plus years trying to reclaim it.

passages from the Empire that its beauty had become mundane to him.

Instead, he was more fascinated by how Catrin herself looked, with the gentle glow of her lantern lighting her from below and the aurora reflecting in her wide blue eyes. The corners of her mouth crept up and then it dropped open. For the briefest moment, he saw an echo of the vibrant, curious girl he once knew. The moment passed quickly, as Catrin set her face and continued down the mountain, calling over her shoulder for him to keep up. Shaking his head with a chuckle, Torsten trailed behind, not the least bit disappointed about the view she presented. In taking the lead for most of the trip, he'd deprived himself of the immense pleasure of watching her hips and arse as she walked.[2]

While he'd appreciated that glimpse of the girl she had been, Torsten knew it was this strong woman that he was truly disappointed in having missed.

---

2. While the lunologists of Sanctuary had always instinctively used their lunula to aid them when ill or to soothe fatigue, Berne had shared how Sirin had taken to training him and a few of the others, Catrin included. She was teaching them how to take more conscious, precise control of their bodily functions. All those intentional changes had allowed Catrin to keep pace with someone much larger, better equipped, and more practiced at overland travel than she was.

A half hour later, they descended to the cove where Torsten and the emissaries had left Aegir's steamship. Once they'd discovered the gap, Aegir and Torsten had frequently traveled together. The ship had significantly sped up the trip to Sanctuary, and Torsten was eager to see his friend.

When she saw it, Catrin gasped. The Lady's Revenge was painted black and blue so that she'd blend into the horizon in the long, deep night of northern winter. She seemed to manifest from thin air. Pulling on the rope that would lower the gangplank, he waved Catrin up onto the deck.

"I've grown up around boats my entire life and I've seen nothing like this..." she said, her voice hushed with awe.

"Well, of course. You grew up with canal boats. The Lady's Revenge was built for the ocean," he said, waving as Aegir came out on deck.

"You remember Aegir?" Torsten asked.

"Of course she does!" Aegir burst out, his bellowing laugh at odds with the covert nature of his work. "We're old friends!"

When stealth wasn't required, Aegir spent most of his time in a half shifted state, somewhere between human and orca. His skin was patterned black and white and retained the slippery texture of his shifted form. His teeth were pointed and his hands and feet were elongated and webbed.

"You *have* been gone a while, eh Torsten?" Aegir chided. "Did you forget Cat and I were the same year in school? We grew up together!"

With a squeal, Catrin moved to give Aegir a big hug. The orca-shifter lifted and spun her in a circle. Torsten growled possessively before he realized he'd done so.

Aegir looked at Torsten questioningly over Cat's shoulder, his eyes shifting between Torsten and Cat. With a curt nod, Torsten confirmed that he considered her his and he'd appreciate Aegir's respect, though he knew Aegir to be a shameless flirt and there wasn't any real chance of that happening. He could only hope that Cat knew it as well and knew better than to take Aegir seriously.

"And how are the girls?" Aegir asked. "It's been a while since I've seen them."

"It has! They miss you!" Catrin said. "They are the most wonderful trial, as per usual. They are going through their orcish first puberty and I feel like every other moment I'm stopping them from gnawing on furniture or helping them pick up something they spilled because they don't know their strength yet. But honestly, I think it's been harder on them than on me. I... I didn't know it would happen, so their bodies just started changing without me giving any warning."

The pain in her voice was a vise around Torsten's heart.

"It's not your fault, kitten," he said, the growl in his voice growing."How would you know to expect such a thing? You'd have no way of knowing... unless of course the girls' father had seen fit to divulge even the tiniest bit of information on orc-rearing."

"Regardless," Cat said, turning to look at him."I'm done being mad at him about it, it doesn't fix anything. If he doesn't want to be an active participant in his daughters' lives, then he's missing out. They have plenty of people who love them more than enough to make up for it. But-"

"They sure do!" Aegir broke in before Catrin could finish what she was about to say next. Catrin chuckled and smiled at Aegir. Torsten would do nearly anything to have a smile like that directed at him. For the last three days, he'd seen her frustration, her indifference, and even the depths of her pleasure directed at him, but not once had he caused her joy.

"Now, get this lovely lady settled, and I'll see about getting us underway!" Aegir said, turning toward the helm.

"This way, kitten," Torsten said, grabbing Catrin's hand. She followed him below decks as he mentally promised himself to do everything in his power to make her smile as soon and as often as possible.

"It's tight quarters, but still a fair bit more comfortable than the ground in a tent. Can't say it'll be more comfortable than my chest, but that's always an option as well."

"Oh you'd like *that* I'll bet," Catrin said, a saucy smile accompanying eyes wide with censure. She could get sassy with him anytime she liked. Hell, he liked it when she bossed him around a bit.

"That I would," he confirmed. A saucy smile wasn't his goal, but he'd take any step in the right direction he could get. She hadn't denied it and she hadn't admonished him, so he'd consider it progress.

Opening the door into the small passenger cabin, Torsten waved her inside."There are six berths, so you're spoiled for choice. Pick whichever you like."

Catrin examined the bunks, two on either side wall and the last set on the hull. As she looked, Torsten noticed her nose twitching.[3] When she reached his usual bunk, the bottom along the outside wall, she shot him a look of challenge and dropped her pack.

"I'll take this one," she said, watching him closely.

"It's the best bunk in here," he said. Smiling broadly, he crossed to drop his bag on the bunk next to hers, rather than the bunk above.

---

3. Even in her human form, Torsten's scent was easily discernible for Catrin, having spent several days with him.

"Isn't this yours? Don't you care that I took it?" she asked.

"Kitten, you've got to know that I am happy to have you in my bed anytime you want."

"Damn, I walked right into that one, didn't I?" Cat groused. She pursed her lips in annoyance but couldn't seem to help the smile that tugged at the corner of her mouth.

"That you did," he said, grinning. "I love when you use that smart mouth on me."

The boat rumbled to life underneath them and the paddlewheel creaked as it began scooping water. Cat jumped at the noise, and Torsten rubbed her back.

"Peace, kitten," he whispered. "She's just waking up and getting us out on the water."

Letting tense shoulders fall, Cat looked up at him, chagrined.

"Thank you, this is all so new..."

"Of course," he said, lowering his voice. "I've got you, kitten. If you'll let me, I'll always have you."

Ducking away from him, Catrin looked at him like he'd smacked her.

"Stop that right now! Goddess damn it, Torsten, the second I think I can just have fun with you, you go and say something like that. Why can't we just enjoy the time we have together?"

"What's wrong with you, woman? What would be so bad about being with me? Are you going to punish me for making the right choice at seventeen forever?" He ran his hand through his hair, and after a few deep breaths turned back to her with a pained expression.

He cut off, his throat constricting. "You can't keep punishing me for what Edrigu did to you. I know I hurt you, but that fucker's the real one at blame here, not me. And I'm not going to let him get between me and what I want, and I want you."

Cat's face was red, and her chest heaved. She stared at him, blinking mutely before dropping her bag on the bed, turning on her heel, and walking out, slamming the door behind her.

Chapter Nine
Catrin

IN WHICH REAL FRIENDS STAB YOU IN THE FACE

T ORSTEN WAS A MENACE. The man was trying her last nerve, and she was seconds from wringing his neck. How *dare* he criticize her about Edrigu? After that fiasco, she had every *right* to avoid relationships. Not to mention the fact that she had *children* who needed her. Children who'd never had a father and were already starting to latch onto him. Getting involved with him would be a horrible idea, because when it inevitably went wrong, she'd be left to pick up the pieces.

Instead of wringing his neck like she wanted, Catrin stomped upstairs —no, on deck, to find Aegir, like a *fucking lady*. They were just pulling away from the mooring and the boat swayed beneath her feet as she composed herself and found him at the helm.

"Well ho there, darling, how are you settling in?" Aegir asked, his head whipping around to check the sides of the boat as it inched away from the dock. Behind him, a smokestack pumped out smoke or steam, she didn't know which.

"Ho, Aegir," she said, giggling.[1] It was impossible to *not* have a little crush on him. Nearly every person she knew growing up had harbored one. He was charismatic and had a way of speaking to someone like they were the only person in the room. Despite his magnetism, she'd never been actually interested in him and had instead watched as he churned through their friends growing up.

"I'm settling in fine. I just wanted some air. How goes the, erm—cast off or whatever you call it?" she asked.

Aegir threw his head back in a full belly laugh. "It's going well." He quieted for a moment, looking at her. "You look a little agitated Cat, are you all right?"

"I'm fine, just dealing with a big green orc that doesn't seem to understand real life."

---

1. For clarity's sake, "Ho" is not a saying that was common in Sanctuary. Instead, it is, shall we say an Aegir-ism. Folks knew and responded in kind, but rarely used it outside of conversation with him.

Aegir shook his head, and rested a hand on the wheel, the other on his hip. "In his defense, his 'real life' has been very different lately."

"Well sure," she said, rolling her eyes. "But he also knows nothing about mine. Did you see the way he was draping his arm around me like he owned me earlier?"

Her friend grimaced. "You mean like he cared about you? Like he could barely stop himself from touching you, you mean? Yes, I did. And I've never seen him like that before, ever."

Lovely, now she got to feel guilty about *that*. "Why are you taking his side? You're *my* friend."

"I'm his friend too, Cat," he said, crossing his arms. "What egregious offense did he commit?"

"He keeps trying to help me with my life, acting like he wants to stick around."

"Oh, I see." Aegir rubbed his chin. "Like he might want a relationship?"

"Yes! Exactly."

"Cat, that sounds like something that should be nice. Am I missing something here?"

"He thinks he can just waltz back into my life and pick up where we left off, with no regard to anything that's happened between."

"As annoying as I know you think that is, I also know he's got good intentions. I've found him to be a man who keeps his word, so if he tells you he wants something, and that he's going to do something, he means it. You ought to give him a chance. He could be good for you. But," he said, stretching tall and looking away."I suppose that's none of my business. What's going on with the two of you is between the two of you. And-"

A growl from her stomach interrupted whatever he was about to say next.

"Do you have any food around here, a kitchen? I can whip something up if you point me in the right direction."

"I was beginning to worry I'd stuck my foot in my mouth," he said."It's below decks. Galleys at the other end of the hall from where your room is. Use whatever you need. I look forward to it. You and your mom have won the solstice cook-off more times than I can count."

"Well, considering I won't have time to prep with her this year, I suppose I should give you two my ideas..." Cat said, heading below decks.

The galley wasn't hard to find. It was small-it was a boat after all-but she found plenty of ingredients. Aegir's mention of her mother twisted in her stomach. She assembled a small pile of supplies, but they all looked disgusting.

She hated the fact that even days away, her mother still had the power to make her feel guilty. After the realization about their letters, any thoughts of her mother *should* fill her with righteous anger. Instead, her guilt weighed on her as she chopped vegetables and dumped them into a pot. Mindlessly, she chopped and scooped, mixed and tasted.

Before she knew it, some sort of *something* was bubbling on the small stove.[2] As was often the case at home, she didn't know what she'd made. While she wasn't currently separating fighting children, or reclaiming balls that had rolled under furniture, the ability to throw something together without thinking still came in handy. Her mother expected her to bring innovative ideas to the meeting every year, but it was really only on nights when Berne and Sirin were over that she had any ability to be creative.

Grabbing a loaf of bread, she slunk into the built-in booth and began slicing it as an accompaniment for whatever it was she'd made. Now, all she had was time and quiet and she'd squandered any hope of being creative because of her stupid mother. When she should have been trying to think about solutions to get through this trip with Torsten.

She'd loved sex with Torsten, but he kept making everything so... complicated. This once,

---

2. The Lady's Revenge, as a steam ship, pumped heat to a cast iron stove, and stayed, when the ship was on, a constant temperature.

why couldn't she have the guy that just wanted to have sex? Sex she could do. Especially sex like *that*.

"Mmm, Aegir, did you suddenly become a better cook? That smells amazing." Torsten popped his head around the corner, his pointed ears wiggling as he sniffed the air."Oh, Cat... I wasn't trying to disturb you. Just thought I could rib Aegir about suddenly being able to cook worth a damn."

Her traitor heart did a little skip at the sight of him. Those little ear movements were dangerously charming.

"It's alright, though I'm sad to tell you that his cooking isn't magically better," she said, tilting her head to express that he might as well come in.

"I'm sorry for storming off..." she said."You didn't deserve that."

Torsten shrugged and ducked into the tiny kitchen, his massive form filling the room."I was kind of a dick about it. What'd you make?"

"I am honestly not sure. You can look if you like." Cat returned to slicing the bread, pointedly avoiding his gaze.

A sharp intake of breath and the sound of the lid slamming back down made her whip her head to look. Torsten turned toward her, eyes squinted shut and his mouth pulled taught.

"Looks like some sort of soup... with dumplings on top. I hope opening the lid doesn't ruin them..." he said, voice strained.

His guilt was admittedly adorable, and the corners of her mouth crept into a smile.

"Don't worry, I think they'll survive. Though, if I made dumplings, I'm not sure what the hell I am doing with this bread," she groaned.

Sliding into the booth across from her, Torsten frowned."You didn't remember you made dumplings? You must be really distracted... someone must be really annoying you."

"Oh, don't be so full of yourself. I was, and I hate to bruise your ego—it had nothing to do with you. I was being a whiny baby about my mother."

"Oh?" He let the question hang in the air, inviting her to elaborate, but not pressing.

"Just the usual, you know, thinking how pathetic it is that I came on this trip to avoid her..."

"Stop it, it's not. It's pathetic the way she treats you. You'd never do that to your kids." Reaching over, he grabbed a slice of bread and began tearing it to shreds.

"Hey! What are you doing? I just cut that!" she shrieked.

Torsten chuckled and grabbed another."I figured you wouldn't take kindly to me holding your hand, so mine need something to do. And, seeing as how you have all this bread cut, I thought we could dry it for bread pudding for breakfast tomorrow. That way, it wasn't a waste, it was prep!"

"Oh," Cat whispered."That's actually helpful...
thank you."

Raising her eyes from where they'd been staring
down the bread, Cat dragged them over Torsten's
hands and arms. Each movement made the
muscles in his thick forearms flex. Transfixed,
Catrin couldn't tear her eyes from the lithe
movements of his hands. How could such massive
hands move so gracefully? He worked with quick
efficiency, each tug pulling at her heart and settling
lower as he built a stack of shreds on the table next
to him.

She looked up to meet his gaze."And what about
your parents? Your sister? How are they?"

Torsten cocked an eyebrow at her when she
changed the subject, but didn't comment on
it."They're good. Ikera was young enough that she's
fit right in with the culture. Ama and Aita are just
glad to be [3] back. They love educating their people
about all of us. I'm... hopeful for these negotiations.
They worked really hard to prepare the emissaries,
and I think we might actually have a chance for a
treaty."

---

3. Ama and Aita are the words for mother and father in

"Us" he said, as if he was from Sanctuary and not the orcish armies.[4] His shoulders had fallen and was refusing to meet her eyes now.

"And well, I whined at you enough the other day about my woes," he finished.

"Mmmm... it must have been hard, not fitting in with your own people, not knowing how to act," she said.

"I caught on. I just-didn't want to... It wasn't me, didn't feel authentic and I think on some level, that grated on people. A few times, other guys would tease that I thought I was better than all of them, that I'd been protecting the enemy. That's how they've thought of Her, the Lady, for a long time."[5] His face was drawn, and the sight of it tugged on her, goading her to make him smile.

"Well surely others were excited to have someone new, someone handsome and big as you?" she said, raising her eyebrows. She quashed the bit of panic

---

4. It should be noted that the orcs do not have a country or even area of Caihalaith that is considered their homeland. Thousands of years of subjugation has resulted in a dispersed people, tied only to their birth village or the one where they settle. As such they previously had no official organization outside of their military structure.

5. I find I cannot fault them for this opinion. In her later writings, our Lady laments how she went about the creation of our world and worries if she's doomed entire peoples. Indeed, her slumber was in part, she says, to remove her influence from the world.

that rose in her chest. Flirting wasn't going to hurt anything. They'd already had sex.

Torsten threw his head back and his laugh shook the table with its force."Oh kitten, thank you for the vote of confidence, but I'm *little* for an orc, my accent is all wrong and I wear glasses when I read. Accent, glasses, reading-any of those things would make me undesirable, but all three was enough to get my pride handed to me on a plate by anyone I had the gall to approach. Thank you for stroking my ego, but to other orcs, I am runty, an unfit warrior, and sound 'annoying' when I speak." He put his fingers up in air quotes when he spoke.

"Orc guys want someone that can give as good as they get when wrestling and ladies want well... not me, I suppose. I can't tell you how many times I struck out or realized in the morning that I was just a quick fuck." He shook his head, chuckling."You might think this is going terribly, kitten, but the fact that you are talking to me again after sleeping with me is a damn good sign as far as I am concerned."

Catrin couldn't believe what he was saying. How could anyone think Torsten, perhaps the most devastatingly handsome man she'd ever seen, was less than gorgeous?

"How... is that even possible? I've been sort of horrible to you."

"If horrible is screaming my name as you come on my cock, I can't wait until you start being nice to me," he said, leaning over the table so his head dimmed the light behind him. Cat could feel her heart beat faster at his nearness. She knew he could *hear* it, that he'd know how he affected her. Luckily, he wasn't the only one with such abilities, and it gratified her to notice that while he might be smiling in that sexy, cocky way, his own heart was racing, too.

"So," he said, not betraying his pulse at all. "I'd say it's going pretty well."

Chapter Ten
Torsten

IN WHICH THINGS GO SHOCKINGLY WELL

"I'M STILL SHOCKED THAT it's going at all," Catrin said, shaking her head. "A week ago, I thought I'd never see you again. A week ago, I would have laughed in your face if you'd told me I'd be on a horse heist with my childhood crush. But here we are, in this strange little bubble of time outside of real life."

Torsten nodded. "We are, that's the point Cat, it's a vacation. We're getting the horses, sure, but it wouldn't kill you to have a little fun..."

His heart was in his throat. It all seemed so much *more* that he'd felt before, like he was putting everything on the line.

"You know, for once, I think I do want to have some fun," she said, looking up to meet his eyes. They were *so* sad, it broke his heart.

"I know I keep cutting you off when you try to talk about real life, and part of me *is* sorry for that. But, I don't want you to promise anything because I'm sick of broken promises. So I'll make you a deal. If you agree to stop talking about what happens after, then I'd like to continue on together, having sex, I mean."

"And after?" he asked, trying to be playful. His heart was trying to beat out of his chest, he'd take any ground she was willing to cede. Because with every inch she gave, she showed him that he meant something.

"If you can't last five seconds without asking about after, then I think we're going to have difficulties with this plan," she joked.

"I'm not asking for forever," Torsten said. "I'm not asking for you to commit to anything. I was asking you to think about it, to be open, to give us a shot. That's all I want." He shook his head, raising his hand to indicate defeat.

"But sure, Cat." he said. "I'll give you your time-away bubble. You can enjoy what it's like to be mine without me bringing up the future. But during that time, you're *mine*. Let me give you your moment away from everything else. Can you do that? Can you give us the rest of this trip to just be together? No expectations, but also no fighting me every damn step of the way."

If all he could have was sex, he'd give her the best fucking sex she'd ever have. She might think she was drawing a boundary, but really, she was giving him the best opening. He'd spoil her pussy and win her heart in the process. It wasn't the tack he'd have liked to take, but he was willing to do whatever was needed.

Because the more time he spent with her, the more sure he became.

"No expectations?" she asked, her voice small.

He wanted to scoop her up and comfort her, but right now, she didn't want sweet, she wanted a good, firm fucking.

"And no fighting," he reminded, nodding.

"Then, yes, let's do it," she surprised him by moving around the table and flinging her arms around him. Was she really so blind to how perfect they were together? The second she let her guard down everything just clicked. He nuzzled into her hair, pulling her close and breathing her in.

"That's my girl, kitten."

I F TORSTEN THOUGHT WAKING up with Catrin on his chest was the best wake up he'd ever had, it was nothing to waking up with her between his legs. For a moment, he registered a distinct lack of warmth on his left side, and movement near his legs. When he cracked an eye, he saw Catrin kneeling down and gently unlacing his trousers. Her eyes were wide and mischievous, her face flushed. Her perfect pink tongue licked her full bottom lip, a devious smile appearing in its wake.

He wasn't certain where she was going with this, but he *was* certain he'd enjoy it. Considering she was going to such trouble to be sneaky, he closed his eyes and pretended to be asleep. To keep his cock from swelling in anticipation, he started working through a mental inventory of his blacksmithing tools.

Double faced sledge hammer, lump hammer, ball peen-nope not that one-flat tongs... With his eyes closed, he was keenly aware of the small tugs of his laces, and the quiet noises Catrin made.

Clamping his lips together, Torsten suppressed a gasp as Catrin's hands hefted his flaccid cock. In seconds, she'd sucked him completely inside her mouth. She rolled his pliable length around her tongue, ringing a moan from him. It was only seconds until he was fully hard, but for those few brief moments, she'd been able to take all of him into her mouth.

His growing length forced her back, but she didn't let up the pleasure she was lavishing on him. Grasping the base of him, she swirled her tongue around his head. Her exquisite tongue toyed with his piercings, the tiny movements sending jolts through him. For a few seconds, he was drowning in pleasure, in the feel of her. He groaned, letting her know he was awake, and she let out the most decadent giggle.

"Fuck kitten, you're good at that," he gasped out. "You suck my cock like you're starving."

Looking down at her, between his legs, gorgeous arse lifted in the air, she was everything he'd ever imagined, and more than he deserved. Increasing the suction, she tugged his foreskin over his cockhead, trapping his piercings inside. She stroked her tongue over them, each swipe undoing him. Over and over she teased him, winding him up and bringing him closer to the edge.

"You feel so good, Cat, you're-" he cut off, he couldn't say everything that he wanted.

You're all I've ever wanted. You're every wet dream I've ever had. I might not have known that until recently, but you're everything I've ever hoped for.

The thoughts sobered him. If he ever wanted to say any of that to her, he needed to prove to her that he was worth the risk, which he wasn't going to do lying on his back and letting her do all the work.

"Come here," he said, leaning down and pulling her up to him, ravishing her mouth as if he could steal a piece of her heart if only he could find it. Once she was breathless he pulled away to work his way down her body. "You're so fucking sweet with the taste of my cock on your tongue. But I know what will taste even better..."

Latching on to a nipple, he pulled the taught bead inside, swirling and tugging on it. He kneaded her other breast, glorying in how its heft filled and overflowed his large hands. She was fucking exquisite, every inch of her was made to be squeezed and massaged, every surface of her yielded to him perfectly.

Working lower, he pressed his fingers into her hips, smiling at the dimples they made.

Better than I imagined. He nuzzled his nose into her soft tuft of hair, whispering against her, "This is the altar where I worship. *This* is where I kneel."

Running his tongue through her swollen lips, he lapped her up, the bright, tangy taste of her flaring through him. Yes, this was exactly where he was meant to be, and he'd convince her of that with each stroke of his tongue.

Catrin squirmed under him, letting out sighs that made his cock twitch beneath him. He could almost see it now, an image starting to coalesce. Catrin, laughing as he chased her through her house, taking her on the kitchen table. He'd pump her so full of his seed that she'd swell. She'd be so gorgeous, round and filled.

"Torsten-please!" she yelled. He latched onto her clit with vigor, sucking and prodding it with his tongue. She was exquisite like this, writhing and flushed, the sheen of sweat glistening over her chest.

"Yes, Torsten," called Aegir's voice, accompanied by a loud banging."Do hurry up, some people have work to be about."

"Aaah!" Catrin shrieked, covering her face with her hands. Adorable.

"You're just mad it's not you, mate!" Torsten called. He tugged Catrin's hands from her face and smiled reassuringly.

"I've had to listen to him fuck plenty of times, he can stand it for a few days."

Catrin bit her lip, nodding, but still clearly nervous.

"He's just being a dick," Torsten called so Aegir would be sure to hear it. He responded by stomping up the stairs, so Catrin would know they had some level of privacy.

"See? There we are," he whispered, tracing his hand along her jaw. He grabbed her drawers and balled them up so she could bite down on them.

"Here, if you're worried about making noise, you can scream into this." He held it near her mouth, an offering, not a command. Catrin blushed, and looked a bit embarrassed, but opened her mouth nonetheless. She clamped onto it, giving a small test squeal, and smiling around the gag.

"Perfect," Torsten praised, kissing down her plush stomach to return to his work. In short order, she was back to making muffled cries and bucking against his face. She dug her hands into his hair, crushing his face to her and he loved every second of it. She tensed beneath him, chanting something into the fabric. In seconds, her body bowed off the bed. She collapsed back down, sprawling out. After a few seconds of recovery she reached a shaky hand out to him.

"Do you want something, kitten?" he teased, running his finger through her slick folds, dipping the tip of his finger inside. She nodded frantically, gods he loved her like this."Do you feel empty? You need my thick orc cock to fill you up? You'll have it, then."

He pressed into her, hissing at the flawless feel of her around him, the deep, penetrating heat that filled him. He dragged in and out, watching her face shift in pleasure.

I could stare at her like this forever.

He ground the piercing at the base of his cock into her clit and in seconds, she was squeezing him. The pulsing ripples of her orgasm milked his own from him and as the sensation overwhelmed him, he pushed harder, and his knot entered and stuck.

He gritted his teeth and growled as he fucked her through it, succumbing to the base desire to fill her full of his seed and trap it there so it could take. Bracing himself on his elbows, he placed a tender kiss on her forehead, shifting a hand to pull the drawers from her mouth.

"Well that was the best fucking wakeup I've ever had," he said, his cheeks aching from how broadly he smiled.

"Me too," Catrin whispered."Me too."

THEY SPENT A FAIR bit of their travel time holed up in their cabin, idling away the hours naked, but Torsten also took time to talk to Catrin about horses and their tack. She was marginally familiar with it all from the books she'd read, but the drawings he made for her helped.[1] They talked through options of what might happen, but really, the actual "horse liberation" part of the plan was the weakest link. They didn't know anything

---

[1]. While it didn't much come up during this excursion, it was interesting to me to see, upon their return, the differences between the saddles Torsten knew. Saddles in Caihalaith have a knob or pommel that fits between the rider's legs and are generally much larger and more ornate.

about the stables or their location. Nor anything about what they could expect in terms of guards or stablehands. They had some sleeping powder from Arndis, which she could administer in a drink, and they thought they'd have the best luck getting the horses out at night.

Otherwise, the plan relied on Catrin's quick thinking. She still didn't seem entirely comfortable with being the sole rescuer, but it was imperative Torsten not be seen, so he tried to reassure her whenever he could. He hated not being able to plan in advance, but Torsten had developed a mantra for her: *get in, find the stables, find the horses, make a plan, execute the plan.*

He showed her what he knew of lockpicking, but they were in agreement that a better option would be to steal any keys she would need.[2] They prepared where they could, and spent some time above deck, but seeing as they wouldn't have a bed again for the rest of the trip, they made the most of the facilities whenever possible. By the time Aegir pulled the boat to moor off the coast of an island, they'd settled into an easy rapport. His hissing kitten had mellowed under his attentions, and he loved seeing how she blossomed at ease.

---

2. Torsten also *graciously* taught all of our children lockpicking which didn't prove much of a problem until they began their training at the Citadel.

Chapter Eleven
Catrin

IN WHICH OUR HEROINE
BLENDS SEAMLESSLY INTO
HUMAN SOCIETY

THEY READIED TO DISEMBARK, as Aegir would bring them to the mainland via a rowboat. After dropping anchor, he stripped and dove into the water. Catrin felt as if she had bees buzzing in her stomach, she was about to set foot in the Compact of Nations! The farthest settlement north, sure, but, to her, they were mythical lands she thought she'd never see.[1]

"Hop in, I'll get you to shore faster than you can blink!" he called from the water, his legs shifting to fuse into a tail.

"I'll go first," Torsten said, smirking at Cat. He scurried down the rope, looking up in time to watch her.

"The view from here is gorgeous!" he called up at her, miming grabbing her ass. As soon as she was within reaching distance, his hands were on her, gliding up the sides of her thighs to cup the full globes of her ass.

"Here, let me help you," he said, wrapping around her waist and lowering her into the boat so that her body slid down his.

Catrin blushed in anticipation of what they could get up to now that they wouldn't have an audience again.

"When you're quite finished," Aegir called from the water."We can get you to land so you can fuck where I don't have to hear it."

---

1. To the people of Sanctuary, the Compact of Nations was often treated as one large country and regarded as such. The fact that it is a coalition of nations was astounding to them. As such, neither Catrin or Torsten realized that they were in the country of Norden for their entire journey and referred to it exclusively as the Compact.

Cat turned away, giggling and blushing. She *had* tried to be quiet, it was just that Torsten seemed to take her silence as a personal challenge.

"Like I haven't had to listen to you fuck your way through every race of the entire Empire. You can listen to me getting some for once!" Torsten said between guffaws.

"I was doing my job," Aegir said, placing a hand over his heart. "Someone had to gather biological samples on all of those peoples! Now sit your arse down or you'll be thrown out when I start."

Aegir hadn't been joking about his speed. Catrin was immediately reminded of when Ingrid had propelled them through the canals of Sanctuary.

I wonder what they are up to... She'd been away a week now, and missed them terribly. They often spent time with Sirin and Berne, and had sleepovers almost every week, but she'd never been away from them for so long.

I hope they miss me. Her chest tightened with the worry that they might not.

"What's wrong, kitten, you look upset." Torsten's brow was furrowed, his strong brow casting a shadow over his eyes.

"Just missing the girls, worrying about them is all," Catrin said, waving her hand as if it were nothing.[2] While she thought of them constantly, she'd done a good job so far of hiding her melancholy."It's silly because they're with Berne and Sirin all the time, so I'm sure they are having a good time and are well taken care of. There's no reason for me to worry."

"Ach, they are, but of course you're still going to worry. I'd worry if you didn't worry! You worry because you're a good mother." He tucked a strand of hair behind her ear, kissing her on the forehead tenderly."I'm sure they are missing you just as much as you're missing them."

"Thanks, but I don't think that's possible. I'll take them missing me almost as much though," she said, tilting her head up to catch his lips in a kiss.

For the first time, Torsten's kiss didn't set a fire in Catrin's veins. She didn't immediately want to climb into his lap and grind herself on his cock. Her pulse didn't speed, nor did she feel every stitch of her clothing. Instead, the kiss settled something in her. She wasn't immediately unbothered about missing her girls, but Torsten validated her worries, and his gentle touch soothed them into something more manageable.

---

2. Although Catrin missed them terribly throughout the journey, I only touch on it when their absence is relevant to the trip or relationship development so as not to confuse the narrative.

Within moments, Torsten shifted their kiss and Catrin was on fire once more. She squirmed in her seat, knowing that she really couldn't do more than enjoy his mouth while Aegir was there.

After minutes or hours, she had no real idea, they bumped against the shore and Aegir popped his head out of the water, coughing.

"Alright, last stop. All sweethearts off the boat before I cast up my lunch," he said, rocking the boat so that they tipped toward shore.

"Hey! That's my sweetheart that you are talking about there!" Torsten said, trying to peel his friend's fingers from the edge of the boat.

Aegir looked over Torsten's shoulder to Catrin."Cat, can you get this moon–eyed boy out of my sight? I knew as soon as he fell he'd be pathetic, but this is just sad."

Torsten reached down and splashed a wave of water into Aegir's face."Like you'll be any better? You can play the swarthy rake all you want, but I know you are going to fall flat on your face when you meet the right person."[3]

They disembarked and in short order, Catrin had her pack strapped back on and she and Torsten were hiking into the woods.

---

3. Do not fret, dear reader, for Aegir's story is already being penned. Coincidentally, it also takes place primarily in lands held by the Pathian Empire.

"From here on out, we'll need to be careful that you aren't seen. Berne says here that we should be in Pershing by tomorrow," Cat said, consulting the map he'd given them.

"It feels itchy, needing to stay hidden," Torsten said."I'm not used to this. Aegir's the sneaky one."

"I know, but I also doubt you want to be the one to alert the entire continent to the rest of the world. I imagine it would end with you in shackles somewhere." Cat smirked at him. The image of him in shackles wasn't entirely unappealing.

"True," he said, tilting his head to the side."But are we sure no one would buy that I am just a lunologist that loves experimenting with skin color?"

Catrin's shoulders shook with laughter as she ducked through the increasingly thick vegetation."I'm not sure... Do you think that's even possible?"

"You'd have to tell me. Last I checked, you were the only lunologist in this forest."

"I don't know.[4] I've never tried. I feel strange about even putting on my costume for the tavern, let alone changing how I look like that."

"You have a costume?"

"Of course, Sirin didn't dress like us when she first moved to Sanctuary. I will stick out if I don't blend in."

"Oh, well I look forward to seeing it."

A FTER A DAY AND a half of hiking through the woods, they arrived outside of Pershing. Cat pulled her costume out of her pack and began dressing. She put on a skirt and shirt, and a very tight vest–like garment that did magical things to her breasts. That done, she stood with her hands on her hips, showing it off to Torsten.

---

4. While possible, it would require a concerted effort and study. I don't know of anyone who has specifically done so, but I suspect that using a sample from an orc the way the Shades of Sanctuary do for their animal forms would be the best bet. All that being said, the layperson's impression of what is possible with lunology vastly overrates what is actually possible, so I assume most people would guess he was a lunologist rather than an entirely "new" race.

"That's your costume?" he asked, eyebrow raised. His eyes roamed over her, a predatory smile dawning on his face.

"Yes, of course," Cat said, fiddling with the low neckline. She'd done a good deal of research for this costume so she didn't understand why he was looking at her so strangely.

"Kitten, is that really how people down here dress? It seems... cold."

She shivered. Sirin had, of course, worn more conservative clothing when she'd first moved to Sanctuary, but she'd been hiking through the Arctic. Cat had seen her sister-in-law's chemises, and they were just like this one. A few books had confirmed that Sirin's more flexible short stays were for rigorous activity and that day to day, folks wore more structured undergarments. Cat wished she could have discussed her clothing with Sirin, but that would have given away the whole plan. Instead, she'd contented herself with several books that described the clothing worn by ladies in taverns.[5]

The top of her breasts were pushed nearly to her chin, and formed a shelf that she was certain she could carry one of those books on.

---

5. As you might have surmised, these were works of fiction. Having seen this outfit, it is the most wonderfully stereotypical outfit that you or I would imagine being worn by a "tavern wench."

"It is a bit cold, but I'm not going to be outside all day. This is obviously an indoor outfit. I'll just pop into the tavern that Berne mentioned and see if I can't hear any news about Sirin. If they have people looking for her, I think we'll have a much harder time getting the horses out than we thought."

Torsten wrapped her cloak around her shoulders.

"Well, if that's what people wear, then I suppose I won't complain about the amazing view," he said, running a thick finger over the tops of her cleavage. "If you're comfortable, I'm comfortable." He bit his lip, and caught her eyes with his. "I will say, there's something very exciting knowing that a roomful of people are going to see you like this and want you. That whoever is going to be in that tavern is going to see you on display like this. The whole place will be filled with people wishing they knew what those lips or those gorgeous tits taste like, but I am the only one who'll know."

He pressed her back against a tree, diving in to ravish her mouth with a seeking kiss. His hands roamed over her body, skimming over her curves and crushing her against his stiff cock.

"I didn't realize that was something you were into," Cat gasped when he moved to devour her neck.

"Nor I," he said. "Though I'm finding it very compelling at the moment."

She couldn't deny that his words had ignited within her. They dripped through her, liquifying and warming her until she was malleable straight through.

"Mmm, it's a shame you won't be able to be there, to see people watch me, or to hear what they say."

Torsten pulled back from her neck, eyes boring into her. "I don't know, with a cape I might be able to wait outside, at least hear what is said, and…" he said, sobering. "That way I will hear if there is any trouble. I'm not going to try to reveal my people's existence to the world, but if you are in trouble? Well kitten, I can't be held accountable for my actions. I'd alert them to the existence of the whole bloody Empire if it would keep even a single scratch from your body."

"Would you now?" Catrin asked, unable to keep the laugh from her voice. When her eyes roamed his face though, he didn't seem to be joking.

"I would."

"Oh." It was such a silly response, entirely unsuited for the monumental statement he'd just made, but she was having trouble grasping the enormity of it. It strayed far too close to things they'd decided not to speak of. Too close to real and lasting feelings. So, she did the only thing that seemed reasonable, she pushed him away.

Catrin brushed her skirts and raised an eyebrow at him. "Well, if you are coming you'd better get a cloak on and control yourself. I'd hate to have to explain the situation to anyone. 'Oh, well we were just going to steal back my sister-in-law's horses when a man bumped me in the street and Torsten disemboweled him.'"

Torsten smirked, one of his canines peeking out behind his tusk.

Sweet Lady, he's gorgeous. I am well and truly in the suds, aren't I?

Catrin turned and began walking away. She was drowning in him, and had no idea how to pull herself out. This was just fun, and she needed to keep it that way. As soon as she was home, and didn't need to smell him all the time, didn't have to watch his back flex under his shirt or drool over his forearms as he prepared the fire, she'd be able to turn him down. Returning home would set her to rights and out of the haze of his pull, she'd be able to think clearly enough to end things. Her children relied on her, and as bad as a breakup would be for her, it would be truly horrible for her children if they got attached.

Torsten's laugh floated through the forest after her, tickling her spine and making her shiver. He was too much, but her resolve only needed to last a few more days. In a few days, it would all be over, and she could go back to her life.

Her quiet, cozy, normal life, which was just how she liked it. She didn't need a partner. She'd made it this far with her support system, and she was raising two amazing, beautiful children just fine. Never mind that she cried herself to sleep some nights, worrying that she wasn't doing enough for them. Never mind the fact that she'd go over to her brother's house to see Sirin just to be held by someone, to have someone stroke her hair and assure her she was doing everything she could.

Behind her, she could hear him hastily picking up the gear he'd dropped when she'd stopped to change. "Cat, kitten, hold on a moment, I know you're eager to get there, but if you'd wait but a moment-"

"If you want to come, you need to hurry, you've worried me with all of your 'burn the world to save me from a scratch' talk. I'm not keen on being arrested," she called back at him.

Within moments the blasted man was jogging up next to her, his hands concealed in gloves and his large body encased in a thick cloak. Dressed as he was, he could have been just a large man, though she worried he might be a bit too large to be believable.

"Perhaps you should slouch. I don't know that I've ever met a human man as big as you."

"And you aren't likely to, either," he said, flashing her a cheeky grin from underneath his hood.

"Oh, get off it, Tor. You know what I meant!"

"I did, but you *also* know what *I* meant, and you didn't say I was wrong, either." The infuriating man sauntered ahead of her, shaking his butt with every step.

Catrin growled and stomped after him. How dare he be so cute and funny?

T HE CONSTERNATED CROW SAT near the outer wall, and Torsten was easily able to boost Cat over and climb it after her once the sun had set. It was apparently close enough to the wall that they didn't need to go traipsing through the whole city, but far enough away to make Catrin nervous. Soon after sunset, the lunula-lamps lit the streets, bathing them in their blue-green glow.[6]

Between the hood and the tint, Torsten didn't stick out near as much as Catrin thought he might. The real issue, she realized, as they wove through

---

6. Many northern towns opt for lunula lanterns over gas lamps on streets. While the lunula in other areas would be far too dear to waste, the people of Pershing need only sift it from the river. As such, it is cheaper to do periodic maintenance on lanterns filled with lunula suspended in water rather than pay for lamplighters as are employed in other settlements.

the end of day trickle of townspeople, was how massive he was.

"Could you stoop a little more? I worry that you're going to stick out because you're so big," she whispered.

Next to her Torsten snickered, which then built to a giggle. "I told you-"

Catrin reeled on him, grabbing the front of his cloak to pull him down.

"Oh you think that's funny, do you? You're going to get us both captured and maybe even killed if you don't pull it together. Now get down here and stop giggling like you're twelve."

Torsten reined in his laughter, his laughs fading to faint gasps. Stooping down next to her, Torsten grasped her hand and tugged her in the direction Berne had indicated.

Just as he'd said, The Consternated Crow was situated in a quiet section of town. Her eyes darted through the dim settlement, careful to avoid anyone's eyes. As luck would have it, Catrin was able to see a horse in real life where it was tied up in front. She studied it for a moment, trying to memorize its scent and the way its tack fit. Torsten didn't let her linger though, because they'd look suspicious standing next to a stranger's horse. Instead, he pulled her away and into a back alley.

"I want you to be careful, you hear me?" he said, brushing a gloved thumb over her lip.

Catrin pushed down the excited flip in her stomach and jerked her head in a nod.

"Of course, I'll get in, see what I can find out, and be out before you know it. If I'm lucky a few folks will ogle me a bit." She went up on tiptoes to kiss him. "I'll be back before you know it, just... act natural."

Torsten leaned with one foot propped back against the wall, his arms crossed in front of him, hood pulled low. Catrin shook her head and walked away.

*L*ADY, *HELP THAT MAN* **remain unnoticed,** she pleaded.

The outside of the Consternated Crow was immediately welcoming. Its windows were frosted over in the chill air, and the warm glow of a fire flickered through them. Music rolled out the front door, wrapping her in warmth as she stepped through the heavy wooden door.

Inside, the room was full of laughing people, who, Cat realized, almost all had colored hair. Here, only the elderly had white hair, which made her twirl one of her own white-curls around a finger, worried that she'd stick out. A few people looked up at her when she walked in, but most went about their own conversations.

Behind the bar, the kind innkeeper Berne had mentioned waved her over. Either she was extremely perceptive, or Catrin really looked that lost. As she threaded her way through the crowd, she felt eyes draw over her, saw interested tilts of lips, and even heard an appreciative hum.

She'd never been away from home, known no one who hadn't known her as a child or seen her with mud covering her face other than Edrigu. She'd mused, during nights spent alone in her bed, when she was at her most vulnerable, if that was her problem. Perhaps she'd latched onto Edrigu so strongly because they hadn't already known everything about one another. It had been exciting getting to discover someone new, to have someone to discover her.

Across the room, a man licked his lips at her, sending a flush from her hairline to the exposed tops of her breasts. She winked at him, confidence thrumming through her, lightening her step. The man leaned over to the person next to him and whispered in their ear. The two chuckled together, their eyes never leaving her. The man stopped a server who was walking by and nodded to Catrin. The server shook his head and moved to leave.

Catrin quickened her step toward the bar. She was fine with looking and even a bit of a flirt, but she didn't like the hungry way his gaze had shifted.

"Hello darlin', what can I get for ya?" the innkeeper said, wiping out a mug. She was a bit shorter than Cat, and the stripes of white at her temples calmed Cat's nerves a bit. Those tiny stripes of home felt like a lifeline pulling her back to safety.

"Oh gosh, I couldn't even begin to tell yeh, what do yeh have?"[7]

"Well, we've got a nice roast this evening," the kind-faced innkeeper said. She continued speaking, rattling off different foods, but Catrin ignored it in favor of listening to the surrounding room. Her instincts prickled as the attitude in the room seemed to shift around her. She wished she had her rabbit ears so that she could swivel them toward different speakers. Instead, she caught bits of conversation. A woman tittering here, a derogatory word there. A deep voice describing in lurid detail what he would like to do with her breasts.

The flush she'd felt drained from her face and her instincts drove her to shift. She shivered with the discomfort of resisting it. Her eyes darted from side to side, uncomfortable with being faced away

---

7. As Catrin is now speaking English, her accent has surfaced.

from most of the guests. When she looked back to the innkeeper, the woman's eyes were wide and her smile gentle as she waited for an answer. Apparently, her list of what was available was done.

"I'll take the pasties and some beer, if yeh please."

"Of course, darlin'. Of course. I'll have it right for you." The tavern keeper walked away from the bar, through a door which would presumably lead to a kitchen. What little comfort she'd given Catrin evaporated with her. Catrin shrunk in on herself, pulling her shoulders in to be as small as possible.

She felt him before she saw him. Her rabbit shivered inside of her.

"What is a sweet morsel like yourself doing here all alone? You look like you could do with the protector, little lady," he drawled. The man's accent was similar to Sirin's, and his words took a moment to filter through her brain. They sounded to Catrin as if he had marbles in his mouth.

The words of their language stumbled out of Catrin's mouth, thick and cloying. "I'm in no need of a protector, thank yeh. I can take care of meself just fine."

She'd thought this would be fun. She thought she'd flirt with a stranger and then flit back to the safety of Torsten's embrace. Speaking with this man, however, felt unsafe and slimy.

With a smooth subtlety, the man snaked his hand to her arm, and before she even realized, he was tracing circles under her forearm. Catrin snatched her arm away, clutching it to her breast, and bored into him with her eyes. She used the look that she used on her girls when they were in trouble, hoping he'd read her admonishment and leave her alone.

Instead, the man chuckled, twirling his mustache and raking his eyes over her in a way that made her feel slimy.

"Oh, a little feisty, I see. I like them with a little fight in them. Let's get some booze into you and see if you aren't a bit more amenable. Because you're all alone, darlin', and every man in here would like nothing more than to take a bite out of you. You may not think you need a protector, but I'm telling you it's only a matter of time before you get yourself into a situation."

His hand pressed into the small of her back and she jumped away from it, feeling like she had bugs coating her skin. In backing up, she bumped into another person.

Shit. They'd boxed her in, and she'd allowed it. Between the two, the rank smell of their alcohol laden breath invaded her nostrils, and the world pressed in on her. The sounds of the tavern overwhelmed her ears, the sharp laughter of the patrons rolling over her in waves. She momentarily dampened her hearing, but instead of helping, it just made her hare feel pinned down. Her animal instincts rebelled against ignoring stimuli. That was how she stayed safe.

The man behind her grasped her arm in a bruising grip. Eyes darting frantically, Catrin searched the room. Some people were purposefully avoiding looking at her, though others watched and chuckled at her predicament.

"Listen, arseholes, I don't know what yeh think you're doing, but yeh need to take your hands off me right now." Catrin kept her voice cold and steady.

"Or what... little lady?" the first man sneered.

"Oh Eliza, there you are!" a voice called out. A tall, muscular woman wrested Catrin bodily away from the men and into a hug. "Just play along," she whispered.

The woman's hug was so welcome Catrin thought she might cry from relief.

"I've been looking all over for you, but you know me. I got the name of the tavern wrong and then I ran into a few people. I'm sorry I was late. Now, let's get our drink. Gentlemen, I'm sure you wouldn't mind giving us your seats?" she said, flexing her neck and setting a hand casually on a dagger at her hip.

The two men scowled and made what Catrin assumed must be a rude gesture. One spit on the floor as they walked away.

"You aren't from around here," said her rescuer.

"What do yeh mean?" Cat asked, feigning ignorance."I live not far from here."

"Be that as it may, I haven't seen you around, and neither has anyone else I reckon. Trust me, looking like that, I'd remember you. Pardon my question, but are you looking for company tonight? I'd gladly take you up on it if you are, but your body language right this moment is telling me that was not your intention."

"Um, n–no, that wasn't my intent. I suppose, well, I was actually trying to blend in?"

"In that getup?" The woman asked, eyes wide and incredulous."Oh sweetheart, I don't think that's possible. That outfit is *designed* to be the exact opposite of 'blending in.'"

"But I thought —" Catrin looked around the room, this time, paying attention to the women. There were a few showing some skin, but most wore high–necked blouses. Indeed, the woman next to her was buttoned up, almost to her chin, and she wore pants. Nearly the exact opposite of Catrin.

"I'm assuming, based on the set of your shoulders, that you are receiving attention that you didn't plan on—"

"No, not quite. I thought it was attractive, to be sure. I suppose I didn't realize people might see it as an invitation. It certainly *feels* like some people are taking it as an invitation."

"Judging by the proprietary way some of these folks are looking at you, and the way others are looking at you like they'd like to sink their teeth into you, I think that's a fair assumption. They've no right to. I'm not saying it's right. I just think folk aren't used to seeing such outfits."

"They aren't? I thought, well—" Catrin said."I thought this was, erm, traditional dress in this area."

Tugging on her shirtsleeve, Catrin grimaced.

"Oh stop," the woman said, waving her hand."Don't worry about it. Now that I'm with you folks'll leave you alone."

The innkeeper returned, plopping a heaping plate in front of Cat. The pasties glistened appealingly, accompanied by a crusty roll still steaming from the oven.

"I'm El and this is Marta, proprietress of the Consternated Crow," the woman said, waving at the adorable innkeeper.[8] "What brings you in, all alone?"

"Honestly, two things. First, I've heard wonderful things about the food, and I'm also looking for a

---

8. As soon as Berne heard El's role in this story, he began animatedly regaling us with stories of their nights drinking together. Apparently, they are old friends who have an ongoing rivalry over who can drink more. Of course, Berne can burn his off with lunula, but he says it would ruin the fun, so he plays fair.

friend. It seems no one has heard of her in a long time, but I think she might have passed through."

"Oh, well, we see a lot of folks, but we can see if we remember her," Marta said."What does she look like? When would she have come through?"

"It would have been a little over a year ago now, so a fair time ago, but she'd be distinctive around these parts. She's about my height, has long dark brown hair and deeper skin. She's from an island off the southern coast, so I doubt you see too many of her people up this far."

A sad look came over Marta's face as Catrin described Sirin."Oh darling," she breathed."I'm so sorry. I remember her. Folk came by from the Citadel looking for her a few days later, came back a week later saying they'd found her dead. I am so terribly sorry, my darling."

Cat gasped, clapping a hand over her mouth. Relief flooded through her, but she played it off as grief. She tapped her lunula to trigger herself to cry."Oh, my gosh, could yeh maybe pack my food for the road? I just think I need to be alone."

"Oh, of course dear, let me get that all wrapped up for you." Marta said, pulling the plate back and wrapping the hand pie and cheese."You aren't traveling alone, dear, are you? That's how your poor friend was lost, you know? She went off on her own...."

"No, no. I've got my erm... well no, I'm not alone." Cat blushed. It was silly, really, she could have just said friend, but Torsten felt like more than a friend. He certainly wasn't her... anything else, but calling him her friend felt disingenuous.

Marta chucked."Well, you make sure your *friend* takes care of you tonight," Marta said."You've had quite the shock, and I don't like letting you leave so suddenly. They're close? Your friend?"

"Yes, he just needed to get some uh..."

"It's alright dear, you don't need to make up something on my account. Folk aren't always up to activities that are easily spoken about and you're a terrible liar." Marta handed her a package of food and clasped Catrin's hand."I am so very sorry about your friend, my dear. Please be safe."

"I will, thank yeh kindly for everything. How much do I owe yeh?" Cat took some of their money out of her purse, hoping she remembered the names for each denomination.

"I'll not tell you of the death of a friend and take your money. El here will see you safe to the door. We don't want anyone else getting any strange notions of how to be friendly."

Catrin squeezed Marta's hand and thanked her. El led her out to the front of the bar, pausing at the door.

"Are you going to be all right out there? I don't want anyone else bothering you..."

"Don't worry about me, my friend is close by. I'll be extremely safe in moments, I promise. Thank yeh for all of your help."

"Course, it's nothing more than what Marta pays me for, but if you want to get a drink next time you are passing through, I wouldn't say no..." She smiled and winked in a way that gave Cat the impression that it wasn't an advance, just a friendly invitation.

"I'll look yeh up next time."

"Be safe out there."

"I will."

Chapter Twelve
Torsten

IN WHICH A RISK IS TAKEN, A REALIZATION MOST PROFOUND, AND A QUIET EVENING

SECONDS AFTER THE OTHER woman stopped speaking, Catrin appeared around the corner. Torsten swept her up in his arms and buried his face in her curls. Her warmth seeped through his clothing, calming him just enough to keep him from barging into the tavern.

"If that woman hadn't come up, I was about to burst through that door and knock some heads in. I'm sorry that happened to you, kitten. I should have been there with you. I should've protected you better."

"Damn, I forget your hearing is as good as mine," she whispered, stroking his hair.

"I couldn't even understand what they were saying," he said into her hair, breathing deep to reassure himself that she was real. "But I've heard that tone of voice before and I didn't like it even a tiny bit. I was holding on to my nerves by the barest of threads."

Catrin brushed a hair off of his forehead, her smooth small fingers caressing his skin. "I'm fine, I was fine, I promise."

Torsten nuzzled back into her hair, crushing her against his chest.

"If anything ever happened to you, I'd never forgive myself, kitten," he whispered, kissing the top of her head. She was safe in his arms, and he said a silent prayer to the Lady in thanks. They didn't talk much, but he'd be grateful for her protection, now.

"Tor, I'm fine, I promise." Catrin pulled back to smile at him. He'd never get tired of her smile.

"I don't want you to be fine," he whispered to her, running his nose up her neck. "I want you better than fine. I want you to be amazing, resplendent, joyful. Or, better yet, I want you exhausted, languid and content."

Torsten loomed over her, caging her gorgeous body against the building. Catrin giggled, biting her luscious lip.

"Well, that could always be arranged..." she whispered.

"It could, could it?" Torsten grasped a thick thigh, hoisting it in his palm, and pressing her against the building so she could feel this erection against her core.

"Mmmhmmm," she hummed."As long as that's something you still want."

"Lady's sake, Cat, I don't think I'll ever stop wanting that. Maybe..." He quirked his eyebrow and devoured her with his eyes. She was so lush, every bit of her filled his hands."Maybe what you really need is to be reminded who you belong to?"

Tongue darting out to moisten her lips, Catrin's eyes dilated and her chest heaved.

"I just might need that." Her voice was breathless, and the heat in her cheeks was unreasonably sexy.

Torsten leaned in, pressing his forehead against hers, the scent of her arousal thick in the air between them.

"You want me to fuck you in this alley?" He growled into her ear."Make you scream so all of those idiots inside know you're more than cared for?"

Catrin's breath came fast, her eyes flicking to the sides of the alley."Please."

Her blush ran down over the tops of her delectable breasts, the cool night air making her shiver as tiny beads of sweat collected there.

Torsten licked his lips, leaning down to taste the sweat on the tops of them.

"Delectable," he whispered. She tasted like warm days in the sun rather than chill nights in a back alley. Though, all things considered, a chill back alley night wasn't anything to complain about. In fact, with her warm and pliable under his fingers, he couldn't think of anywhere he'd rather be.

Catrin's lip trembled, and it occurred to him it was a damn shame that her lips weren't already swollen from his kisses. He caught her plump lower lip between his, sucking and laving at it, sliding his tongue inside to plunder her mouth.

His people had a reputation for pillaging, but she was the only treasure he meant to covet. Sliding his hand up her thigh, he squeezed, earning a gasp. Catrin writhed against him, already bucking to seek the friction of his cock.

"Patience, love," he purred. "We'll be quick, but we aren't in *that* much of a rush."

Catrin's head fell back against the tavern wall.

Lady, she's beautiful. The blue-green light of the lunula-lanterns reflected at him, lending her an ethereal quality that elevated her beyond a mere woman. Here, she was the goddess's own avatar, something divine to be worshiped.

Torsten slid his thick fingers along the leg of her split drawers and up to her folds, sliding inside to her already swollen clit. He devoured her throat, sucking kisses along its length and growling into her ear."Already so wet for me. You're *always* wet for me, aren't you, precious? This needy little pussy knows what she wants, and it's always me. She wants my thick cock plugging her up, shooting my cum into her and nothing else will do."

When are you going to see that I was made to fill you? When will you see that yours is the only cunt I ever want to fill?

His mind flooded with the image of her, belly swollen with his child, their other two children, Ingrid and Ursule, climbing over him. He could imagine it so easily, how he'd fit into their life, how he'd help her and she'd give him something to live for again. All he needed was to get her through this trip and she'd see. She'd see how they needed each other, how their lives were so perfectly matched to intertwine that he refused to believe it wasn't orchestrated by the Lady's own hand.

Right now, all he was allowed was her body. Her mind and her heart were closed to him, so he was determined to play her body as an instrument, to win her heart by exhausting her mind with pleasure until she couldn't think of any more ridiculous objections.

In fairness, he allowed, they weren't *entirely* ridiculous. She'd been left, over and over, initially by him. He didn't know how he could prove to her he *wouldn't* leave her, but the only option available to him at present was overwhelming her with pleasure.

He swirled a finger around her clit, applying pressure and luxuriating in the sounds she made. He heard each squeak, each whine as a small victory, a sign that he was proving how much he wanted her.

Her small, frantic hands unbuckled his belt and his cock sprung free, eager for whatever attention she chose to lavish on it. She wasn't, it seemed, in any mood to faff about. She bucked herself against his hand and wrapped her fingers around him, sliding from root to tip.

His body coursed with adrenaline, the threat of being found speeding his heart. It was thrilling, but he knew their time was limited. Grabbing Cat under the ass, he lifted her against the wall and lowered her onto his cock.

She moaned obscenely, and he shifted a hand to cover her mouth. He loved her sounds, but didn't fancy spending the night in jail because of them.

"Ssssh, kitten," he whispered into her ear. "We don't want someone hauling me away from you just when things are getting good."

He lifted her up, pumping her on his cock. Catrin wrapped her legs around his back, the heels of her boots digging into his ass. Days of fucking had made it easy for him to slide inside, and he'd made a perfect home for himself there. When they were like this, everything felt right, everything clicked, and he wasn't sure why she refused to admit how completely they were made for one another. So much in his life was uncertain, amorphous, but this? Here was something that he felt sure of, that he felt deep inside could be an anchor, a mooring place for his soul. He grew desperate in his motions, slamming her up and down, hand covering her mouth as he filled her.

"Gods, Cat, you are perfect. So fucking perfect. This cunt, these gorgeous breasts. All of you was made to tempt me so perfectly. You are everything I-no, fuck, you're *more* than I ever wanted, ever thought to dream of. All of those people in that bar wanted you. They all wanted to suckle these sweet tits, feel the warm, tight home between your sexy thighs. But only I get to. Only I get this sweet cunt, only I get to hear your sweet mewls."

Cat squirmed against him, seeking friction on her clit.

"I'm going to move my hand so I can rub your needy little clit," he whispered, "but you have to promise to be quiet. You have to be my quiet good girl and later I'll make you scream. Can you do that for me, precious?"

Catrin nodded frantically, and he snaked his hand down her body, slipping it under her skirts. Even though his cock was slick with her, she was still dripping.

"Fuck you're drenched precious," he bit out.

"We're supposed to be being quiet." Her words came between clenched teeth and her eyes bored into him. She was so fierce, his little rabbit, her reactions lightning fast, her emotions equally so. He leaned in to suckle on her neck, loving the way her breath hitched when he bit down just slightly.

"Yes ma'am. You're right. Quiet," he whispered."I just have trouble not running my mouth with you. I always need to tell you how fucking perfect you are."

Her channel squeezed him so sweetly, and while she'd scolded him for talking, he could feel how much she liked it. She pulsed around him as he spoke. Her body teased, thighs squeezing around him. Twisting the fabric of his cloak, her nails dug into his shoulders. Her pussy clenched him like a vice and she buried her head into his shoulder. She bit down on his neck to muffle her sounds as she came.

His own need was a raging fire within, a tingle that built at the base of his spine and shot through him. The feeling of her teeth on him sent him over the edge. His balls tucked close and then he was shooting into her, hips stuttering as he fucked her through his orgasm. Like every time, his brain screamed at him to knot her, to breed her, to tie her to him irrevocably. But an alley was not the time, and they needed to leave quickly.

They clung to each other, sharing their air. Slowly, Torsten noticed the sounds of the tavern behind them. He reached into his back pocket and pulled out a handkerchief, and lowered Cat gently to the ground, holding her skirt away from the splatter. Once she'd drained most of his spend on the cobblestones, he gently wiped her pussy and let her skirts fall. Her huge eyes looked up at him, so achingly tender. He pressed a soft kiss to her lips and whispered, "Let's get out of here."

They left the city silently, sneaking out and walking for an hour into the forest before settling down for the night. When they left, Cat held his hand, her stride easy next to him, but as they walked, she changed. Once they were out of the walls, she dropped his hand and hiked ahead, face set in determination. She'd had a difficult experience in the bar, and he figured she was working through her feelings about it.

That night, she was quiet while making camp, volunteering to assemble wood for the fire while Torsten cleared a space and set up their tent.

"I have a wee surprise," she said when she returned with an armful of wood."Marta, the innkeeper sent me with two hand pies and some extras."

Pulling out a small package, she unwrapped it to reveal two pasties, a large hunk of cheese, some bread, two small apples, and a couple cookies.

"That was kind of her. Did she know there were two of us?" Torsten asked.

"I think so… she said you'd better take care of me," Cat said, a coy smile telling him exactly how she expected to be cared for.

"I intend to take the best care of you," he said. *For as long as you'll let me.*

"Let's eat," Cat said, patting the log next to her. He settled next to her, deciding that he liked quiet moments like this with her. He enjoyed needling her, loved seeing her fired up and feisty, but this felt like the Cat he knew, the Cat that had always belonged to him more than anyone. She'd been quiet and trusted him to defend her, to include her. This was the Cat who would leap fearlessly into a river, confident he'd catch her.

Each easy touch of their hands brought her closer to him. Each touch was a victory, a sign she was feeling what he did. That perhaps she was seeing how he'd fit in her life, to understand how she could have as many easy, quiet dinners like this as she wanted.

Well, maybe not this quiet, considering orclings... he thought with a secret smile.

"What are you getting the girls for solstice?" he asked as the girls came to mind. "Do they tend to like the same things, or different?"

The corners of her mouth rose. "Different, though of course they'd fight over things if I only got one of anything so I still get doubles. They're at the age where they'll start thinking about their shifted forms. Currently, they're torn between polar bear or arctic hare, since they can't decide if they'd rather be more like me or Berne-though Ingrid has also thrown moose into the mix of late.

"He and Sirin helped me build two little dollhouses. I've made them wee dolls for inside, all different animal people, though of course there are two of each. So far we have a pair of polar bears, hares, reindeer, foxes, owls, moose, and seals. I've made them all with little clothing, though I still need to make some of the furniture."

Shoulders lax, she was at ease speaking of her children, musing and popping bites of food into her mouth between words. It was gorgeous how she blossomed when speaking about her children and he smiled to himself, watching her.

"The table and chairs were easily fashioned from wood, as were the little beds, but other things, I just worry that wood or clay won't be quite right, for the stove, for example, or the icebox." Catrin's brow furrowed in thought.

"Sounds like we could make those things out of metal. If I start right when we get back, I could have them done in time," he offered."I'd be happy to help, if you'll let me."

"Well, that, I—" Catrin began, tucking a hair behind her ear."You don't have to help, I'll finish it as soon as we're home."

She waved her hand and he caught it with his, speaking low."Cat, this isn't about us. No matter what happens with us, you and Berne are my family, so you can all expect solstice gifts from me. So either you let me help or I will figure something else for them on my own."

"Fine, you can help then," she conceded."I suppose the stove and iceboxes would be good in metal."

"Anything else? Little lamps maybe? I could make adorable little fire-pokers if they have chimneys. Perhaps a post box?"

Cat was giggling now, rocking back and forth on the log."We can't have the wee animals' mail getting lost."

"Oh no, they'll be quite cross with us otherwise."

"They would! Imagine if they had an important letter, and it never arrived."

"Or," he said, tucking a curl behind her ear."Imagine they wrote letters and never got a response. They'd be heartbroken, I'm sure. And their recipient, too. They'd spend years never knowing that the sender didn't hate them."

Joy swelled within him, coalescing into something that had toyed at the edges of his mind for days. A deep, abiding sort of happiness that could only mean one thing. He loved her. This hurt, complicated, gorgeous, caring woman was all he'd ever wanted.

"Kitten, if I'd known this sweet cunt was waiting for me, I'd have been back years ago. I'm so fucking stupid. I'm so dumb for not telling Berne I was writing to you, for letting them get bundled in. We could have fallen in love in letters. I didn't know what it could be like. Lady, if I'd known this, that you could be mine, I'd have said fuck it to my job, to everything and been back to you so fucking fast..."

He'd meant it to be sweet, tender, but instead tears glistened in her eyes, threatening to spill over onto her lightly freckled cheeks. She blinked rapidly, and he moved his thumbs up to catch her tears as they fell. Thumbs wet, he kissed her eyelids.

"That does sound terrible," she whispered.

"True, but, eventually, I think it would all work out. Eventually."

Chapter Thirteen
Catrin

IN WHICH A WALL IS REBUILT,
HORSES ARE HEISTED, AND A
RESCUE IS EXECUTED

TORSTEN'S WORDS LINGERED IN Catrin's brain long after he fell asleep. He laid curled around her, his warm steady breathing at her back. She couldn't get her brain to quiet enough for sleep.

Eventually, I think it would all work out. Eventually.

With each thing he said, he was hacking away at the wall around her heart. No, not hacking, he was carefully and methodically wearing it down. He was a steady wind or constant rush of rainwater. Perhaps that was why she felt so panicky about it?

Torsten wasn't careening into her walls, he wasn't smashing through them. He was examining each stone's placement, acknowledging its purpose, deeming it unnecessary, and wearing it away. And she had been dumb enough to tell him he was allowed to do so.

She'd truly thought that telling him he couldn't talk about "after" would help. Instead, she'd given him a dedicated section of her wall to work on. Sure, there would be less to patch in the end, but he'd get through before long if she didn't do something, and soon.

Perhaps the worst part was, she was starting to ache with want for things she couldn't have. She could see how good he'd be with her girls. That tiny glimpse of her girls climbing all over him while he laughed stuck out, making her wish she could manipulate her brain the way Sirin could. Perhaps then she could be rid of the image altogether.

Instead, she was doomed to think of it. From her previous heartbreaks, she knew it would fade with time. She'd get over him, eventually. But until then, little things would remind her of him.

The smell of a cold crisp winter morning, or the spray of the ocean. The scent of a fire, or the expanse of a clear starry sky. Chicken and dumplings, pasties, and Sirin's fried rolls were surely all on the list, as were, she realized, caves, just in general. To top it off, she thought the sound of her girls' laughing might also be on the list. She hadn't heard them laugh and play with such excitement and abandon as they had with Tor in far, far too long.

Of course, as they'd talked about the girls' gift, she'd imagined the stupid little rabbits she'd made, and their fingers as they'd toddle the dolls to their tiny postbox.

A familiar tingling started in the center of her face, a tightness that heralded tears. Her brows felt heavy and she silently cursed herself. She'd let herself do this, again, and she'd pay for it, she knew.

Torsten dripped sweet words, and if she let him, he'd make promises of forever. But she'd heard those before, romantic and platonic both. Over and over again, she'd been told she was loved; that her parents or Edrigu would be there for her. And over and over, she hadn't been enough.

After Annika's disappearance, her mother had told friends and neighbors, "We go on because Catrin and Berne need us. We've lost one child, but we have two others."

All the while, she'd cry every time she hugged Cat, had barely been able to look at her without sniffling. At first, because she looked so much like Annika, and later because she wondered if that was how Nika would look at the same age. Over time, Cat had thought, and had been reassured by Berne, it would get better. Instead, her parents only grew more distant, more obsessed with the daughter they'd lost.

They'd give lip service to how much they loved them both, but she could still see the differences with how her parents interacted with Berne and her. Over time, things with her parents and her brother returned to normal. Or at least they didn't look so heartbroken when they looked at him. Their looks at Catrin had never changed.[1] Her mother always looked as if her heart were actively breaking, and her father would set his jaw and pointedly look at her hair, rather than her face.

About a year before she'd met Edrigu, she'd gone through a desperate stage. She'd moved out, had started her apprenticeship and had hoped that not seeing her all the time would help. It didn't. So, she'd spent countless hours changing the shape of her features so that she wouldn't look so much like Annika. She'd swapped the nose she shared with her mother for her father's, and purged much of her fat to thin herself out. She'd gotten to the point

---

1. Catrin and Annika were born a year apart, and as luck would have it, looked very similar. As children, people would always remark how they looked like twins, and Annika, it seems, resented that. She avoided her younger sister and any association with her.

where she'd look in the mirror and been entirely unable to recognize who she saw.[2]

Curled up, safe in Torsten's arms, shame flooded through her as she remembered that time. She distinctly remembered looking in the mirror, seeing someone else, and feeling *joy.*

She'd felt fucking *joyful* that her own parents wouldn't recognize her. That perhaps, if they could separate her entirely from Annika, and by extension, herself, they'd be able to even look at her.

Instead, her mother had bypassed looking like she was on the verge of crying and progressed straight to wails. Her mother had flung herself into her father's arms, all the while howling how Catrin was "robbing them of the little bits of Annika left to them." How she was "betraying her sister and her whole family."

It had been a colossal failure.

Just like Edrigu had been.

Torsten might *think* he wanted her, might think he loved her even. He hadn't said it, but she'd seen it behind his eyes.

She was painfully familiar with that look, too.

He *might* truly believe that. But it was only a matter of time, she knew, until she wouldn't be

---

2. I am truly *so* vexed that they didn't have calotypes during that time. I would pay a great deal of money to see a depiction of Catrin during this time. I've yet to meet someone who passed gracefully through the "finding oneself" stage.

enough. Who knew what it would be, or when, but she'd learned that it always came.

Only Berne had loved her through it all, only Berne had held her while she cried after every hurt. Only Berne who had acknowledged that she'd also lost a sister. Only Berne had never expected her to be anything other than who she was.

Berne was the only one she could depend upon.

Truly, she was lucky. In finding Sirin, Berne had gained Cat a second person she could depend upon. Berne would never reject her, and by extension, Sirin was stuck with her.

It was too late, though, with Torsten. She could feel it. Already, she knew she'd made a grave mistake. She'd fallen in love with him. She'd be miserable when it was over. And he *would* leave, she was under no delusion that she was worth sticking around for.

She'd never been enough, never would be. Eventually, he'd see that because while he didn't seem to fit in among the orcs, someone so well traveled, with such an exciting life, could never be happy with the domesticity she could offer.

He would leave eventually, but she couldn't afford to wait for eventually.

Because as dangerous as he was to her, he was even more so to two little girls, desperate for a connection with their culture, and for a father. She was in too deep, and she would shatter, but she had a duty to make sure they didn't.

Sleep was hours in coming. She wrestled with her emotions until she could no longer keep her eyes open. Try as she might, she couldn't wrestle a quiet, hopeful part of her that insisted on whispering... *What if?*

TWO NIGHTS OF SLEEPING next to Torsten, laughing at his jokes, and drinking in his kisses later, they arrived outside the Citadel. Each time she'd fortified herself against him, he'd flash her a cheeky smile, or look at her like she'd hung the moon and she'd melt.

She was no closer to being free of him, and vastly closer to losing herself.

By the time they arrived, she'd crumbled and decided that instead of pushing him away, she'd drink as much of Torsten in as she could. She'd lived on happy memories before, and she'd have to again. In their limited time, she'd build up a store of memories to get her through the dark times ahead.

It was mid-afternoon when they approached, the sun from the west lighting its gates. They peered at it from the depths of the forest, Torsten covered in his cloak.

"We need to figure out where the stables are," he whispered."Do you think you could hop in there and find them?"

"Of course, though it might be a good idea if you rub some dirt on me. Bright white isn't exactly stealthy." Catrin squeezed her eyes shut, hating the thought, but knowing it was probably for the best.

"I already thought of that. Berne gave me some brown dye for your fur. He said some of the other rangers use it when they have to go deeper into the Compact." He pulled a small dark bottle from his bag."Go on kitten, I'll see you camouflaged."

The briefest of thoughts began her transformation, her bones shrinking with the familiar burst of energy she felt when shifting. In moments, she was looking up at Torsten's calves. Torsten leaned over and scooped her up, cradling her in his arms as he lowered himself to the ground. With a small brush he pulled from his bag, he smoothed the dye through her fur. Turning her to coat all her sides, he whistled a song she remembered him loving when they were young, a silly ditty about children making progressively bigger messes when they were supposed to be cleaning.

Catrin's small frame shook with laughter.

"There you are, back to your summer coat, or at least what I assume your summer coat looks like," he said, blushing a deeper green and looking away."Oh, I suppose you should be off now, I'll just be here."

He picked her up, bringing her to his face so that he could nuzzle her fur."I want you to be careful. Don't take any risks, not one. If you need me, just scream, and I'll be there as fast as my legs can carry me. Remember, get in, find the stables, find the horses, make a plan, execute the plan," he said, reminding her of the plan they'd worked out. If she needed him, she'd leave and they'd regroup.

Running a hand through his hair, he spun them in a circle, making Cat feel dizzy."I know nothing's gonna happen. I know you're not in any real danger—I know that."

Catrin wasn't sure who he was trying to convince, because his argument wasn't exactly compelling. She nipped lightly at one of his fingers, admonishing him, and struck a bold and confident pose. Head lifted to the sky, ears tucked back. She hoped she was portraying the amount of confidence and dignity she intended.

Torsten chuckled and rubbed his knuckles into the top of her head."You're right, precious, I have all the faith in the world that you are going to do beautifully."

He sat her down, tying Sirin's kerchief around her neck, and tapped her lightly on the bum. "Don't forget, inside is the baggie with the sleeping powder from Arndis."

Catrin nodded her head and hopped away. After a few hops, she turned back to him and twitched her ears. Having grown up in Sanctuary, he'd know the gesture was a temporary sort of goodbye.

Breaking the treeline as the sun dipped below the horizon, Catrin staggered at how tall the walls of the Citadel were. They towered over her, hundreds of times her size. It sat atop a hill, towering over cliffs that led to the Lady's river. On Catrin's left side, a series of fields led up to the intimidating walls, and to her right a road wound its way to the main gates.

Keeping as close to the edifice as possible, Catrin rounded the wall, her tiny heart providing a quick tempo to hop to. Her ears perked at each sound she heard, a group of young people laughing, a man taking the trash out, and what must be the dinner bell. The final sound explained the relative silence of this compound.

Get in, find the stables, find the horses, make a plan.

After ten minutes of sneaking, Catrin hopped under a fence and into a series of fields. The whole place smelled of horses, which was a good sign, to be sure.

Not long after, she discovered a gate with a small gap at the bottom. She was barely able to squeeze herself through. Once she was on the other side, she hid behind some crates and looked at the gate, which had a sturdy iron lock on it.

Please, dear Lady, let me find a key. I don't know if I can pick that thing and the horses will not fit under it.

Hopping atop the crates, she peeked out of the alleyway to survey her location. From a distance, the Citadel had looked like a large, walled fort, unified in form and function. Inside the walls, the true nature of the settlement emerged. There was a large central structure made entirely of a dark stone. Attached to it were a multitude of other structures, in an array of states of construction. On one side, there was an intricate building held up by buttresses next to a smaller wattle and daub building with timber beams that reminded her of home. To their right was a bright red, brick building, shaped like an H and covered in ivy. Across a large courtyard sat a collection of smaller white-washed brick buildings with signs hung out front.[3]

---

3. As one can imagine, it was imminently fascinating to hear this described through someone else's eyes. I'd spent the better part of my life regarding the Citadel as home, and had entirely habituated to these oddities.

The scale of the place was astonishing, even if she hadn't been a foot tall. While the grounds were massive, she could barely fathom the amount of people that buildings this tall could house. Sanctuary had blocks of flats to house single people, but they were all only three stories tall. The tallest building in town was the Council Hall and several buildings at the Citadel could house at least four Council Halls stacked atop one another.

She circled to the right, behind the brick buildings. The row curved around the outer wall and Catrin picked her way through the small alley they created. Littered with discarded pallets and crates, she darted through and around them, grateful for the cover.

Her thickly-furred paws dampened what little sound she made. Focusing on the smells of the settlement, she sifted through them to find the scent she'd smelled on a horse in Pershing. Through the riot of scents, she faintly detected the warm aromas of a horse and hay. Hopping quickly along in the direction of the scent, she arrived at what she assumed were the stables.

So far, she'd had good luck with staying out of sight, but here was where she knew she'd have a good chance of exposure.

She twitched her nose, seeking the scents of humans among the horses. She only detected two, at the far end of the building. Each end of the stable had large double doors which were rolled back to open the building to the night. Inside, the interior was brightly lit with lamps posted at regular intervals. The building was full with the sounds and smells of horses—unfamiliar, but a relief.

Get in, done. Find the stables, done. Find the horses, make a plan. Two down, two to go. It helped to think of that last massive task as just one thing, at least until she got that far.

As far as she knew, Butter and Biscuit were a brother and sister draft horse breed, which apparently meant large. They both had a black stripe that ran down their mane, which may or may not be cut into intricate shapes. Butter was a warm rich tan, while Biscuit was darker.

Hopping on a few boxes to get a better vantage point, Cat looked down the line of stalls. The first few housed sleek-looking horses, and all were dark. At the far end, there was a small room. Voices floated to her, sounding deep and male. Across from the room, in stalls next to each other, were horses that could only be Butter and Biscuit.

Damn, that's inconvenient. Still, she was in no real rush. After all, they'd agreed that leaving late in the night would be their best bet. Cat made her way back to the floor, keeping close to the wall in case the men left the room. Once she was immediately across from the room, she scurried under the nearest gate, deciding she'd rather chance the horse over the men.

The first thing Catrin saw was feet. Huge, massive feet-no, hooves-that could crush her in an instant were inches from her head. She pressed herself back into the corner of the stall, getting as far away from those hooves as possible. From a distance, it looked as if she had managed to locate Butter's stall.

The massive horse in Catrin's stall slowly swung her head around. She ambled over to Cat, lowering her head and sniffing. Catrin's heart beat quickly in her chest and she froze, her hare's instincts insisting it was her best chance at survival.

Noises from the room across the aisle interrupted her shaking. She dashed across the stall, ducking under a feed trough for shelter.

The men left the room, and Catrin tracked their footsteps as they shut the large doors, and moved down the aisle of horses. At the far end, they shut the doors again, but this time, she heard a lock being bolted. With them gone, the stable was nearly silent, letting her pick out the breathing and heartbeats of the surrounding animals.

Slowly, Cat left the safety of the trough and positioned herself once more at the far edge of the stall. She dipped into her lunula and forced her body into a very controlled shift. Slower than she'd done in years, she stretched her form, doing everything she could not to startle the horse.

Butter watched her intently, leaning in instead of backing away. Catrin stretched, returning to her human form. She was startled to realize that the horses still towered over her. Butter's head could easily swing over her own, and she figured that the horse must be of a size with Torsten.

"Well hello there, lovie. I'm Catrin, your… auntie, I suppose. I'm going to get you out of here and take yeh home to your mama. Just as soon as I can figure out how." She was careful to speak in Sirin's tongue, not wanting to scare Butter with her own, and held out Sirin's handkerchief for her to smell.

Butter eyed Catrin, ears swiveling. The horse curled her upper lip, breathing in and out forcefully. Catrin froze, but at once, her animal instincts assured her that these actions were friendly. After a few repetitions, Butter cocked her head to the side and lowered it, inhaling the smell of Sirin's handkerchief. Relaxing visibly, she moved to bump Cat with her muzzle.

From the stall next door, a huge head peeked over the fence. Sleepy eyed and grumpy, he let out a huff, blowing Catrin's hair. Butter bumped her brother, making a small noise that sent him back into his stall.

"You showed him who is in charge, eh?" Catrin giggled and rubbed Butter's warm nose. She liked the horse, but had no time to dally while the stablehand was out.

"I'll be right back. I need to go investigate this room."

Holding her breath, Catrin eased the gate open. She crept across the hall and poked her head inside the room. The walls were lined with saddles, each bearing a name plaque. Next to the door was an empty nail she thought might be the regular hanging place for a set of keys. Her eyes scanned the saddle labels for the horses' names. Butter's was on the far end, easily located. Biscuit's, on the other hand, was missing entirely.

Damn, is his out for cleaning? Why is it missing, it's not like anyone is taking him out, right?

She didn't know much, but she did know that you couldn't ride a horse without a saddle. There were probably millions of reasons it could be missing, foremost of which, she realized, someone *could* be taking him out regularly.

An uneasy lump grew in her stomach, augmented by the anxiety coursing through her. It was entirely reasonable that they'd sell Sirin's horses, or at least that the Citadel would assume ownership of them.

For the first time, it occurred to her that she might not just be liberating Sirin's horses and returning them to her, but that she might, instead, be committing a crime.

Shaking her head, she pushed the thought away. What did it matter if she was a criminal in a place she'd never be again? Since Sirin wasn't dead, the horses were still rightfully hers, and Butter at least seemed to want to return to her owner.

Close to the door sat a small desk and chair. On the desk was a small mug, a pitcher of wine, and a pile of dirt as if deposited by a pair of boots. In a moment of genius, Catrin drew on her lunula in the conscious way Sirin had insisted she learn. With it, she sped her mental processes and quickened her movements, lest anyone interrupt her.

First, she dumped the sleeping powder into the mug, and poured in the wine, pleased that the powder wasn't visible. That done, she hefted up Butter's saddle and gear and swapped it with the set closest to the door where it would be easily accessible when she left. Taking note of the buckles, she tried to imagine how they might strap around the horse. She double checked the labels, but there really didn't seem to be one for Biscuit.

Outside, she heard the sounds of voices laughing, an abrupt reminder that she was on a schedule. She scurried back to Butter's stall, suppressing a giggle when the horse immediately bumped her with her snout.

"Ssssh, you goose, I'm not here. Act naturally, else we'll be caught. If you want to see your mama, you'd best pretend you have no idea there's a small hare in your stall."

Catrin shifted back, and tucked herself away once more.[4]

With the click of the lock, a single man entered the stable, greeting the horses and dousing the gas lamps.

"Time for sleep, children, everyone take your naps. 'Fraid there won't be a bedtime story tonight!" he called. He sat down at the desk, thunked his boots onto the table, and took a loud slurp of his wine.

Catrin shook with nerves. The night was *somehow* proceeding well, but it was still early and if she was honest with herself, the plan was still entirely vague in her mind. Curling up underneath the trough, she settled in to wait.

AFTER SEVERAL HOURS, SHE heard the sounds of snores coming from the small room. It was time to act. Several hours of thought hadn't furthered the plan nearly as much as she'd like,

---

4. Careful to preserve the dye on her fur, which was a slightly more complicated operation than she usually performed.

but she at least had a heading. She shifted back to her human form, and set about getting out of the Citadel as quickly as possible.

She'd noted little harnesses hung up next to each stall. To the right of the gate, there was a small label that read "Butter" and hanging next to it was a hook, a length of rope, and a harness. Looking at the harness, which she thought might be called a bridle if she remembered correctly, she noted it had two loops with straps that seemed like they'd fit around the horse's head, which matched the drawing Torsten had shown her on the boat.

Sneaking out of the stall, she tiptoed toward the small room and confirmed that the stablehand was sleeping. He was a youngish looking fellow, surprisingly well-dressed, though his boots were quite muddy.[5] The mug lay on the floor next to him, only a few drops spilled. Holding her breath, Catrin lifted the huge saddle and took it into the hall, and took the ring of keys which were indeed hanging by the door. As quiet as she could, she closed the door and rolled a wagon wheel over to jam the door

---

5. From Cat's description it sounds as if this was Edmund, who was the stablehand when I was there. Edmund, I am terribly sorry for any and all turmoil you experienced as a result of these events. I've tried to find you, but I fear you may have perished in YPS 1001, among so many others. If you are still out there, please get in contact so I can make any reparations needed beyond the letter I sent in 981.

handle. Once she felt a modicum of safety, she set back to getting the horse ready to go.

The harness was easy enough to get on, as Butter dipped her head and flicked her ears through the straps. Once it was on, she shifted from foot to foot, eager. Cat tied the rope around her bridle and walked over to the next stall to get Biscuit. As she'd been told, he looked sleepy and annoyed to be disturbed. She'd only just grabbed his harness when she felt a rush of warm air at her back. Butter waited close behind, having followed her out of the stall.

"I think your sister's eager to see your mama," she whispered. "Now if we can just put this on yeh, we can be on our way!"

Biscuit had no interest in the handkerchief, ignoring her completely to mouth some hay out of a hanging net.

"I'm coming in, we need to get yeh ready."

Big eyes blinked at her slowly and she eased open the gate. Other than shifting his weight, Biscuit was immobile. Getting his harness on was a bit more difficult than Butter's, and required her to tug a hay bale over, as he wouldn't deign to lower his head to help. His harness received a rope as well and shortly, she was at the end of her extremely short plan.

"Alright, well. Erm. Horses are for riding... so I suppose that's what we should do, eh?"

Dragging a hay bale over, Catrin hefted the massive saddle onto Butter's back. Once it was on the horse, the buckles seemed to make a bit more sense, and she did the best she could. She secured them, grabbed the handle, and put her foot in the foot strap to mount.[6] She heaved herself up, but the saddle spun around Butter's chest, and in seconds Catrin was tumbling to the ground. Laying there, Catrin's arse hurt and her head spun.

Butter swung her head down to sniff at Catrin, nudging her to stand.

"You two seem to have the routine down... Sorry if I am a cog in the works. Seems I will not be riding out of here." She spun the saddle back to neutral and decided that her time might be better spent getting herself less... conspicuously naked.

A quick scan of the room yielded a large brimmed cap and a long coat. A pair of large boots stood by the door and they swallowed her feet the second she stepped into them.

She grabbed a random blanket from a hook next to the tack room, and secured it around her waist with another horse's bridle rope. The coat and hat were next, and she tucked her stark hair inside.

---

6. Of course this is not a "foot strap" it's a stirrup, but one must remember, Catrin didn't know a great deal about horses at the time.

From a distance at least, she'd look less conspicuous than she would naked.

Since Butter was so much more agreeable, Cat tied Biscuit's lead to his sister's harness. It seemed like between the two of them, Butter was in charge. Taking a deep breath, Catrin slid the wide doors open a crack and peeked outside. She winced at the noise of the door opening, leading Butter and Biscuit into the night.

The night was still as they approached the door, the sleeping settlement around her seeming entirely unawares that a horse thief was about. The problem with stealing a ring of keys was that you never knew which key was the one you needed. She closed her eyes and tried to remember what Torsten had said about identifying keys for locks. The lock itself was a thick iron thing with a large opening. That eliminated any of the smaller keys. Of the larger keys, three were iron, and the rest seemed to be brass. Holding the them tight to minimize the noise, Catrin tried the first iron key, and cursed when it wouldn't go in all the way.

A cough in the night startled her, and she fumbled with the next, the keys cluttering against one another. The Lady's luck was not with her any longer, because the second key didn't fit either. Her hands shook as she heard footsteps approaching. The final key slid in, and Catrin released a sigh of

relief. A flick of her wrist popped the lock, and she
hastened to open the gate.

While she could hear activity in the distance,
the immediate area was clear. A vast field spread
before her. The horses happily meandered out,
lowering their heads nigh immediately to clip the
grass with their teeth. Shutting the gate, Catrin
spotted a loop for a lock on the outside. She
threaded the lock through the loops, securing it.
She dropped the keys in the grass—she didn't want
to inconvenience anyone forever, and truly didn't
want the stablehand to get in trouble.

The horses were happy to follow her across the
paddock, and when she reached the edge closest to
Torsten, she paused, unsure of how she'd get the
horses out, as the fence didn't even have a gate
anywhere. She pursed her lips, considering. First,
she tried the fence, rattling the sections to see if
any of the posts or cross ties were wiggly or weak.
She bolstered her strength with lunula, a trick she
was still working on mastering. Even with her
increased strength, she shook and shook it, but the
ties held fast.

Cries from the city cracked across the field
toward her. Her eyes darted to the gate, waiting
for it to burst open. The reflected light of torches
moved back and forth in front of the gate, sending
jolts of fear through her. Catrin raised her leg
and kicked the cross-brace, funneling her fear and

her anger into her leg. The brace cracked, hope springing up within her. She kicked again, and the wood clattered against the brace beneath it. The horses stepped back, agitated, and she smoothed her hands over their heads, reassuring them that all was well.

Butter pushed at her shoulder, gently nudging toward the opening. Cat furrowed her brow, but Butter walked toward the fallen fence, neatly stepping over and tugging Biscuit alongside her. Catrin giggled, grateful that the horses, or at least Butter, were as eager to leave as she was.

In the distance, the loud clatter of a gate echoed through the night, quickly followed by the sounds of horses galloping out of the city. Catrin picked up her pace, her heart, thundering, and her chest, echoing their hoofbeats. She knew that their vision would likely be as good as her own, so they needed to get to the tree line as quickly as possible. Thankfully, Butter seemed to sense her urgency, and followed, close behind, tugging Biscuit along with her. Catrin stumbled as she ran, every rock on the ground interfering with her gait.

It sounded as if the riders had split up, fanning out in a search party. One set of hooves came from directly behind her, gaining on her quickly. As she ducked past the first tree, she heard the guard call out for her to stop.

Bile rose in her throat, her stomach contents, threatening to come up. She weaved through the trees, hoping an irregular path might throw him off, but she was leading two horses on foot, and in moments, he was upon her. The guard leapt from his horse, and seized her arm before she could register it happening.

"You're under arrest," he said, spinning her to face him. His face was a blur as she shrank to the ground, surrounded by her coat. The man screamed and stepped back as she poked her head and small twitching nose out of the pile. Involuntary shifting was becoming a truly annoying habit.

"What - how? A rabbit?" the guard stuttered. He shook his head, reaching down to pick her up. Catrin tried to scurry away but he was just too fast. His arm blurred as it shot out at her, grasping both her ears and lifting her off the ground.

"The lads will never believe me when I tell them a little rabbit stole the horses, but something tells me that's not all I'm dealing with here." he said.

In the woods behind him Catrin heard a twig snap. The guard whirled around, making Cat feel sick with the speed of it. He was *far* faster than he should be.

"He-hello?" he called into the forest."Jimmy? That you? S'not funny."

A sound from the opposite direction had him spinning them again, the smell of fear permeating the forest around them.

The sounds of the forest suddenly quieted, not even a twig snapped nearby. No birds chirped and even the other guards in the distance seemed to fade away.

Then, as if from the heavens themselves, Torsten dropped out of a tree in front of the guard.

"Boo" he said, lifting the butt of his great sword over the man's head and bringing it down swiftly. The man crumpled to the floor, and Torsten caught Catrin from the air as he fell.

Torsten's eyes roamed across the horses. "One saddle."

A yell in the distance drew his attention before he turned back with a nod. "We'll make better time if I ride and carry you. I think we should make ourselves scarce."

Torsten's fingers flew across the buckles of the saddle, tightening the thick strap underneath Butter's belly, and securing another around her neck.

"Let's get out of here before he wakes up."

Chapter Fourteen
Torsten

IN WHICH THERE IS ONLY ONE HORSE... THAT IS RIDEABLE

RIDING BUTTER, TORSTEN PICKED his way through the forest at a trot, away from Pershing and the Citadel toward where they were to meet Calida. They had a good forty miles to go, as they needed to be far enough away from civilization that anyone from the Citadel wouldn't see her. A dragon was difficult to miss.

The sounds and lights of the citadel faded behind them, though he took them over several streams in attempts at ruining any pursuit. Catrin shivered in his arms for the first two hours, but by dawn, he was confident they'd lost their pursuers.

The adrenaline must have worn off quickly, because Cat snoozed in his arms for several hours before getting fidgety. She burrowed into him, repositioning herself repeatedly; first under his arm, then snuggled into his neck, and finally, flattened against him. Her movements were jerky with many frustrated flicks of her ears.

"You alright, precious?" he asked as morning light spilled through the trees. "You seem fidgety."

Tiny eyes squinted up at him. Her nose twitched and she thumped him with her back foot causing him to rumble out a chuckle.

"I'm pretty good at reading body language, precious, so I'm getting that you're irritated but I'm not sure why..."

She sniffed at him, and nuzzled further into his coat, shooting him a grumpy look. He frowned down at her. What in the world did she want? She bumped his hand with her head and gave a little kick with her back foot. He reached his hand out and as soon as he started petting her, she fell into sweet slumber, her small warmth a quiet reassurance against him.

They ambled along, the crisp slants of light between tree branches marching across the ground until they pointed nearly straight down. Catrin, who'd been sound asleep for hours, stirred against him. A twitch of her leg was the only signal before she started growing, weight exploding out of her to press solidly against him. He blinked as her head of curly white hair was shoved under his chin.

"Auuuugh!" Catrin flailed against him, windmilling her arms until she toppled from Butter's back. Arm shooting out, Torsten managed to catch her before she hit the ground. He gripped her tightly, shifting his weight, and pulled her back to sit in front of him.

"You alright, precious?"

"I'm sorry, it's just a little disorienting waking up naked on top of someone."

"You do seem to be making a habit of that," he said. "Is this a problem you've had in the past?"

Catrin turned her head away from him. "I can't say that it is."

"Oh, I see. So this is a problem exclusive to me then?" he said, a broad smile splitting his face.

"Oh, I'm sure you'd like that. This has nothing to do with you, Torsten. It's probably some issue with sleeping in strange environments."

Torsten pulled his bottom lip between his teeth, but decided that he'd let her tell herself that.

"Do you want to put some clothes on?" he asked.

Patting Butter's neck, he considered their options. Normally, he'd never ask a horse to carry himself and someone else. Orcs were big and normal horses would flounder under the weight of two. But Butter and Biscuit were the largest horses he'd ever seen. She wasn't winded, and stepped lightly. If she could carry both, they'd move a great deal faster.

"Miss Butter here seems to be doing just fine with both of us." The horse in question turned her head to look at him. She let out a gust of air from her nostrils, a huff that seemed to say, "Of course, it's no problem, don't be insulting."[1]

"That would probably be for the best, yes." Catrin shivered, confirming his suspicions. He reined Butter in, and helped Cat slide to the ground, following her and looking anywhere but at her gorgeous curves. They didn't have time to stop for a tryst now, and there was something that bothered him about ogling her when she was uncomfortable. As she rummaged through the pack, he busied himself with giving the horses each a carrot from their food stores, he'd made sure to save one for each of them. It was one of the first things he'd learned about horses in the Empire—food goes a long way to earning their trust.

Once Catrin was fully dressed, Torsten helped her back onto Butter. The horse's stirrups seemed adjustable, with a little handle to allow for mounting. He'd never seen such a thing, but

---

1. Butter and Biscuit's weight tolerances, and indeed those of other Fjerd horses is significantly more than other draft breeds. I've a theory that it's the result of proximity to the Lady, though less pronounced than those animals in her immediate area.

considering Sirin's height, and how massive Butter was, it made sense that Sirin might need to have a bit of assistance when mounting.

Once she was seated, Torsten situated himself behind her, and Butter took off almost immediately. She was a willful thing, often acting as if she knew better than her riders.

"Now, these are the reins," he said, picking them up. "We will use them to tell her which way we want to go." Catrin watched his movements closely.

"And if we want her to stop?" she asked, her voice rising in pitch.

"Well then, we pull back on the reins, just a little bit. We don't need to go yanking on them." He demonstrated, pulling gently on the reins, and Butter obligingly stopped. He urged her forward, and they started on their way again. In front of him, Catrin was stiff, resisting Butter's movement.

"It seems like you're working hard to stay stable there," he said.

"Well, when the thing you are sitting on keeps moving, it takes a lot of attention. I'm trying not to fall off!"

"Funny thing, there, kitten. The best way to stay still, when riding, is to move."

"That doesn't make any sense at all, Tor." Her hair whipped him in the face, her head turning toward him to scowl.

"Well, I can't rightly say if it makes sense or not, but it's what I know to be true. Here," he said, resting his hands on her hips. He rolled them with the movement of the horse. "I know you know how to do this, precious. You ride me like a champion." He whispered to her, letting his warm breath linger on her neck. Chest reddening, Catrin huffed at him.

"That's something else entirely."

"Yes and no," he said. "Both are a partnership, requiring you to work with your partner instead of against them. Feeling them out so you can match their movements. You've been doing it for a few seconds now. Doesn't it already feel better?"

"Well, yes, but now you've got me all flustered. How am I supposed to concentrate on riding when you have me thinking about *riding you?*"

"Mmm, that's just the thing. You need to think less and just let your body move. Trust me, it knows the exact way," he purred. "The second you start thinking about it, you tense up, you lose the rhythm, but when you just *feel*, you're doing beautifully."

Catrin relaxed in his arms, her body losing its tenseness and finding a rhythm with Butter. Torsten sat behind the saddle, its high seat pressing into his growing thickness. Catrin wasn't the only one worked up. He snaked his hands around to her front, cupping the roundness of her belly, and just grazing the crease of her sex.

She was so mouthwateringly tempting, and he was sure she didn't have any idea of how much of an effect she had on him.

"I think I might be torturing myself a little bit here," he whispered into the top of her head. He pulled in a deep breath, relishing the scent of her.

"In that case, I'm glad I'm not the only one." Catrin giggled and leaned back into his chest.

"This seemed like such a good idea, 'I teach you to ride and tease you a little bit.' And I suppose I did do those things, but now I'm hard as granite, and we won't be able to stop for hours yet."

"We can suffer together then—"

At the word suffer, a tempting idea took root in Torsten's head. His mind filled with the image of Catrin writhing against him in the saddle, coming over and over again as they rode.

"You know, kitten," he said. "You don't necessarily need to suffer. In fact, I could make you come right now... if you want..."

Catrin's breathing hitched and sped at his words. The pulse in her neck, racing against his lips as he spoke the words into her neck.

"That doesn't exactly sound very fun for you," Catrin said. "It sounds like I'd be having a wonderful time and you'd be getting sore fingers. We'd get three orgasms in, and I bet you'd be ready to be done. And then you just have to wait and suffer for the rest of the day, as I assume we're not stopping until nightfall."

"I love the idea of you collapsing back against me, spent because I've wrung you dry. The thought of watching you come over and over and needing to hold off until we get to camp is extremely tempting. By the time we get there, you'll need me to hold you up to fuck you, which I'll be more than glad to do. Because not only does that sound like the absolute best time I'd ever have, but it sounds like something that I'd want to repeat over and over fore—"

He couldn't say it.

Their agreement stopped his words short. He didn't like not being able to tell her, but he wouldn't break his word to her. Her acceptance of him hinged on proving that she could believe his word and that when he told her something he meant it.

He still had every intention of talking about their future the second their feet were on the ground in Sanctuary, but until then, he'd honor the bargain. In the meantime, he would give her plenty of reasons to consider a real relationship.

Resolved, Torsten snaked his hand up her leg, hiking her skirt with it. He toyed and caressed the soft skin of her thighs.

"And then, precious, when you and I had more than enough, and when you're soft and pliable and sated, I'll lift you up, flip you around, and sink into you."

When his fingers reached her pussy, they slipped through her swollen folds with a squelch.

Gods, she's divine. He hummed in approval and pressed wet, sucking kisses to the side of her neck."Oh kitten, you are so perfect for me," he said, as his thick fingers slipped into her with ease."This gorgeous pussy is so perfectly molded to me now, she craves the shape of my cock. Do you think if I reach high enough, I would find a little indentation where my piercings press into you?"

Catrin whimpered against him, writhing as her pussy clenched around his fingers.

"Oh love, you want me so bad you're about to come already. Did all that riding get you worked up? Or were you thinking about how much you love riding my cock? As soon as you did, you got the rhythm beautifully. God's Cat I—"

His eyes widened in horror. He'd called her *love.* She hadn't seemed to notice, and it had just slipped out. Not that it was untrue. He knew she was worried about him leaving her. He growled, thinking about all the things that had happened to her that led her to believe that it was even a remote possibility. He'd wanted her from the second he saw her again. But over the past week, he'd fallen in love with the beautiful blend that was Catrin. Remnants of the girl he knew so well, and the inspiring woman she's grown to be.

Even her cunt knew she belonged to him. Her body was primed and molded to him. Ready and soaking for him to take her, to welcome him inside. Surely she couldn't experience this level of connection, this intimacy they shared and throw it all away? Already, he didn't see how he could go back to a life devoid of her. She'd seeped into his psyche, giving purpose to the yawning hole that had been his future. Couldn't she see that she was the answer to all of his questions, just as he was the answer to hers?

When he turned his attention fully back to her, she was on the verge of her first orgasm. His body knew hers so well that he'd continued pumping into her, grinding the heel of his hand against her clit while he'd grown increasingly frustrated by their situation. He nurtured her through it, slowing her a second, easing off her sensitive spots while she was overstimulated. Instead, he reached into her bodice and cupped her breast with his free hand, gently lifting it free from its confines. Her already pert nipple hardened in the cold air, and he smoothed over it with his large hand, loving how she filled his grasp. Her lush breast spilled out between his fingers, unable to be contained by his fingers as they dimpled into her.

He kissed her head, her white curls tickling his nose. He closed his eyes, trusting Butter for a moment, so he could savor the sensations of her. The steady rock of her body against his, the delectable squish of her in his hands, the scent that was so *Catrin* it made his chest hurt.

"Beautiful, kitten," he whispered into her hair, guiding Butter with his knees. She writhed and whined against him as he wrung orgasms from her. He immersed himself in her sounds, the feeling of his fingers encased in her warm, wet channel, the calm she brought to his soul. He was exactly where he needed to be, wrapped up in her, drowning in her in the best way. Before he'd returned, he'd had nothing to look forward to, no *real* plan for the future. She was the softness he needed, just as he was the stability she lacked.

"Torsten-I-I don't know if I-" she said, head lolling onto his chest.

"You can, precious, I know you can give me a few more. Can you give me a few more?"

Catrin whimpered, but nodded her head. Torsten smoothed a thumb over her brow, gentling the determined frown she'd put on.

Several orgasms in, she began to whimper, the sweet mewls punctuating her labored breathing. He eased his demanding fingers, stroking with tenderness, letting her know with his movements that he'd flex with her. That he'd adapt to her needs if only she'd let him.

But would she let him? He was sure, so sure of what they had and she... wasn't. Or she was just scared? He'd been telling himself she was just scared, but perhaps she really didn't want this. Perhaps she knew her mind and he'd been overconfident and arrogant assuming he knew better.

She *was* extremely capable. Her life was stable, she was raising two amazing children, had a successful career, and a community that valued her. Perhaps she truly didn't need him, didn't want his messy aimless self tearing into her tidy life.

It was one thing to want an escape, a holiday from responsibility's pressures. It was something else entirely to upend one's entire life for an aimless brute. Suddenly, he saw himself from her perspective. A bachelor, whose only value he could bring was a knowledge of orcish culture. Worse, he wasn't even *good* at being an orc. How arrogant and puffed up must he seem, going on about how he'd help her with the girls when she knew his difficulties? He was the farthest orc on the planet from an authority on their culture and society and she was an angel for not laughing in his face when he suggested tutoring the girls.

"Please," she whispered after her next orgasm. "Please, I can't take any more. Just fuck me because I think I am about to pass out. Please Tor."

His eyes stung and he grit his teeth. "I'm all set, precious, sleep now. You did so well, you've earned your rest."

This he could do for her, though it was the only thing. He could wrest orgasms from her and leave her shaking and spent, but that was all.

Of course she didn't want more with him. Of course she didn't want him messing up her tidy life. Of *course* she was the only one of them to see this for what it was-a fling. A fling that was ending as soon as they met up with Calida. He'd savor her tonight, sip at her fount and cherish what little time they had left. He'd squandered this experience with his horrible realizations and self-pity, but he wouldn't do that again this evening.

BY THE TIME THEY camped, Torsten was convinced this fucking deal was perhaps the worst decision he'd ever made. He plastered a smile on his face, the last thing he wanted was to ruin their last night together.

"Tor? Are you all right?" she asked, her voice tight with concern. "You've been so quiet."

Had he? He hadn't noticed, though he'd been so wrapped up in his head since earlier that he must have been. "Sorry, precious. I've just been doing a lot of thinking. You've got a lot of reasons to be excited to get home tomorrow and I've just got a lot of questions. It's getting to me a bit."

"Of course it is," she said. She reached over and rubbed his back."Everything was still up in the air when you left, but umm... I was thinking, that-well I know we said we wouldn't talk about after until we got back-but, do you think you could try not to kiss me in front of the kids? I don't want them to get any ideas."

Any ideas. Ideas like he might be in their life for good, like he'd been having about how amazing it would feel to be a dad."Course-of course," he said, nodding.

Of course. There it was. He'd been a one night stand more times than he could count, but this was the worst. With her words, she implied that there might be a next time, but then immediately let him know where he stood. There could be a next time, as long as no one knew. His chest felt like there was a massive hole in it, sucking in everything around him, crumpling and caving in.

Is this how she'd felt? After he left? This deep gaping emptiness? He'd known he'd hurt her, but this was the worst thing he'd ever felt. He-

No. He'd had something wonderful, something beautiful and magical and special, and he'd be damned if he wasted another second of it.

Tomorrow. Tomorrow he could go back to the sad flat he'd been assigned and wallow. Tonight, he'd told himself, he'd savor her and the time they had.

With a fierceness that surprised even him, he pushed the vegetables aside and grabbed her, clutching her to him and smashing his mouth against hers. He would devour her. He'd focus and concentrate on every sound, every taste, every slide of her lips to keep him company in the months ahead. Tonight, he'd be fully present, fully in the moment with her, for tonight was all he had.

With a surprised squeak, she yielded to him, humming her approval at his roughness. Once she was breathless, flushed, and pliable he pulled back, chest heaving. He'd always remember her like this. She was the most achingly beautiful thing he'd ever seen, every soft surface he'd ever dreamed of, and tonight he meant to savage her.

"Eat," he gasped, surprised at the desperation in his voice. "Quickly, I'll not wait long."

He shoved the salad he'd made onto a plate and thrust it toward her, removing a skewer of meat from the fire and placing it atop. The rest of the salad came straight from the board he'd cut it on into his mouth, chased with the dripping hot juices of the other two meat skewers. Finished before she'd even properly started, Torsten stood from the fire, cleaning and packing up their gear.

"Oh, you're *serious,*" she said, doubling down to her meal with gusto.

He made quick work of their kit, stowing it before heading for the tent. "You get used to eating quickly in the army," he said over his shoulder. "I'm going to get the bed laid out, I expect you to be here and naked in five minutes."

Catrin giggled behind him, and he hadn't even finished the bed before she pulled the tent flap aside. Their small stove sat in its allotted corner, chasing the chill from the tent and Catrin buttoned the several door flaps after she entered.

"I don't know what's gotten into you, Tor," she said. "But I like it. You can boss me around anytime." Clothes fell off her in agonizing layers, revealing the verdant dips and valleys of her body to him. He studied every inch of her, stoic despite the desire raging through him. She'd always be like this in his mind, luscious and pink. Flushed from her hairline to her navel, nipples furled tight from the cold, the drugging perfume of her arousal filling the tent.

"Why don't you let me finish making the bed," she asked. "You're still wearing far too many clothes..."

Turning fully toward her, he rose and waved her over. Catrin scurried over to resume his place, and he grabbed a full butt cheek when she walked by. She knelt over their bedding, spreading it out and offering him a choice view of her succulent ass. He shed his clothing quickly, diving down to the bed as soon as he was naked, and buried his face between her legs. Catrin fell forward into her pillow with a moan as he slicked his tongue up through her wet slit. She tasted like every bright summer day, every happy memory, every lusty dream he'd ever had. She'd become his everything.

And he was going to lose it all.

He ate her with renewed ferocity, coaxing out her moans until they morphed into screams. Over the last two weeks, he'd studied what made her come, and he wielded that knowledge with excruciating precision.

Lady, please, let her remember me like this.

Once she'd come twice, he rolled them onto their sides, and entered her from behind, squeezing her softness to him, relishing in the slow drag of her pussy. He couldn't speak, like he normally would, for fear she'd hear the misery in his voice.

He was sure, so sure of what they had and she… wasn't. And tomorrow they'd go back to town, and it would all be over.

He'd said he would savor their last time, but even so, it was bittersweet. He couldn't fuck her face to face as he'd like-he knew there'd be no hiding his sadness that way. Instead, he clutched her, grasping her breasts as a lifeline, wiping his tears into her hair and masking his sniffles with grunts and growls.

She came quickly, squeezing his cock so sweetly that he exploded. He filled her, thrusting his knot inside. Once the silence of the aftermath settled, he lost his ability to conceal the sounds of his misery, anxiety rising in his chest and cursing himself for a fool.

"Torsten? Are you well?" Catrin's voice cut through the darkness and straight to his heart.

"I'll be fine, kitten. It's been a long day for both of us. I'm tired and got a bit too introspective." He would be fine, he knew, eventually. He had to be. Cat was, and she'd gone through so much more.

It just wouldn't be soon, and it wouldn't be pleasant.

She tightened her arms around his, wrapped around her middle. She nodded and reached back to grasp his head, burying her fingers in his hair. "I've been there. I'm here if you'd like to talk about it."

"No, I'd rather get some sleep. We'll meet Calida tomorrow, and I want to be alert for that."

"Very well," she said, turning her head to kiss him gently on the mouth, wiping a tear from his cheek. "I'm happy to listen if you change your mind."

Yes Cat, I'd love to tell you how I'm a pathetic idiot who doesn't deserve you. That I've only just now seen how fucking ridiculous the idea that I could actually contribute anything to your life is.

"Thank you, sweetness, but let's get some rest."

"Thank you, sweetness, but let's get some rest."

Chapter Fifteen
Catrin

IN WHICH CONFUSION PERVADES, A DRAGON KNOWS WHAT'S BEST, AND THE JOURNEY ENDS

THERE WAS SOMETHING OFF. Cat could feel it. Perhaps Torsten was just tired, or nervous about transporting the horses, or worried about his job, like he'd said, but that didn't feel accurate. The previous night, he'd clearly been upset, and she'd hoped she could provide some comfort to him. The ride yesterday had been exceedingly fun, and she was starting to admit to herself that perhaps she wanted this situation to continue when they returned to Sanctuary. At least until he left.

She couldn't see herself seeing him around town and not wanting to *immediately* tackle him. Of course, the girls couldn't see them together, but otherwise, she didn't see why anything had to change.

And maybe... eventually... she might be able to believe that he'd stay. The idea had occurred to her on the ride yesterday, that she didn't have to end what they shared. She was already in love with him, so continuing on wouldn't make it hurt any less when he left. All she could do now was protect the girls. If they grew to see him as a father figure and he left her, she'd never forgive herself. It was a risk she just couldn't afford to take.

Except that morning, though he was kind and attentive, gave her little kisses on the head and squeezed her hand when he passed by, he'd been reserved as well. She'd gone to sleep in the arms of her orc, hopefully comforting him through his difficult thoughts, but she'd somehow woken to a different man, and was now presented with... distance. There were no playful gropes or cheeky smiles like she had grown accustomed to, no jokes or teasing. Only short sentences and touches that felt like goodbye.

Once they were mounted, the deep rumble of his voice vibrated her back.

"Should get there in an hour or so, if you want to get some sleep in."

"Torsten, I've been sleeping for the better part of the last twenty-four hours, while you've only had a single day's worth of sleep in the last two. Do *you* need more rest? I'm sure we could figure something out."

"No, I'll sleep on the flight. I'm used to flying with Calida," he said.

Cat pursed her lips. There was *something* off and she wouldn't abide it. Of course, he was allowed to feel however he wanted, but not knowing what was bothering one of her people made her skin *itch.*

"Do you want to talk about last night? It seems like maybe something is really bothering you..." she offered. Perhaps he just needed an invitation and a reminder that she was willing to listen. Perhaps he needed to see that she was going to support him, that she wanted to be the shoulder he sought when times were hard. She needed time to make sure all would be well with them, but knowing that she *wanted* to see where this went gave her peace. Riled up parts of her had settled with the decision, and now, she wanted to help him find the same.

He huffed. "I'm at a crossroads in my life. I think I've been trying to pretend that I'm not, and yesterday I realized I need to face facts and stop deluding myself. I spent my whole life preparing for this trip back to Sanctuary. Well, not *this* trip. The one with the envoy last week, I mean. So, I've got to find a new purpose for my life. I'm a good blacksmith, but I don't want to make weapons forever."

She could hear a smile dawn on his face as he leaned down to pat Butter and continued."I've sort of been thinking about farriery. I like horses, I have some of the skill required, and I've shod a few before. It's something I could be good at."

What little joy had built in Catrin drained from her face, down her stomach, and plopped onto the ground. Why should that upset her? He *was* good with the horses, and she knew the orcish armies were notoriously good horsemen. He'd have plenty of work, and not have to make weapons... but that was it. It struck her like an arrow. He'd have plenty of work... elsewhere. There were only going to be two horses in all of Sanctuary, he couldn't only shoe two horses. He was an active sort, and needed lots to occupy his time.

He'd said he wanted more, but here he was, talking about leaving. Her throat burned at the reality. She shouldn't be surprised. And she wanted to scream for letting herself be taken in again.

"Torsten dear? That you?" A voice called from the forest ahead. Catrin turned and saw the most gorgeous purple woman she'd ever seen. Opalescent scales shimmered in the sunlight. Her deep purple hair fell in thick, loose curls to her waist and cupped full breasts tipped with deep purple nipples.

Oh, she's not wearing anything.

"Who is that?" Catrin hissed.

"Calida, our ride... the dragon."

"Oh, of course, of course. She's just... different than I expected," she whispered.

"Different. Well, that's one way of saying it. She's something else, I tell you."

When they neared, the woman beamed at them, reaching strong arms up to help Catrin off the horse. She lowered Catrin with ease, placing her gently on the ground, and immediately level with her breasts. Catrin gasped, blushing and turning away. She wasn't a prude, but anyone would react to have a pair of such perfect breasts thrust in their face.

"Catrin, this is Calida. Calida, this is Catrin my... friend."

Friend. His friend. The words stuck in her heart. She'd thought that she meant something to him, but maybe he'd just pretended or... or had she done this? Had her agreement driven him away?

"Torsten! She's precious!" Calida squealed, squeezing Catrin to her in a hug. "I see why you were so eager to go on this trip... hell, I'm sad I wasn't invited but for this little bit now."

The dragon crossed her arms under her considerable bosom, propping them in what looked to be a *quite* intentional way and stuck out her bottom lip.

"Instead, I was stuck in Sanctuary with a bunch of old busybodies. They have me staying with the head of the village and she's a sour old prune. I'm trying to think of *any* way out of the matter without offending her. She's such a bore in the worst way and I might die if I don't figure something out, soon. Perhaps our dear friend Catrin might have an extra room? Catrin, does anyone call you kitten, dear? They should..." she continued.[1]

"Sorry, no," Catrin stammered out. "No extra rooms, I'm afraid. Plus, I have five-year-old twins, which can be a handful and a trial to live with. I'm sure you'll have plenty of wonderful options. No one wants to live in my house when the shrieking starts, I assure you."

Torsten climbed down and started wordlessly sorting through the bags packed onto Biscuit.

"Grumpy?" Calida mouthed.

Grimacing, Catrin wobbled her head. She wasn't sure if grumpy even began to cover it. Torsten seemed miserable.

---

1. Of course, Torsten had spoken of Cat when he arranged the flight with Calida, she's just as much of a meddler as Berne is, though.

"Here we are," Torsten said, pulling out a vial and a collection of syringes from the bag."Here, kit-Cat."

Catrin took them and Torsten unbuckled the bags with a vengeance, his movements erratic and jerky. Calida raised her scaly eyebrows to Cat, a silent question within. Shrugging a shoulder at Calida, Catrin turned to dust off her skirts. She had only an inkling of the issue and didn't even know where to begin explaining it. The forest clung close around them, trees blotting out the horizon in all directions.

"Are you going to have room to shift? It all seems very tight here..." Cat said.

"There's a clearing a ways ahead, I just got too excited when I heard you. From what Torsten said, I just *had* to meet you and see what-"

"Calida, can you help me over *here*, please?" Torsten interrupted.

"Of course, darling, you know I'm always happy to help you with whatever you need!" Calida said, rolling her eyes at Catrin.

She ambled over to Torsten, where he had some low, harsh words for her. Catrin didn't listen. It would be horribly rude, and she was honestly terrified of what she might hear. He'd been angling toward an end, and she thought she preferred not having to actually listen. The last thing she needed to hear was him telling his friend that he wasn't interested anymore and she could quit trying to help.

Instead, she wandered to Butter's front, petting the horse's warm muzzle. She picked some leaves she'd seen centaurs eat back home and offered them to her. Butter daintily accepted the leaves, gently nudging Catrin with her head in thanks.

"Well then!" Calida called out, startling her. "We'd best be off! It isn't far, but I'd like to get out of here before those clouds blow away. They're good cover."

The dragon led, leaving Catrin to follow, leading Butter. Biscuit ambled along after her, and Torsten bent to pick up the bags that had been on the horse's back. Looking back at him, Catrin let out a disappointed sigh. He was beautiful, and she'd miss the feel of his skin, the ripple of his muscles under her fingers.

An arm slipped through hers, and she was surprised to see Calida at her side.

"Well dear, do tell me about these sweet little ones. I know you say they shriek, but I assure you they have *nothing* on dragonets!" The tall dragon rested a hand with perfectly manicured claws on Catrin's arm.

"Um, well, they're five, like I said. They love playing outdoors and building little houses. Ursule is interested in clothes, and Ingrid loves drawing. They're constantly fighting over what their shifted forms will be, and whether or not they are going to match. Ingrid is considering a moose, but Suley-Ursule, isn't sold on a moose but desperately wants to match."

"They sound just precious, dear! And I bet they take after their mama, just gorgeous," Calida said. Her voice sounded a little loud to Cat, and she dampened her hearing. Perhaps she'd left it heightened.

"They are lovely, truly. Suley is interested in fashion, and Ingrid lets her dress them both each day, which just tickles Suley. She's started developing opinions on what I wear each day, though I have to remind her that I'm a potter and I'm not going to be wearing my best dress to throw clay."

"A potter? You're an artist, then! I've always admired artists, myself. I have a bit of a... what is the saying? A green thumb when it comes to art," Calida said.

Catrin burst out in a giggle."No, a green thumb is for gardening, and it means you are good at it!"

Calida's mouth quirked in a sly smile."Let me tell you a secret, I know that. I just wanted to see you laugh, dear. You looked so melancholy."

The dragon rubbed Cat's forearm and gave Catrin space to speak, should she want it.

"It's been a very tiring few days," Cat offered.

"I should say so! I haven't scented someone smelling this strongly of Torsten, well... ever. I think he's kept you busy," Calida whispered, her head tucked close to Catrin's. "And I know he has a tendency to be a bit of an arse sometimes, but these things tend to work out as they should."

Catrin smiled politely. She wasn't sure if these things *actually* tended to work out, but it was a nice sentiment.

Before long, they crested a small hill that led into a valley clear of trees. Calida waggled her eye scales at Catrin. "Now you'll get to experience my true beauty," she said. The dragon leapt away, dissolving to mist that sparkled in the air. The shimmer expanded larger and larger, until Catrin could scarcely see where its edges were. With a pop, the dragon appeared, larger than before, and as she said, even more beautiful. The purple iridescent scales that had previously served as mere decoration now covered the vast majority of her body. Catrin hadn't been sure how anything could be large enough to carry two horses, two humanoids, and all of their gear, but Calida was definitely large enough. Catrin gasped at the sight of her. Even though Catrin lived somewhere extremely magical, she'd never seen anything even remotely close to this.[2]

Calida stretched her large wings, one of them blotting out the sun.

See, little one? This is where I truly shine! Calida's voice sounded in Catrin's mind, startling her. The tone of Calida's voice broadened, and she felt like that meant she was including Torsten now. *Well then, hop to it you two, let's tranquilize those horses and get on the road!*

Tranquilizing the horses wasn't nearly as easy as Calida made it sound. Each of them would inject the tranquilizer into a horse, and stay with them for the entire flight. Arndis had emphasized how important it was that they administer the sedative slowly, to ensure they didn't harm the animals. She'd been fairly certain that this tranquilizer would work, and of the amounts. She'd administered it to plenty of centaurs before and thought it might transfer over. Torsten must have prepped the packages on the walk, because he handed Catrin a completed setup. There were three syringes for each horse, the first containing

---

2. Lunology, as a magical art, evolved organically from the Lady's magic, and as such, has strict rules and boundaries. The magics each of the magical populations wield are significantly more amorphous. Their talents are in-born, and as a result of strict segregation, there has been little intermarriage or even information transmission between the groups.

Arndis' best guess at an initial dose, the second to be administered throughout the flight if the horses begin to rouse, and a third as a contingency.

"You take Butter," Torsten said, walking away without another glance.

Catrin was sure she didn't know this man. Torsten was confident, silly and flirtatious. Not whatever this was.

Catrin crooned softly to Butter as she located where she'd insert the needle, speaking softly to Butter as she slipped it inside. The large horse recoiled in pain, and for a moment Catrin was worried Butter would hurt her. A few soft words quickly settled the horse and soon Cat felt comfortable administering the sedative.

Pushing the plunger in, she carefully monitored the amount of the liquid she pushed, stopping at the intervals Arnis had marked and waiting for specific signs. When Butter's lower lip started drooping, Catrin continued the push until the horse's head hung low to the ground. After a few minutes, Butter lay down on the ground, the final push sinking into her.

To the side, Torsten was fighting with Biscuit, who was neighing and flailing his head. Torsten was shushing and holding him, and eventually, Biscuit too was asleep on the ground.

"That was hard won," she said, hoping he'd respond in his lighthearted way. Instead, he nodded his head solemnly and turned from her. Wrapping his body around the horse, he waved Calida over.

"Alright Calida, one horse to a claw. We'll keep them sedated for the flight, but get us home as fast as you might. Cat, there's snacks and water in her side bag. Let's get this over with."

Let's get this over with. Catrin wasn't sure she'd ever heard anything worse.

Chapter Sixteen

Torsten

IN WHICH A DRAGONFLIGHT,
DIFFICULT CHOICES ARE
MADE, AND AN OFFER MOST
UNEXPECTED

FLYING WITH CALIDA WAS one of Torsten's favorite things in the world, but the entire flight, he just prayed it would be over soon. Within her claws, her warmth kept them cozy and out of the wind, but it was a hell of a lot less interesting than riding on her back.

Halfway through, he needed to administer more tranquilizer to Biscuit, but generally, he was alone with his thoughts. Without anything else to do, he was forced to confront his dark thoughts. His stomach and mind were fetid masses of festering emotions writhing within him. His love for Cat, his hurt, and his insecurities twisted around each other, intertwining into a tangle that he could scarcely begin to unravel.

She didn't want him to show her affection in front of her children. It felt like a slap in the face of all they'd shared. Had he not shown her his dedication? Had he not shown her with everything but words that he loved her? He'd thought, for a brief time, that she might be starting to love him back, but if she did, would she have asked him to hide like that? No. He'd never ask that of her, so he could only conclude she must not, or at least not to the depth of feeling that he felt.

Which, truly, how could she? He wasn't a dependable father figure for her children, he had no job, no real home, and no idea what he was going to do moving forward. He didn't even know where he planned to live if he wasn't staying specifically for Cat, let alone anything else.

If she didn't feel the same, could he stay in Sanctuary? See her around town and not have his heart break each time?

He thought about returning to the Homeland, where his cooking didn't please anyone's palates, where he was the slowest at chopping wood, and where he spoke his own language with an accent. His faults would forever label him a foreigner in his own land. He'd never find a partner among them, but the thought of ever being with anyone else abhorred him, he found. Once again, he was at sixes and sevens, adrift with no direction. Perhaps, if nothing else, Aegir would take him on and he could just man the ship, travel between Sanctuary and the Empire, interfering with supply lines where they could.

For the briefest moment, he cursed his parents for putting him in this position. Because of where he'd been born and raised, he was a stranger among his people. And because he'd left, he'd missed any chance he and Cat would have had at anything simple and easy.

The flight felt hours long, his very being protested at being separated from Catrin. Did she truly not feel this longing? Surely, after all they'd shared she'd feel it? As his thoughts continued to storm darker, they made their way north. The air grew steadily colder as they neared Sanctuary, and even Calida's heat wasn't enough to keep him from shivering. Eventually, the cold and his exhaustion conspired against him and he fell into a fitful sleep of dreams where he chased Catrin but could never reach her.

WARMTH WASHED OVER TORSTEN'S body, waking him, as they flew through the dome of magic that protected Sanctuary. His muscles relaxed, and he heard Calida release a spurt of flame, a signal to Berne that they were coming.

Prying two claws apart, Torsten peeked out. On the ground, in a large clearing near their house, Berne and Sirin played in a field with the twins. Unexpectedly, Arndis waited with them, too.

Ingrid froze, her small green hand pointing up at the sky. The group turned, their faces lighting with surprise, and Berne's with relief. Calida circled the clearing and landed softly on her hind legs, turning away so that she could deposit Cat, Torsten, and the horses where they'd be hidden from view.

Small joyous voices rang through the air as the twins came barreling around Calida in search of their mother.

"Mama?" Ursule called. "Are you really back?"

"Mama!" Ingrid's voice was more sure, but both children attacked their mother in a hug. Tears streamed down Catrin's face as she held them, kissing their curled hair.

"Oh my loves, I have missed you so much!" She finally squeaked out. "Did you have a nice time? Did you learn anything new?"

Ingrid launched into an explanation of the new dish Sirin had taught them, while Ursule mentioned something about Berne's bees.

Torsten ran over to meet Berne, who pulled him into a tight hug.

"Everything well?" Berne asked."Did you get them?"

"Went off fine. They're well, just asleep."

The air whooshed behind him as Calida shifted back into her humanoid form, revealing the pair of horses on the ground.

Sirin stopped walking, her eyes wide and her mouth hanging open.

"They're sleeping." Berne assured her immediately."And I know it's not solstice yet, but this was the best thing I could think to get you. I'm sorry that they are early but-" Berne cut off as Sirin launched herself at him, eyes glistening. She pecked kisses all over his face before jumping down and running over to each of the horses. Sirin flung herself over Biscuit's back and belly, arms spread over him. Her mouth was stuck in a permanent "o" of surprise, and she blinked rapidly. Next, she repeated the process with Butter.

Behind her, Arndis slipped over to Biscuit and used a large syringe to administer what he assumed must be the antidote to the sedative.[1]

Sirin returned to Berne, hugging and kissing him frantically, blubbering her gratitude between kisses. Berne stroked her hair, his eyes tracking her every movement. The twins squealed about the horses and Catrin was holding tightly onto each of their arms, trying to keep them from bothering the sleeping animals.

Torsten, however, stood alone. He looked to Calida, trying to find solidarity in his loneliness. Instead, she was chatting with Arndis near the horses.

Each look at Catrin made his throat squeeze in pain. She held each of her children on her voluptuous hips, face alight as she listened to them chatter on about their adventures while she was gone. He pressed his lips together, forcing his gaze away from them to Berne and Sirin. They were, after all, the whole reason he'd gone on this trip.

As he looked, Sirin's happy sniffles grew into a wail, Berne's face instantly bewildered.

---

1. Sedatives, at least those used in horses, do not have antidotes other than perhaps adrenaline. However, when I inquired later, this antidote was an extremely concentrated dose of lunula. While they are not lunologists, this dosage does seem to negate the sedative they use, which is also home-grown.

"Sirin, what's wrong, love?" he asked. Sirin gripped the front of Berne's jerkin.

"I can't ride her," she said, her voice transforming from her wail into unstable laughter.

"What? Are you missing something, do we need to commission some gear?"

"No, no," Sirin said. "Pregnant women aren't supposed to ride horses!"

The entire field froze as everyone turned their attention to Sirin. After a moment of stillness, Catrin squealed and ran over with the girls to hug her sister and brother. Berne wiped tears from Sirin's face and whispered to her.

"This isn't how we wanted to tell you," Berne said to Cat as she crashed into them. "We thought we could tell you over dinner instead. You're still invited of course! You too, Torsten."

Watching them, Torsten was very aware that as much as he wanted to be, he wasn't *actually* a part of their family and he had no business attending.

"Oh no, actually I need to check in with the contingent. See how negotiations are going and all that. I'll catch up with you all tomorrow." He unbuckled his pack from Catrin's and the rest of the horse's gear and waved. "Let me know if you need help carrying anything or getting their stable assembled."

The look of confusion on Catrin's face hurt more than anything. Why was she acting as if this wasn't the plan at all, like he'd made this up? Regardless, watching this family he was not a part of celebrate was a vise around his throat, and he needed to be away as quickly as possible.

A hand landed on his shoulder, and he knew before turning from her smell and familiarity with her touch, but it was Cat.

"Yes?" he asked.

"Torsten, what is going on with you? You've been acting so strange."

"What's going on?" he whispered, turning and shoving his hands in his pockets so he wouldn't touch her."What's going on is I'm doing what you asked. I'm acting like I don't know what your cunt tastes like in front of your family, since I'm your dirty little secret."

Recoiling, Catrin blinked at him."That is not what I said. How could you think that? There's a difference between you being a dirty little secret and protecting my children from growing attached to someone who still doesn't know if he's going to leave or not!"

"Cat, you know damn well that if you asked—" his eyes flicked above her head as Inigo appeared behind her, running across the field. He raised an arm to wave at Torsten.

"Tomax!" he called, causing Catrin to wipe her eyes and plaster on a smile."I saw Calida overhead. I need to speak with you, it's urgent."

Torsten looked between Inigo and Catrin, torn between his duty and the conversation he knew they needed to have.

"Go, it's fine," she said.

"I'll be right back," he said. They'd been getting heated, sure, but her words gave him the tiniest bit of hope. He stared into her sad eyes, trying to impress his sincerity.

"What's the word?" he asked, jogging over to his buru.

"We'll, we've received a letter from the Berggeheimnis," Inigo said in their native Orskara. "Now that dragons are cleared for entrance into Sanctuary, we've started the new mail service. Anyhow, in the first batch, the dwarves wrote and requested you as their next placement for ambassador. They've been impressed with your interactions in the past and ability to adapt to their cultural norms. We've got Calida scheduled to leave the day after tomorrow bright and early. So, if you agree, be ready to be on that flight. I know I told you that you didn't have an obligation to come back, but I think this could be really good for you, career-wise. I could set you up to be in a leadership position in a few years. They've never specifically requested anyone, and as you know, they're a really important faction for us."

Inigo's excitement was plain in the way he bounced on his toes and words spilled out of his mouth. He was right, it was a wonderful opportunity. It would mean, for the first time, he'd be chosen for something based on his own abilities rather than an inherited duty. He'd have real impact on the future of his people, and a respected position in the revolution. Two weeks ago, it was everything he could have ever wanted. A way to serve and represent his people without needing to live under the constant reminder of his own differences.

Torsten opened his mouth to answer but couldn't think what to say.

So much had changed in the last two weeks. What he wanted in life had shifted so drastically. As much as Cat had hurt him, as much as he still felt unworthy, he couldn't help but hope that their current troubles were a temporary hiccup. That through hard work, he could become worthy of her, even though he wasn't already. This though, would complicate matters at best and could ruin it all at worst.

"I—thank you, Inigo," he said. "I'll let you know this evening, if that's all right? It's an amazing opportunity, I just need to make sure it's the right fit for me right now." The words sounded too formal, like something his father might say, but falling back on his training was easiest in the moment.

Inigo clapped him on the back. "But of course!"

His commander walked away, unaware of how he'd just thrown Torsten's already tenuous life plans into chaos. In a daze, Torsten walked back to Catrin, who'd watched the whole exchange, it seemed, clutching her hands under her chin.

"What did he have to say?"

'The dwarves," he said. He shook his head, still unbelieving."He said the dwarves requested that I be placed as their next ambassador."

Catrin's eyes went wide, blinking slowly."That sounds like an enormous opportunity."

"It is," he said.

The minor distance between them stretched until it felt like a chasm he couldn't cross.

"Do you want to go?" she asked. Her eyes darted around him, and she fidgeted with her hands. Her voice had a high, false quality he'd not heard from her before. It stretched the distance even wider.

"I don't know. I loved visiting the dwarfs, and there's actually a pretty good reason for me to be there, should the Empire find out. They have some of the best blacksmiths in the world."

The dwarvish blacksmiths had techniques he'd never dreamed of and built the most delicate looking weapons and armor that were stronger than any he'd ever made. Thinking back, no one there had made him feel odd for being different, they'd been excited to hear about the rest of the world and the things he'd seen. They'd clamored for news and his thoughts. He could be happy there, but it all paled in comparison to what he'd have with Cat if he had the opportunity.

"And..." His voice sounded steady to his ears, an accomplishment considering the emotions roiling inside him. "I don't know if I have a reason to stay here or not. Do I have a reason to stay?"

"I can't be a reason to stay, Tor, Edrigu was staying because of me and we see how that worked out. You need to go wherever it is you actually want to be, not wherever I'm trapping you, and then... And then I guess we'll figure out what we are once you do." If not for the tears streaming down her face, he'd never know she was upset. Her voice was steady and she held her chin high.

"You wouldn't be trapping me, Cat," he said. "You could never trap me. But, this is also the opportunity of a lifetime. And I think..." He pressed his hands into the small of his back, looking up at the sky and breathing in and out. "I think I deserve to be where I'm wanted."

"You do, you do deserve that." Catrin whispered "You know, if it was just you and me, it would be different, right? So, what does that mean for us?"

What did it mean? The answer came to him, in one fell swoop, he didn't like it, but he could see how it could work-could solve both of their problems.

"I think it means that I'm going to take the post with the dwarves, and you can have some time to figure things out—Letters—we're going to *actually* write letters. With the dragons flying back-and-forth, as often as they plan, you won't have to wait months to see if I'm actually going to do it, maybe just a few days. And then... we'll see how it goes."

Her face was a mess of emotions, and she didn't speak for a long while. Every muscle in his body was screaming at him to go to her, but he held firm, hands shoved into his pockets once more. Her eyes flew around, looking anywhere but at him. He'd give so much, anything really, for her to look at him again the way she had the last week.

Eventually, she cleared her nose with a deep sniff, and nodded. "I'm going to miss you so much and I —" she shook her head.

"I know, kitten," he whispered. "I know, but I really do think this is for the best. It will give you the time you need. And hells, anytime you want to see me, I could just hop on a dragon and be back in a day or so. We can visit... while you figure things out."

"I'm-I'm not saying goodbye." Curls tumbled around her as she shook her head violently. Her eyes flicked over to her kids and Torsten felt his stomach drop.

"I'll devise a plan for the girls' tutoring. I still want to do that for them-for you. If it's all right, I'll come by tomorrow and we can get a head start..."

Catrin nodded, sniffling. "So, I suppose I'll see you tomorrow then?" she asked, her voice small and tender.

"Yes, kitten, you'll see me tomorrow."

Chapter Seventeen
Catrin

IN WHICH A MISERABLE NIGHT, A JOYOUS DISCOVERY, AND A MIDNIGHT FLIGHT

CATRIN SPENT THE NIGHT putting on a happy face and celebrating with her family. She was overjoyed for Sirin and Berne, but she knew they sensed something was wrong. While Sirin introduced the children to the horses, Berne pulled her aside.

"You were crying earlier, do I need to punch Torsten's head in?" he asked, putting both hands on her shoulders.

A wry laugh burst from her and then she immediately started crying. Shaking her head, she buried herself in his embrace, her brother's huge arms enveloping her the way they always had.

Here, she was safe. It was instinctual. Here was the one man who had never disappointed her, had always shown up for her, and always cared for her unconditionally.

"Ssssh, there now," he said, patting the back of her head.

"He's leaving, and I think I hurt him, and I was just thinking maybe we could figure things out and now he's leaving," she said, the words falling from her in a tumble.

"Oh, poppet," Berne said, cradling her head."He is leaving, but things will work out. I figured something might have happened while you were away. Do you want to talk about it?"

"No, not really." Catrin couldn't see how talking about it with her brother would be helpful. He was a great listener, but he was still her *brother*. There was no way he actually wanted to hear what they'd been up to.

"Though, don't even ask me to talk to mom and dad right now," she said.

"Why?"

"They were hiding his letters. He *did* write me, they just took them."

Berne tensed and a low growl built in his throat."But you cried every time for two years! They saw you going through that and just *let* you?"

He squeezed her tighter, crushing her into his chest. "I should have opened those damn packets. Fuck state secrets and confidentiality."

Through her tears, Cat giggled. "You don't mean that. You couldn't have, but I appreciate the thought."

"Like hell I couldn't have, I defied them to get a wife, I could've opened a little packet to protect you."

ON THE WALK HOME with the girls, in the twilight, the lunula lit up the canals, casting everything in a familiar teal light. It was good to be home, it was familiar and comfortable, but it also felt so *small* after spending so much time outside. The mountains ringed the valley, and she found she missed being able to see things she'd never seen before. She missed the feeling of discovery that she had barely noticed while she was away. In Sanctuary, she'd seen every house, every tree, every person ten thousand times. It *chafed* her now, where it had always calmed her before.

"Mama, what was it like, outside?" Ingrid asked, toying with Cat's hand in hers. "What was it like being where no one knew who you were?"

"It was scary, at times," she started."But it was also exciting. I could say or be anything I wanted and no one knew any different."

Ursule gasped, swinging Cat's left arm."I could tell everyone I was a princess, cast out from my kingdom because of an evil queen!"

"You could, though I hope I'm not the evil queen in this tale..."

Ursule giggled and shook her head.

"I could even tell people I was a boy and no one would even know!" Ingrid chimed in.

"That's right," Cat confirmed, squinting down at Ingrid from the corner of her eye. Something about that seemed... worth asking about."You could."

"I know you were scared," Ursule continued."But you had Torsten with you! He's so big and strong he could beat up any bad guys if they were mean to you!"

"He could," Catrin confirmed, tightness building in her chest."Though in the Compact, they don't know that orcs exist, so we had to be careful he wasn't seen. He didn't even come with me into the Citadel to get the horses, because it was too risky."

"They don't?" Ursule asked, face screwed up in horror."So, we can't ever go there?"

"Well, no, probably not," Catrin started."Unless you learn to shift yourselves to look fully human."

"We could *do* that?" Ingrid asked, eyes wide.

"Of course, darling. We can change almost anything about our bodies, though, your auntie Sirin knows more about controlling those changes than I do. If that's something you'd want, we can work with her on it, once we know you've come into your lunula control."

"Oh yes," Ursule said. "I want to explore the world someday!"

"Me, too," Ingrid said, though her face was more thoughtful than excited.[1]

Everything with the girls seemed... easier. She hated that she'd been away, but being back with them it was like she'd regained a piece of her heart. It wasn't like she felt like an amazing mother overnight, but perhaps she wasn't entirely inept.

While her girls provided a lovely distraction from her melancholy, thoughts of Torsten kept drifting into her mind. Quips he'd make in response to questions, or how if Ursule wanted to explore the *whole* world, she'd need a guide for Caihalaith.

Once they arrived home, the twins drifted off in the middle of their bedtime story and as Catrin tiptoed out of their room, her misery hit her full

---

1. Looking back, more than twenty years later, it's fascinating to see how their personalities were forming and have translated to their adult selves. It also heals something in my soul to see how their childhood dreams have been realized, though perhaps in ways they could never have anticipated.

force. Her once comfortable home felt too quiet and tidy. She still smelled of the road and horses, so a bath was in order. She'd always loved baths, and made an affair out of them whenever she was able. She took a quick shower to get clean, before filling her large tub with hot water, scented oils and lighting a few candles.

Hissing as she lowered herself into the water, Catrin tried to let all of her worries float away. Instead, they came roaring to the forefront of her mind. Torsten had reacted... much more strongly than she'd expected, and she was beginning to think that his behavior the night before hadn't been purely lust driven. He'd been so forceful with her, so demanding, and she'd assumed it was just a reaction to it being the last night of their trip. But as she sat with it, perhaps he'd been acting as if it were their last night *ever.*

Had she read his feelings so wrong? Many times while they were away, she'd have sworn he was on the verge of saying he loved her. Now, she might never know. He said they'd write, but the distance was *so* vast and if his new post went well? He certainly wouldn't want to abandon it to return to Sanctuary. When he'd first told her of the dwarvish cities, hidden beneath the mountains, his eyes had been bright and dancing. He'd clearly loved it there. She couldn't see asking him to leave somewhere he so obviously loved, to stop doing something he was so excited by. Perhaps, she needed to let him go... perhaps she needed to let him reach his full potential, instead of trapping him here with her.

A broken sob burst from her, the very thought abhorrent. She didn't want to be someone that trapped him, she wanted to be someone that *freed* him.

With a frustrated grunt, she stood from the bath, rubbing herself vigorously with a towel. The bath wasn't helping. It was only giving her time for her mind to wander and fester. Balling up her dirty clothes, she snuck upstairs to her room, tiptoeing as to not wake the girls. Her room would soothe her. It was a space she'd designed specifically to be serene and exactly as she liked. As she walked in, the familiar scents of her lavender sachets in drawers greeted her, mixing with the subtle cedar of the wood. While it should have comforted her, instead it felt... unfinished. Like there was something missing from the aroma. It was flat instead of complex.

Her bed, vast and pristine, loomed across the room. She scurried across to it and climbed in, willing it to dampen her misery, wrap her up in its thick layers of blankets and blot out her feelings. Turning the knob that doused the gas lamps, she lay alone in the dark, squeezing her eyes shut.

Her stomach felt hollow, a bone-deep emptiness that she feared would become her new normal. Perhaps, emptiness was better? Abject misery would be exhausting, but maybe emptiness could be endured. Letting it wash over her, Catrin caught the hint of a scent. Suddenly, it snapped into place, slicing through her and lodging into her heart. The faint smell of Torsten teased her from where she'd dropped her travel pack, mingling with the lavender and cedar to form a complex, drugging bouquet. Before she quite knew her intent, she was sprinting across the room in the dark, tearing through her pack and clutching a skirt to her. It was the skirt she'd worn to the tavern, her costume. Clutching it to her chest, she climbed back into bed, burying her face in it to huff in the remnants of him. She wanted it everywhere, wanted to be surrounded in him, if just for a little while. For a week, she'd smelled like him, and now, she realized, she'd washed it all away. She'd as good as washed him down the drain with the bathwater, leaving her bereft of him.

Perhaps it wasn't healthy to cling to him so, but she couldn't help herself. Perhaps it would all be fine, but in that moment, she couldn't imagine an outcome that made sense and allowed them to be together. So, she shrank down into her hare form, and made a little nest of her skirt, burrowing inside until he surrounded her.

At least, she thought, *this way I can't cry.*

THE FOLLOWING MORNING WAS only marginally better, at least some of his scent clung to her. She'd see him, briefly, and the thought cheered and tortured her. The kids babbled excitedly over breakfast, eager to spend the day with him and learn as much as they could in the time they had. When the doorbell clanged, her heart leapt to her throat, the children tearing downstairs hollering. By the time Catrin arrived downstairs, they'd already wrenched the door open, revealing Torsten and another orc, who carried an instrument she didn't recognize.

"I uh, asked Kemen here if he wouldn't mind working with the girls after I left, and he said he was happy to help..." he said, rubbing the back of his neck. "If that's something you'd want."

Catrin blinked quickly, keeping the tears that sprang up at the sight of him at bay, and nodded. "Yes," she said, her voice squeaky. "Thank you, Kemen, that would be lovely."

Catrin met Torsten's eyes and the sadness she saw there echoed her own. Whatever semblance of emptiness she'd cultivated fizzled away by seeing him. He fidgeted with a packet, she'd never seen him fidget. How much damage had they wrought together?

"I uh-thought you might like this." He held the package out to her."It's some clay, and mineral pigments from the dwarves. We brought samples of goods from the Empire. I don't know much about it, but it sounds like you can heat it immediately or something."

Cat's brows rose and her mouth dropped open, her potter's mind alight. Normally she had to wait a few days for things to dry.[2] If this clay worked half as well as he said, she'd need to order this clay in bulk. She took the package from him with shaking hands, turning it over as her mind raced with possibilities.

For a moment, their awkwardness fell away as he smiled at her."You like it then? I hope it's useful."

"I love it," she whispered."Truly, I can't wait to use it."

Briefly, all of the complications faded and they were just the two of them again. Transfixed, she fell into his eyes, forgetting things were a horrible mess, but then he grimaced and broke the spell. Their troubles rushed to the forefront and he

---

2. While I am not a potter, according to Catrin, this is a marvel. This clay is extremely special, though it just looks like a blob to me.

shook his head. Torsten turned his attention to her children, giving them a big smile that equally melted and broke her heart.

"Well then, we'll be off," he said. "Cat, we'll just be outside, in that field there, if you need us." He pointed to a field she'd be able to see from her potting bench.

Still reeling from their brief connection, she plastered on a smile. "Thank you, and I'll just be here, if you need me." Despite her efforts, the statement carried entirely more weight than she'd meant, but Torsten only nodded, a sad smile tickling the edges of his mouth.

They cleared out, and soon, Catrin was alone with the silence of her studio. She ripped into the package and found a set of pigments, a large lump of clay and instructions for use. Her fingers *itched* to play with it. Under her postbox was a stack of letters, orders mostly, so she worked through them, organizing them in stacks of what people wanted until she found something she thought would be a good test of the clay's properties. The order was for a vase, something tall and skinny she could throw in her sleep. As she pulled off hunks of clay from her block, strains of a song filtered in from the field. It was an upbeat melody, happy and joyous. Her children each held one of Torsten's hands as he taught them footwork. She squeezed her eyes shut and turned away from the window, though the song persisted, permeating her space.

She sat down, spinning her wheel and pulling up the clay to form the vase, Smoothing up its length, she was immediately reminded of pulling on Torsten's cock, the thick heft of it in her hands. His rich laughter sounded outside and between the column in her hands, and his voice filtering in through the window, she was immediately transported back to nights on their journey. His cock wasn't chilly like this of course, but she would warm it up. She shook her head, trying to focus on her work.

If only clay weren't so gods damn slick...

Her hands slipped along the clay, destroying the vase she was meant to be making. Instead, she lengthened it until her hands fit to a now familiar circumference. Bulbous at the bottom, long and thick, with a prominent head. She added round balls for where his piercings poked through. Before long, she had a surprisingly accurate replica. She mixed the pigments and painted them on, disbelieving that it would work.

With a blush and sheepish look out the window, she shoved it in her kiln. The instructions said to bring the kiln up to temperature with it inside. She waited impatiently while it fired, rationalizing her creation. She had every right to see to her own pleasure, and with Torsten away, it might help with missing him.

HOURS LATER, SHE PULLED out her creation and inspected it. Her hands shook as she examined it for flaws.

It'd *worked!* For a moment, she was jealous of Torsten, that he'd have ready access to such supplies. She'd just have to order as much of the stuff as Calida could carry. It probably cost quite a bit, but she had a bit of savings stashed away and she'd make it back easily with time saved. A brief trip upstairs proved that it worked amazingly well. She'd sized it perfectly, though it only served to rile her feelings further. Afterward, she tucked it into her bedside table, wiped tears from her eyes and trudged back downstairs feeling worse than before.

She'd actually accomplished some work by the time her children tromped through the door, happy and exhausted. Torsten trailed after them, lingering in the door frame. Her children babbled excitedly over one another, so that she barely caught two words.

"You both need a shower desperately," she said, refusing to look at Torsten."Head upstairs and get cleaned up."

Immediately, Cat realized what a mistake that had been. Now she was alone with Tor, the day before he left... five minutes after she'd ridden a replica of his cock.

"Well," he began."They-"

"How were-" Cat started."Oh, you first."

"They were great," Torsten said."Sucked it up like little sponges... They're great, Cat. They're really great kids. You've done well." As he spoke, his voice got hoarse.

Cat's throat and eyes started stinging. It was like he always knew what to say to expose her fully.

"Thank you," she whispered."Tor- I..."

What could she say? She couldn't ask him to stay, she couldn't ask him to give that up and yet her heart felt like it would fall out of her chest the second he walked away. She wanted to run to him, to beg him not to leave, but she couldn't get in the way of his opportunity. It's not like she was enough for him to stay for, anyhow.

"I'm going to miss you," she settled on."So, so much.'"

She couldn't stop the tears that pooled on her lower lid from running down her face. His last memory of her would be with a beet-red nose and tear-streaked cheeks, and yet, she couldn't stop.

"You're going to write, right?"

"I will, I promise," he said, crossing to her and sweeping her into a hug.

She buried her face in his chest, drinking in the warm, sun-soaked scent of him.

Because the truth of it was, she was already so irrevocably in love with him.

He kissed the top of her head. Grasping her chin, he tilted her head to look up at him."I swear it, kitten. You're going to get sick of my letters."

Lady bless this man and his stunning smile. He might be getting teary eyed, too, but his smile could melt her in a second every time. She still had no idea how anyone could ever *not* want him.

"What if you meet some gorgeous dwarf?" she wailed, unable to contain it.

"Then," he chuckled."I imagine they'll be sorely disappointed." Fingers running down the side of her face, he grimaced.

"Just, tell me, kitten," he whispered."If you get to the point where you don't want this anymore, so I can try... to-fuck I don't know. I certainly don't see myself moving on."

He cleared his throat, looking at the ceiling."Alright, precious, let's not belabor it. I hope you'll come to see me off in the morning... sounded like the kids wanted to... but, things as they are, could I get my goodbye kiss now?"

Like so many things with Torsten, she didn't even need to think, she felt. Wrapping her arms around his neck she allowed him to lift her off the ground. The soft press of his lips was the sweetest memory she'd ever gotten to relive. Soft and giving, he opened his mouth and coaxed her tongue with his. He slipped along it, and with each caress she could feel the care he poured into each touch he gave her. Every pass, every stroke seemed designed to seduce her. Though, it was a very different kind of seduction. This wasn't a seduction towards sex, instead it was far more dangerous. He seduced her to hope—to believe, to envision a future where she could have this, have him, with her always.

Eventually, she had no idea how long, it turned frantic. His sips became desperate, and she responded in kind. She tried to catalog the feeling of his tusks as they pressed into her, the taste of him, the smell, for her long nights alone ahead. More, she willed herself to remember the indescribable feeling of joy she felt when she was with him.

When they pulled apart, seconds, minutes, hours-she had no idea-later, they were both gasping. Their breaths came in heavy pants and Cat knew her lips were swollen.

Torsten looked into her eyes, his deep brown transfixing her own. She was frozen, trapped, waiting to see what he'd say, what he'd do.

Say you're staying. Say you want me, say you won't leave me, too.

He opened and closed his lips, squeezed his eyes shut and shook his head. "I'm going to miss you, precious. Your letters will be the highlight of my day. I'll write to you every day, and hopefully, someday, you'll fall in love with me back. This isn't goodbye, kitten, I'm gonna fight."

Without waiting for a response, he kissed her head, slipped from her arms and hastily made for the door.

Love him back? Didn't he know she already loved him more than she'd ever thought possible? Didn't he know... she'd-she ran through their interactions and... no how could he know? She'd certainly never told him once she'd come to the realization herself and now? Telling him in a letter didn't feel right, so she might have to wait months. Perhaps she could tell him in the morning? That would be romantic, right? She could hug him, whisper it in his ear? Though, she'd need to think of the perfect way to say it. She *had* to find a way for him to understand that this was entirely about not wanting to risk the kids' feelings and nothing to do with him.

As if they knew, she was summoned upstairs by shrieking.

Duty called.

When she arrived, Ingrid, dripping wet water all over the floor in a towel, was pushing Ursule into the bathroom. Ursule was shrieking about the mess and Ingrid was telling her to shut up.

"Hey," she said, holding her hands out to calm them."What is going on up here?"

"I need to talk to you, but Suley won't get in the shower so I can!" Ingrid yelled.

"Because!" Ursule said, grasping the door frame to resist Ingrid."*She's* getting water all over the floor and making a mess and I don't want to get in trouble!"

For some reason, Ingrid burst into tears and sat on the ground in a puddle of drips.

"Okay, okay," Catrin soothed."Suley, please get into the shower, you will not get in trouble. I need to have a chat with Sissy."

Again, Ingrid's wails increased in volume. Ursule hesitated, her brow furrowing in concern.

"It's alright sweetheart. I'll handle it, please get into the shower." Catrin turned her attention back to Ingrid. The poor thing looked miserable. Shushing, Catrin picked her up, wet body and all, and carried her upstairs to the master bedroom. Whatever was going on seemed private. Ingrid sobbed the entire way up, and it was only after a few moments of rocking in Catrin's rocking chair that she calmed down. Once she'd settled into quiet whimpers instead of wails Catrin broached the subject.

"Now, whenever you're ready, I'd love to hear what the problem is," Catrin said, smoothing Ingrid's hair from her face.

Ingrid sniffled and wiped her eyes."I don't know why I couldn'ta been born a boooooy."

Catrin hadn't had any idea what to expect, but it certainly wasn't that.

"What makes you say that?" she asked, voice calm and quiet so as not to further upset her child.

"Because, I just always felt like I should have..." Ingrid started playing with the edge of Catrin's blouse."Girl words feel... yucky. Today Torsten called me 'Bud' and it felt real good. It's not *fair* that 'sissy' feels yucky and my *name* feels yucky but 'bud' feels just right!"

For entirely too long, Catrin was shocked into silence. She should've said something to comfort her child. She should've dispensed kisses or assurances beyond holding her-or was it them?

But instead, her brain flashed through the last several years, scanning for hints and was disappointed to find that there were, in fact, many. Ingrid had always expressed a great deal of interest in things that would make them "more like uncle Berne." Further, recently, Ingrid *had* been expressing a distaste for certain clothing items, or terms.

An overwhelming tide of shame threatened to swallow her whole. Her baby was going through something monumental and she hadn't even *noticed?* She must be the worst mother in the world! Nevermind not knowing orcish things, this was something fundamental to her child's self image! How could she have-no, she stopped herself, shaking her head. This wasn't about her, this was about her baby, who needed her.[3]

"Oh, darling," she said, pulling them close."I am so, so, sorry you've been dealing with this all alone. I'm sorry you've had these big feelings all bottled up."

She kissed Ingrid's head and whispered conspiratorially."But, I think I might have some good news..."

"What?" Ingrid said, sniffling.

"Being born a girl doesn't mean-" she stopped. No, that wasn't quite right."Just because we thought you were a girl, doesn't mean you have to keep trying to be that way, or that you ever really were."

"What?" Ingrid said again, this time sounding confused and maybe the tiniest bit hopeful."Really?"

"Really, really," Catrin said, kissing them on the head."Sometimes, we just don't know, until you tell

---

3. In hindsight, of course we could all see the signs, and while we all felt guilty, we can't go back and change things. Instead, we move forward.

us, so we make mistakes. Do you want to tell me more?"

Ingrid blinked at her several times and started speaking."Well, um, I don't like girl stuff... like 'sissy' or 'her...' I don't like my hair long, or dresses. I don't wanna get big boobas like you have..."

They shuddered, causing Cat to smile at how cute it was.

"Well, all of that is fixable," Catrin said.

"Really?" Ingrid was shrieking, eyes wide in shock. Catrin nodded her head, smiling broadly to reassure them.

"Yes, lovie! You actually know several people who changed all of that. For example, Edard, the barber, his parents thought he was girl at first, too."

"No!" Ingrid gasped, eyes wide in awe.[4]

"Yes!" Catrin kissed their curls."Now, you said 'she' feels yucky. How does 'they' feel?" Now that they'd made some progress Catrin was eager to see if they could make more.

"Um, normal?" Ingrid's face was screwed up in confusion.

---

4. In the intervening years, we, as a community have ensured that we have several children's books in our library dealing with children transitioning. Our local librarian leads storytime for children who are too young for school and tracks which stories each child has heard to ensure that all complete our pre–school curriculum over time.

"What about 'he?'" Catrin asked as gently as she could.

A slow smile crept across Ingrid's face. Biting a lip, *he* nodded his head."That feels real good."

"Yes? Good." Catrin squeezed him close, pouring all of the love she had into the hug."So do you feel like you are a boy instead of a girl, or something different?"

"A boy," he said with a definitive nod."So I think I'd like it if you called me that. I'd like being "your little boy." He blushed and buried his face in her chest.

"Well, that bit is an easy fix, I will gladly call you 'he' if you like, and we can tell everyone else to as well," she said, kissing the top of his head."We can figure out a new name, if you like, too. The rest will take some time, and hard work, but we can make littler changes the second you want to."

Tears pooled in her eyes again. She was so proud of him and truly honored that he'd felt comfortable telling her. She also felt horribly guilty. She was his *mother*, how could she miss such a thing?

"And... thank you so much for telling me, honey. It was so, so brave," she whispered to him.

Thinking back, there were some small clues, though she'd dismissed them as preference. In the light of new information, it honestly made a great deal of sense.

How long had he been stewing on this?

He looked up at her, eyes wide and trusting, and Catrin melted. Maybe this wasn't a complete failure on her part... maybe him feeling comfortable enough to say something, to trust her to tell everyone else was a good thing? Tears pricked at the corners of her eyes. Maybe this actually meant she *wasn't* a terrible mother.

"But Mama?" Ingrid's voice was hesitant. "Can I tell Ursule? I... just wanna tell her."

"Of course," Cat said, stroking his hair. She needed to focus on him, not her own mess of feelings. "We can do whatever you like, okay? Do you want to tell anyone else?"

He shook his head, burrowing into her chest. "No... could you? I kinda hoped you would?"

"I'd be glad to. If you want I can tell everyone so to you it will seem just like everyone magically knows. Is that what you'd want?"

Ingrid nodded, just in time, as thumping footsteps came upstairs.

"I'm done, are you done?" Ursule yelled through the door.

"Yes, you can come in!" Ingrid yelled back.

Ursule pushed open the door, and sashayed across the room, hair twirled up in a towel, and flopped dramatically on Catrin's bed.

"I always feel *so* much better after a shower, don't you?" she asked. "So what did you need to talk to Mama about?"

"Ummm, Torsten!" Ingrid blurted out. Catrin blinked at him, where had *that* come from?

"Oh? Did you ask her about our plan?" Ursule asked.

Catrin's eyes flicked between the two of them, what in the world were they talking about?

"Plan? What sort of plan"

"Well, you see," Ingrid said."We really quite liked learning from Torsten today and so Suley and I were sad he's leaving. So then-"

"So, then I said," Ursule interrupted."I wished we could go with him. The dwarven city sounds *so* beautiful. We wouldn't even have to go forever, just until we learned enough."

What is it with these children and the surprises tonight? As much as she wanted to be with Torsten, as amazing as that initially sounded, it just wasn't possible.

"Gi-darlings, we can't just pick up our life and move across the world so you can continue your studies, I'm sorry. And anyhow, Kemen will be here to help you."

"Aw but Kemen's not as fun!" protested Ingrid.

"Quite," Ursule agreed."And anyhow, that way we'd be close enough that Papa could come to visit!"

"Did you miss the 'halfway across the world' bit?" Catrin said, sputtering out. Truly they were being ridiculous.

"Torsten said he's leaving in the morning and the dragon will get him there by nightfall, so it's not even *that* far, Mama." Ursule sat up, crossing her arms over her chest.

"And how would it go over, hmmm?" Catrin said. "A human and two half-humans just casually in the Pathian Empire of all places?"

"Oh!" Ingrid said, sitting up this time. "Torsten said that the city is all underground. He said that the dragon's live up above and keep watch to tell the dwarves when someone's coming. The dumb ol' Pathians don't even *know* about the city because they have a *pretend* city up above! When the Pathians come, bunches of people stay underground so the Pathians think there are less of them!"

He waved his arms wildly, illustrating the dragons above and dwarves below. Now that he'd shared his feelings, there was a lightness to him. She'd not noticed that it had been weighing on him. Honestly in comparison to Ursule, he'd always been the quieter twin, the more subdued one, but now he seemed positively effervescent.

"All right, well, our whole life is here and we are not going to pick up and randomly move to the Pathian Empire because Torsten is going," she said, standing up to set her son-her *son*-on his feet. "Now, you two need to get some rest if you want to be up early to see him off in the morning."

Ursule got up off the bed with a frustrated sigh and grabbed Ingrid's hand.

"But the dragons!" Ingrid said as Catrin herded him toward the door."They could fly us back and forth whenever we needed! It would be so fast and easy!"

"Oh and Mama!" Ursule squealed."You could fall in love with Torsten. It would be *so* romantic!"

"Oh yes!" Ingrid piped in, clapping his hands."He's so wonderful Mama, I just know he'd make you so happy!"

Apparently her children were done teasing her and had somehow decided it was time to cut straight to the issue, though they had no idea how right they'd been.

"And we are done. Downstairs, in bed, the pair of you!" She pushed them out of her room and shut the door behind her. Her mind was a whirling mess and she needed them in bed before she had any hope of sorting through it all.

They didn't stop babbling until they were in bed, though Cat barely heard any of it. Ingrid's confession had let her ignore her unsettled feeling about Torsten, but it was roaring to life again. She kissed them both goodnight, whispering "goodnight, my son," to Ingrid. He beamed at her, and it soothed a bit of her tumult.

Shutting the door, she set about making some tea. A warm drink always helped her think and she had a massive amount of thinking to do. Torsten was currently a tender spot on her heart, though one she couldn't avoid touching. First she'd had to endure that aching kiss, and then her children had ambushed her with a request to go with him.

Really, they were so silly. Moving across the world? On a whim? Preposterous. As much as she wanted to be with Torsten, she had no business in the Empire and neither did they. Nevermind their orcish heritage or how magical the dwarvish city sounded. It just wasn't reasonable. She couldn't just up and move, she had children who needed her. Who needed stability, and not adventure gallivanting around the Empire.

Besides, it would be *dangerous* there. It was the Pathian Empire for Lady's sake. They'd be closer to their father, sure, and they could potentially even visit their other family, but they didn't need to *live* there for that.

Picking up a mug, Catrin's now clammy hands slipped on it. She set it down on the counter, realizing her hands were shaking.

A part of her obviously thought all of it sounded like an amazing idea. Of *course* she wanted to go with him, to be with Torsten, to support him in his exciting new endeavor. And obviously she wanted to do more traveling, now that she'd left Sanctuary. True, she could probably blend in as a dwarf easily if she needed, she *was* short. And yes, she'd already thought about having folks send orders via form…

The kids said they wanted to go. They'd brought it up. They surely only meant it as a whim. A move might sound exciting to a five-year-old. It must. *That* was really why they wanted to go.

The whole idea was preposterous.

Why though, was it also so dratted enticing?

For a brief moment, she allowed herself to imagine it. New experiences in an underground city. That stunning clay at her fingertips every day. If she was there, she could work so much faster, hell, she could probably ship orders home faster than she'd be able to make them with regular clay.

Not to mention, no parents to randomly pop over and interrogate her? That would be a dream. Her children wouldn't need to grow up in an isolated frozen wasteland. Sanctuary was a charming town, but she'd always felt stifled, especially after Annika's disappearance.

Most of all, though, Torsten.

Waking up to him each morning. Seeing him thrive in a position that he'd earned on his own, watching him blossom as he realized how smart and capable he was. To be able to be there for him, during the times when perhaps he didn't believe it so strongly and needed a reminder. Truly, they could be so good together.

It hit her like a wall of wind on a cold day. Her kids hadn't said she'd fall in love with him so he'd be their dad, they'd wanted it because he'd make *her* happy.

They wanted her to be happy. She wanted to be happy. She wanted to show them that *they* could be happy. Did she want them growing up and living a life like hers? Pushing away anything that might make her happy because she might also get hurt?

No. She wanted them to take every chance at happiness they could, to take risks to get what they deserved. And if those risks failed? If Cat's did? Then she'd give them an example of going on after taking a risk that was worth it.

Protecting them was a priority, to be sure, but being an example was also important. Loving Torsten was a risk, letting him in was a risk, but with hysterical laughter and tears building in her eyes, she realized it was one she *needed* to take.

Her kids wanted to go and she wanted to be with Torsten, wherever that was.

On light feet, she rushed downstairs. She couldn't let him get on that dragon tomorrow without a plan. She didn't know if they'd go in the morning, that felt unreasonable. But she knew, in the depths of her soul, she *felt it*. To the ends of the earth, to the depths of the Empire, she'd follow him, because he'd follow her. All at once, it was that simple, that easy. She grabbed her cloak and wrenched open the door, running out into a rainy night, locking it behind her and praying her children didn't wake.

When she turned around, there he was.

He was drenched, his white linen shirt clung to him, and strands of hair were sticking to his face. The light of the canals reflected off his green skin where he stood at the end of her walk, tucking something into her mailbox. He was beautiful. A story made flesh.

Turning his head, his eyes met hers. In contrast with the entrancing figure he cut, his face was tired, his eyes looked bloodshot and his mouth was set in a grim line.

Now she'd done it. Was this what it looked like when someone lost hope? Is that what it looked like when you gave up? She hated it.

His eyes widened and he pulled a letter out of the postbox clutching it briefly to his chest before holding it out toward her, wordlessly.

"Torsten," she called, running to him. "Please. I need to speak to you. You were right. You deserve to be loved the-"

"Cat," he said, shaking the letter.

"No, Torsten, please. You deserve that kind of love and I-"

"Cat, read the letter."

"No, I'm not done." Why wasn't he listening? She was trying to make a big gesture and he kept interrupting. She knew that letter was bound to say he was giving up, she could tell from the look on his face, but she wasn't having it.

"Cat, please just read the letter," he said, thrusting it into her hands.

"I am trying to tell you that-."

"Kitten, if you don't read that fucking letter, I'm taking you over my knee right now."

Chapter Eighteen
Torsten

IN WHICH A LETTER IS FINALLY DELIVERED, AND A NAUGHTY SECRET IS UNCOVERED

CATRIN GAPED AT HIM and finally took the letter from his hands. Her own shook as she opened the seal and unfolded it. Her eyes flew across the words, chest heaving as she read what he'd written.

Kitten,

I can't control what I did in the past, or what other people did to you. All I can promise is that the second I saw you again, I knew that I would do anything to have you. That might sound ridiculous if I didn't know you so well, but I know your soul, Cat. I know who you are—who you were before the world ground you under its foot. I might not have been in love with you then, but I've always loved you Catrin, it's just changed in tenor.

I'm going to stick around. I realized that I can't be that far away from you again, not while I know you might love me back.

I'm happy to chase you to the ends of the world if that's what it takes. I'm happy to wear you down and prove to you that I'm not going anywhere. I'll prove to you that I want you and everything that entails. I want to prop you up in times of trouble, help you raise your girls. I want to fix your damn kiln if it breaks, and shoe the ponies I know the girls will want now that they've seen those horses.

Maybe it's just that you want to be chased. Maybe you've been hurt so many times that you can't trust that I really want you, but I think we have something special and I refuse to give up on that. So, in the morning, instead of meeting me to see me off, please, I beg you, get breakfast with me. I know it's a risk, and I know why you can't tell the girls yet but I thought I could leave, I thought I could stay away from you and I just can't.

I need you, Cat. You're the only thing that feels like home, you're the only thing that makes me feel like I'm worth something. All this time, I've been looking for home, but I've realized I could search the world over and I wouldn't find it anywhere but at your side.

Please, let me show you that I can be worthy of you. Please let me show you that I can be worthy of those children calling me Aita (father in Orskara). Please, kitten. I'm sorry, for making you think, for even a second, that I'd leave you, because the only way I'm leaving is if you tell me we are done and you never want to see me again.

I'll be by at eight and we can drop the girls off with Sirin and Berne and we can get breakfast. Please?

Yours, always,

Torsten

Rain and tears mixed on her cheeks, but at least she was smiling. The rain pattered down around them, splashing on the paper. With a hand on her back, Torsten steered Catrin toward the overhang by her door, so it wouldn't get ruined.

As she read, emotions flashed across her face, and eventually she started laughing, of all things. He'd poured his damn heart out in that letter and she was laughing?

"What's so funny?" he said, trying not to be annoyed.

"He's not a girl," she said, giggles pouring out of her as fast as her tears.

"What?" he asked. She wasn't making any sense and that was decidedly not the reaction he'd hoped for.

Shoving the letter into her bodice, she grabbed his face and dragged it down to her. Eyes bloodshot, nose red from crying and hair sopping wet from the rain, she was the most beautiful person he'd ever seen.

"You know what? I'll tell you in a minute. More importantly, I love you. I have no idea where we are going to live, hopefully not in a hovel, but I refuse to be parted from you. I need you. I was coming to tell you that we'd go with you."

Had he ever heard sweeter words? Torsten scooped her up so she could wrap her legs around him and kissed her. If he'd thought their kiss earlier had been the best kiss he'd ever had, this was better. It was pure joy and desperation, need and want and exultation. Her plush lips were the softest thing he'd ever felt. Tears stung the corners of his eyes and he tried not to cry. Catrin pulled back and continued.

"I'm sorry I was scared and I kept telling myself I was protecting my kids, because they don't need protecting from you. Hell, I think they might need you too. We are worth the risk. *You* are worth the risk. Tomorrow, you could get sick and die, and I would be just as crushed as if you left me. But I wouldn't regret the time we'd spent together. I'd still want it and I want to do whatever it takes to convince you that I mean it."

Catrin's chest heaved and she shivered. He needed to get her out of this rain.

"Let's get inside and you can convince me all you want. I'm still having trouble believing this is real. I've dreamt of you and this exact moment so many times."

Fumbling in her pocket, Catrin wiggled for him to release her and unlocked the door. Once inside, he scooped her up under her knees to carry her upstairs. As many times as he'd felt happy over the last few weeks, it was nothing to the rapture he felt now.

Torsten buried his nose in her hair, breathing in the sweet scent he'd come to love so much. Catrin was still sniffling, so he tipped her chin up to him and wiped tears off her face as she blubbered adorably.

"It's real, I promise. I'm so sorry, I didn't mean to make it all so messy," she said.

"It's all right, precious, as long as you truly mean it." Settling on the floor in front of the fire, he removed her sodden cloak. He ran his fingers down her shoulder, savoring every bit of freckled skin.

"I do. I want to be with you. Forever, if you'll still have me." Big blue eyes clouded his vision and occluded his mind. He could never imagine leaving her.

"That sounds perfect, kitten. I definitely, absolutely, want forever. I'd marry you today, if you'd let me."

Catrin's face broke and her body shook with sobs. He surrounded her with his arms, enveloping her with as much love and safety as he could impart.

"I know you're scared, and me saying that I want forever probably doesn't actually help, but I am going to spend every single day showing you how lucky I am to have you."

"I think I'm the lucky one here. After all, I'm the one with all the baggage," she joked, wiping tears from her eyes.

"You think you are the only needy one here? Cat, when I came here, I effectively completed my life's work. I was a stranger to both of my homelands and had no reason to want to be either place. Do you know how horrible it feels to know you have no home? It's like floating alone in the middle of the ocean, waves sloshing you about and you just want to get a breath."

"A storm. Trapped in the middle and you can't see the sun," she offered.

"Aye, and then, like a lighthouse, I walked around a corner and there you were. You were everything I remembered, just *more* in all the best ways. I love that you need me, Cat, because I need you right back. I needed you so bad. I had no home at all, no direction. You are my home. You are my direction. I was spinning because I hadn't found my heading."

A slow smile spread across Catrin's face, her luscious lips, stretching to a sparkling smile.

"Fuck if you're not the prettiest thing I've ever seen, kitten."

In seconds, her hands were in his hair, and her mouth met his in a crash of passion. She was fast and eager, his little bunny. He caressed her tongue, savoring the fresh taste of her across his palate. When he pulled back, she whined and chased him with her lips.

"Does this mean I'm cleared to call you kitten?"

"Please. Kitten, precious, anything you want. I've missed it so much. I've missed *you* so much."

"Wait," he said with a start. "What were you laughing about earlier, with the letter?"

"Oh!" It felt like years ago, she'd forgotten entirely. "Well, I guess you called Ingrid 'Bud' today. It gave *him* the courage to tell me he's actually a boy. So it's not the 'girls' and I anymore."

"Really?" he asked. "Well I'll be damned. And I helped by calling him Bud?"

His chest was bursting with happiness. He'd helped the little tyke? It was like he was already settling into being a dad, and he could run for miles on the feeling of it.

"You did." She kissed his cheek. Lady, he was grateful he wasn't going to have to leave her.

"You know, precious, we do need to figure out where we're going to live..." he said, voice suddenly uncertain. Catrin turned onto her back so she could look him in the eye.

"I meant what I said, we can talk to the kids in the morning, and as long as they were being serious, we could go with you. The special clay and pigment, they were... amazing. If we went, I'd get to work with them all the time! And, I want you to get to do this, if you truly want to."

Toying with a curl, Torsten blushed."You know, I sort of do? I don't want to ask you and the kids to upend your lives for me, but if you think you'd truly want to..."

"I would, I do, and to be frank, I think they do, too. As long as you think Calida could transport my equipment?"

"She'd be glad to, I'm sure."

"Take me to bed, please? I need you."

Holding her to him with one arm, he pushed off the ground.

"I'd like nothing more. Where to, sweet tits?"

"Sweet tits?"

"You said I could call you anything I wanted," he teased, playfully nipping at her neck.

Catrin giggled and then slapped a hand over her mouth."Upstairs, you brute. Here, put me down."

He lowered her to the floor, dragging her body down his front, ensuring she felt every inch of him and his need for her. Flashing a suddenly shy smile, Catrin doused the fire in the hearth, giving him a prime view of her gorgeous ass.

"Kitten," he asked. "Did you wear a thin little nightgown on purpose?"

"Maybe... all right no, but it's a lovely coincidence don't you think?" she said, slipping through his reaching hands to grab her lantern from the table. Backing toward the stairwell, she beckoned him.

Her finger crooked and he could only obey. The minx sashayed her way up the stairs to a landing with a single open door. Catrin opened the lantern and slotted it into a metal shielded depression in the wall and turned a knob.[1]

In a wave, down and around the room, sconces on the wall flickered to life. The room spanned the width of the house, with slanted walls that told him they were partially inside the roof. Everything about the room was so perfectly Catrin. An easel stood near a window, with canvases propped against the wall. The room was decorated in blues and creams, both cheery and serene. When he stepped inside, Catrin nudged the door behind him.

---

1. Years of stability in Sanctuary have allowed for the invention of such marvels. I still think the Lady might have suppressed our technological advancement, considering the boom currently in process, but during the time it was intact, the people of Sanctuary refined it to a level unrivaled elsewhere.

She stepped back into his embrace, wrapping her arms around him.

"Good," he said, lifting her to walk her over to the bed. When he lowered her into it, he was shocked to see how it dwarfed her.

"Kitten, this is an awfully big bed..."

She giggled, pulling her legs up. "Berne had already cut everything when Edrigu left, so I've just had this big, lonely bed all to myself."

Cat's eyes went wide and she reached behind her to swat a pile of clothes onto the floor. She looked back to him, smiling casually.

"Now what was *that*, precious? You're making a mess here." Torsten crossed to pick up the clothing and Catrin scrambled across the bed to beat him there. Shrieking, she swiped them off the ground and stuffed them under her stomach.

"It only gets more interesting the more you hide it, love." He turned her over, easily manhandling her so that the clothes were now piled on her stomach. "Is that your skirt?"

At first, he was perplexed, why would she be sleeping with her own skirt? After a moment though, his sensitive nose picked up a scent. His scent. She clutched her skirt, covered in his spend, her face and chest flushed.

"Oh kitten, did you cuddle this last night when you couldn't have me? Did you breathe in my scent as you slept? Fuck precious, even when we were apart you were perfect, weren't you?"

She was going to damn near explode his heart. His head was spinning, his cock was rock hard in his trousers and he thought he might die of joy.

Catrin bit her lip and nodded, letting him pull the fabric away. The brighter light of the room revealed her rosy nipples, which were barely visible through the thin fabric of her nightdress.

"Look at you. How could I ever leave this? I'd be starving for you for the rest of my life." He towered over her, sliding his suspenders over his shoulders and letting them hang at his sides. Bending down, arms on either side of her, he sucked her nipple, chemise and all, into his mouth.

"I didn't call you sweet tits for nothing," he said."You are the sweetest thing I've ever tasted."

Catrin's mouth pursed as she failed to hold in a laugh.

"It's just not sexy!" she burst out through her mirth.

"It's not supposed to be. It's supposed to be silly. It's *supposed* to make you relax."

"I suppose it did do that," she conceded.

"Mmmhmm," he hummed, kissing up her neck.

Catrin gasped and when he turned his head, she was tearing up again."I'm sorry, I just... how are you so perfect?"

"Ah, you see, that is a specialty adaptation we orcs have, it helps us breed reliably. As soon as we're done having orclings, my face will shrivel..." he contorted his face into a horrible visage."And overnight, I'll just be repulsive."

He smiled in triumph as Cat was smiling and chuckling again.

"Lies, I've seen your father. He looked exactly the same after Miren was born."

"Fine, fine, you've got me," he said, kissing her on the nose and standing."But I wanted to see you smiling again."

He peeled his pants down and toed off his boots, whipping his shirt over his head in one smooth motion.

"Wow, that was quite the maneuver," she said."Are you quite practiced at this then?"

"Well, when you're the smallest and least desirable orc in the horde, you have to be good at getting naked quick. If I had an opportunity, I had to take it."

"That is still absolutely unfathomable to me, but I can't complain about the skill set." She blushed and turned her head."It might be of interest to you, that I bought this chemise specially, in case."

Catrin toyed with the lace at the edge near her cleavage. Now that he could see the top, it was highly impractical as an everyday clothing garment.

"I see..." he said, crawling up the bed toward her. Smiling mischievously, her fingers trailed to a line of buttons down the front. Gingerly, he unfastened them, careful with the tiny, delicate things. Someday he'd likely rip a nightie to shreds, but this one was special and he wanted them to have it forever. After what felt like a thousand buttons, he slid the sides down to reveal her perfect breasts.

"Gods, it's like every time I see you is better than the last. Do you know what I am most excited about, precious?" He asked."I'm most excited to be able to say everything I'm thinking. I don't think you had any idea how much I was holding back."

"No, I guess I didn't," she said, eyes alight."What haven't you said?"

"I haven't said that you've given meaning to my sad, sorry life. I haven't said that loving you sustains me. I haven't said that I can't wait for a life with you. I look forward to spending my life supplicating to these lips, and worshiping this body. When I think of a perfect day, it begins and ends right here, with you." He lowered himself to suckle her breasts."More specifically, a perfect day starts with savoring all of the tastes of you."

He rolled her nipple around his mouth, toying with it until she gasped. The other deserved the same treatment. Taking her firm bud in his fingers, he fondled and pinched it lightly. The other he licked and savored. He pressed into it, his tusks dimpling her perfect orb.

Once her arousal had built to fill the air around them, he hiked her skirt up, running his blunt fingers along her thigh to where she was wet and ready for him. It might have been his imagination, but he could swear it was shaped to him.

"Precious, it's like my cock was made to fit you, like you formed it in your hands to the perfect outline of your cunt."

Catrin looked away, refusing to meet his eyes."Well, um—"

"Kitten, look at me, what is it?" Concern was a vise in his stomach. She shook her head, shoulders shaking."Fuck, precious, what is it?"

Grabbing her chin, Torsten turned her to face him. She was biting both of her lips and was flushed red. The minx wasn't upset; she was embarrassed.

"Oh kitten, what have you done?" he teased.

Catrin's eyes darted to the bedside table, a move so slight, he might have missed it were he not watching so closely.

"Catrin," he teased, enjoying the blush that grew on her cheeks."Is there something in that drawer?"

Before she could react, Torsten flung himself toward the drawer, toppling her off him. He *needed* to see what was in that drawer. He wrenched the drawer open revealing what appeared to be a copy of his own cock.

Grabbing it, he turned around to Catrin. She was curled up in a ball with her hands covering her face.

"Kitten... what is this?"

"Oh stuff it, you know very well what it is!" she called from between her hands.

"Oh love, you've even got the piercings," he said, delighted. "You *did* form my cock to fit your cunt perfectly, didn't you?"

It truly was a remarkable likeness. Holding it next to his own, he was quite pleased with it, really. The color, a deep green with a purplish head was nearly identical. She'd sculpted his thick, branching vein in remarkable detail, had embedded two metal barbells, and even crafted an impressive knot at the bottom.

He guided it over to her, placing a hand on her knees to keep them at her chest. He dragged the head of it through her folds, giggling gleefully when she gasped at the chill of it.

"I suppose that's one difference there, kitten," he said. "It's a bit cold. Though I'm sure you'll warm it up quickly enough."

"Wh—what are you doing?" she asked.

"Oh precious, if you've gone through the trouble of making my cock to play with, I'll be damned if I don't get to play with it, too."

The thick head of it breached her and he was awed to see how the girth of it stretched her. Her folds pulled taut around it as she eagerly sucked it in. She moaned as he filled her with it and his greedy eyes drank in the view of her taking his cock this way. He moved the hand holding her knees to tease her clit, wresting a moan from her.

"There's my good girl," he encouraged."You've made me so happy. Even when we were apart, you kept yourself ready for me. Gods Cat, I'm dripping, imagining you fucking yourself with this, wishing it was me. Did you do that, precious?"

"Yes!" she gasped, nodding her head frantically."Please Torsten, I want you, I've had that thing earlier!!"

"You did, did you? Been missing me?"

Catrin whined as he sped his finger, bucking in a most satisfying way. He loved watching how her muscles tightened, how her face flushed, just before she came. She bucked one final time and held, back bowed off the bed, forearm stuffed in her mouth to stifle a moan.

Torsten pulled the toy out of her with a wet slurp and held it to her mouth."Would you clean this off for me, love? I have other cleaning to do."

His perfect girl took it inside her mouth, lapping her own taste off of the slick ceramic. Torsten thought he got the better deal, though, because from between her legs, he got to taste her from the source and watch as she cleaned the facsimile of his cock. The tangy taste of her coated his tongue. He licked through her sex, suckling her lips and caressing her clit. It wasn't long before she was coming again, chanting his name in a whisper.

"Tor..." she whispered."Do you think I might show you what a good rider I've become? I want to come with you inside me."

His stomach fluttered and clenched.

"You're sure, kitten? I need you to be sure. I don't need you to commit to forever, but I need you to understand that's my goal. We're not *testing this out*. We aren't 'just fucking' anymore. If you take me inside you now, it's because you're putting me through my paces so I can prove to you that we're forever. I want to raise children with you, I want yours to be mine and then I want to fill you with more. I want to see you grow round and lush with my seed and I need to know you want the same."

"Oh fuck, Tor, I *really* do." Her dilated eyes locked with his, nodding slowly and certainly.

Cock twitching at her suggestion, he flopped down on the bed next to her."I would like nothing better."

She had no idea how much this meant to him, how it would soothe his soul and wash clean the moment when he'd decided he wasn't worthy of her.

When she'd regained her wits a bit, he rolled onto his back and positioned her atop him once more. He gasped at the first feel of her slick cunt as she slid over him. Her eyes locked to his as she rolled her hips against him, grinding down into his pelvis. "Now, love, back to your riding lesson." He grasped her hips, frozen, as he saw his fingers dimpling their ample curves.

This.

This was what he'd wanted from the moment he saw her again. The second he'd seen those hips, his hands had longed for her. Now that he had her, he was never letting go. She sank down on him once more, the sublime feeling of breaching her rushing through him, emanating from his cock and suffusing his body.

He was exactly where he was supposed to be. She ground and rocked over him, his gorgeous goddess, holding her hair atop her head. Her rolling movements reminded him of the boat, of how delicate they'd been and how sure they felt now. His eyes stung with the wonder of it. Just yesterday, he'd been convinced it had all been nothing but a mild amusement for her, a brief interlude he'd cherish forever.

Instead, he was blessed with her warmth wrapping around him, her clit grinding into his piercing as she sought her pleasure, and the words that she'd carry his child fresh on her lips. Over the past week, he'd imagined it so often, but nothing could compare to the reality. It was more than the feel of her, it was her belief, her passion that he succeeded that undid him. Somehow, she saw how important his new opportunity was and cared enough to risk everything for him.

His body tightened, pleasure building with each movement she made.

In moments, she was coming again, dragging him with her and chanting once more, though this time, with the sweetest words he'd ever heard.

"I love you, I love you. Gods, Tor, I love you."

Catrin slipped down over his knot, squeezing him with her walls, clenching around him and milking his seed. He bucked up into her, unable to stop the primal need to fill her as full as possible. He'd keep her plugged and full for as long as he could. He'd flood her womb so full and so often she'd need to keep a towel between her legs. Or a plug... perhaps she could fashion a plug.

With a roar, he pumped again, splashing against her walls, relishing the image of her eternally filled with his essence. She collapsed atop him, burying her face in his neck and peppering him with kisses.

"Darling, are you crying?" She sat up, face twisted in concern.

Wrapping his arms around her to tug her back down to him, Torsten chuckled. "Yes, kitten, but only in the best way. Getting everything you've ever wanted is a little overwhelming."

"It rather is. Isn't it?" She nestled against him once more, fingers twining into his hair. When she spoke again, her voice was thick with the beginnings of tears."It truly is."

Chapter Nineteen
Catrin

IN WHICH CHOICES ARE MADE

B Y THE TIME TORSTEN slipped from her, Catrin was deliciously well used. He'd carried her, still knotted, wrapped in a blanket, down to the bathroom and ran a shower. When they'd disengaged, she'd splattered all over the floor of the shower and nearly clogged the drain.

Laying in bed after, she was curled up in his arms, drifting on a sea of happiness. Instead of leaving her in the morning, she'd wake up next to him.

Gasping, Catrin sat up. "Do you need to tell Calida that you aren't going?"

Wrapping his arms around her, Torsten dragged her back to the bed. "I went to see her before coming here, actually. She told me to get my arse over here and talk to you, and she'd wait until things were decided." He raised his vocal tone in an imitation of the dragon."She said: Inigo might be in a rush, but if I know one thing, dwarves hate anything hasty, they won't even notice if you, or your polite letter of decline, get there a few days late."

Catrin relaxed and giggled at his imitation."Thank you, for speaking with her about it. The kids seem to think we'll just be able to hop a dragon back and forth."

"Well, maybe not at a moment's notice, but Calida did mention she's making one run a week, so at least once a week we'd have a ride, so we'd be able to come home for lots of visits. The dwarves, from what I remember, take time off work *very* seriously, so I doubt it will be an issue."

"What are they like? What is the city like? Tell me about them?" she asked, unable to stop her yawn.

"Well," he said, resting his head on his pillow."First off, Calida is right, they hate anything fast paced, and everything just moves slower. The feast we had when I was there last took all day. Let's see, what else... Similar to how we often use lunula for light, they have glowing crystals. You know, I think the Lady might have a thing for shiny things..."

Catrin drifted off listening to him describe the magical place they might call home.[1]

THE SOUNDS OF FEET running up the stairs woke Catrin. Her eyes flashed open and she barely had time to throw a blanket over Torsten's green arse before her door burst open.

"Mommy!" squealed Ursule as she bounded across the room."It's a glorious day, and I have big news! Ingrid says, 'surprise, I'm a boy'! I said I wasn't sure it worked that way and we should come ask you."

Torsten raised his head to squint at the ruckus.

"Oh hi, Torsten." Ursule said, flopping down at the foot of the bed, hands pressed under her chin."So, does it work that way?"

Catrin looked at Torsten, bewildered, and he raised his eyebrows to the door. Clutching the doorframe, Ingrid peered into the room, eyes rapt.

"Actually," she said, to Ursule."It kind of does. You see, he knows himself better than we do, and he

---

1. The crystals of Berggeheimnis are truly one of the wonders of the world, should you ever have the opportunity to visit, dear reader, I cannot encourage you enough.

knows what feels right. And if this is what he is saying feels right, then it's just our job to help him feel comfortable. Do you want to come join us, Ing?"

Nodding, her son brought himself into the room and gingerly sat down on the bed on Torsten's side.

"Hello," he said to Torsten.

"Hello, Bud, how's it going?"

"All right." Ingrid's face lit up with a smile at the nickname.

Catrin reached over and grabbed her son's hand."I'm so proud of you. I love you so much, no matter what. And in a few days, we can talk about what I could do better to make you more likely to share things with me in the future. But for right now, I want to know what we can do to make you feel more like yourself. Is that something that you've thought about? What changes you might like to make?"

Her son furrowed his brow, "Well, Ingrid is a girl's name, so if you called me something else that might be nice. I like Ingrid, but it's for girls."

"You have a couple options. There is always Ingrund, which is the masculine form of your name, or there's Halsten, which was the boy name I had picked out for you when I was pregnant. Considering that you *are* a boy, that's always an option. Another option is that we could call you a nickname like Bud while you think about what feels good."

"Could we try Halsten? It still kind of feels like me," he said.

"Of course, darling, and if that doesn't turn out to be the right fit, we can try something else." Under the covers, Torsten squeezed her hand. Ursule gasped and bounced up and down on the bed.

"We should throw a party! Like when you have a new baby, and your family throws you a party so everybody can come over and meet the new baby!"

While Ursule was throwing her arms in the air, and bouncing around, poor Halsten was squinting his eyes.

"Well, sweetheart, I think that's something we should ask your brother if he'd want. Is that something you'd want?"

"I don't think so. It would be nice if a lot of people knew all at once to call me my new name, but a party sounds really embarrassing."

"Does the Sanctuary Sentinel still run the life events column?" Torsten asked, snapping his fingers."You could always put an announcement where the births are listed so that people will know, but you don't have to throw a big party. Does that sound like something that would be helpful?"

Halsten nodded shyly."What about my hair or my clothes...?" he said, trailing off.

"We can change your hair and get you some new clothes if that's something that would make you feel better. I could take the day off work if you'd like to do that today? I don't want you uncomfortable for longer than you need to be."

"That would be grand," he said."Wait, Mama? Why is Torsten in your bed?"

Catrin looked to Torsten for help, but his eyes were wide and dancing, a curious smile on his face. Lovely. He was going to let her handle this one alone.

"Well, you see, Torsten came over to talk, and it was very cold and rainy..." she started. While it was all true, it felt disingenuous."And while we traveled to get Auntie Sirin's horses, Torsten and I found we quite liked each other. And that we missed being around each other. So, we decided we'd like to have a sleepover."

"Do you like each other in the smoochy–smoochy way that Auntie Sirin and Uncle Berne do?" Ursule asked.

"We sure do!" Torsten said as he made kissy noises and lunged toward Catrin.

Catrin and both of her kids started screaming, Cat from abject mortification.

"Does this mean we get to go with him?" Halsten yelled over the din.

"Well, it means we have a lot to talk about..." Cat answered.

"Yay! We're moving!" Ursule yelled, clasping a beaming Halsten's hands and swinging them.

"That's not what I said!" Cat said. Shooing the twins off her bed. "All right, everybody else out! These are discussions to be had after we are dressed for the day and have had coffee. So the two of you run downstairs. Sule, I am charging you with finding your brother a good outfit that makes him feel happy. Torsten and I will be down momentarily."

"And I'm making waffles," Torsten said.

"Yes!" Halsten cheered.

Ursule grabbed her brother's hand and tugged him out the door, chattering at him about clothing options.

With a heavy sigh, Catrin collapsed into Torsten's lap. "Well that went differently than I expected, breaking things about us to the kids."

"Better? Or worse?" Torsten brushed a few hairs off her cheek.

"Better, actually. I'm not sure why I thought it might be some big deal to them, but I suppose, considering that they have never known me to be in a relationship before, they have no memories of me with their father. When you add that to how much they like you, it sort of makes sense that they'd be excited."

"I've had a feeling it would be fine. I do think I'd like to have been fully dressed for the conversation, but I'll take a good outcome over my discomfort any day."

"Good, because something tells me if you wind up married to me, you will experience lots of discomfort."

"Is that you proposing to me, kitten?" he asked, twining a curl around his finger.

"Oh, so *that's* what you're going to take out of that statement? Not the fact that you're going to be uncomfortable for the rest of your life?"

"Precious, you keep talking about how supposedly uncomfortable I've been, about how badly you've treated me, and I'm still waiting for that to start. Honestly," he continued, a surprised look on his face, "If I'm uncomfortable at all, it's because I'm extremely torn between two activities."

"Oh? And what would those be?"

"Well, the first option has a whole lot to do with the gorgeous woman being poked in the back of the head by my cock. And the other has to do with waffles that aren't going to make themselves. I need to continue my quest to make your kids love me more than you! But, considering I fucked you a *great deal* while we were gone, and it wasn't until your kids liked me that I got you to commit, I think I figured out where my priorities need to lie."

Torsten jumped up from the bed, rolling Catrin over onto her face as he sashayed over to where his clothing lay on the floor. He wiggled his butt as he bent over to pick up his pants, turning toward her with a smirk once he had them.

"I don't know, sir. Your cock there begs to differ..." she said, licking her lips. Two could play if that is what he wanted to do.

"He and I have an understanding. I'm in charge. I'll get him taken care of when I can, and treat him right, but he can get grumpy if he hasn't had something he really, really wants for a long time."

"Oh? And is there something he really, really wants that he's not getting?" she asked, scooching back on the bed so that her chemise hiked up over her ass.

"Ach, aye. There's a seductive little kitten that's ripe for the taking that he wants *real* bad. But, what I know is that while she might like to tease me, what she *really* wants is for us both to prioritize her kids. And if I want the honor of someday calling them 'our' kids, I'd better get my arse downstairs."

He pulled on his pants and tucked his considerable erection inside. Crossing to the bed, he squeezed her arse cheek and kissed her head.

"Ugh, you're right, damn you," she said, rolling onto her back and getting a searching kiss as a reward. "What do you think? About moving and all? You're really all right if we tag along?"

Torsten sat on the bed next to her. "I was serious when I said I'd marry you today. I want to sleep with you in my arms every night, and wake up to you in the morning. I want to be where you and the kids are, and if you're willing to come on a wild adventure with me, then I'm happy to have you. Thrilled."

How did she get so lucky? He knew her so well, and really understood how scared she was. Now that she had him, she was terrified to lose him. Once he was dressed, Torsten winked and walked downstairs, eliciting a roar of excitement from her kids.

If she set her fear aside, Catrin found she really was excited at the possibility of moving. Separate from the excitement of travel, she was secretly excited to live somewhere where no one would compare her to her sister.

Catrin dressed quickly in a frock with an over-apron. After putting her hair up in a bun, she descended to the kitchen.

Torsten and her kids were all wearing aprons, Halsten's hair up in a hat. She mentally added a trip to the barber to their list of errands.

"Hi Mama! We're making *Orcish* waffles this morning! They are a little different, but we think you'll still like them," Halsten called. The change in his demeanor was remarkable. He was still himself, of course, but there was a lightness to him she hadn't seen in longer than she'd like to admit.

"I'm excited to try them!" she said, walking over. Torsten grabbed her around the waist and pulled her in for a kiss on the cheek. Her kids giggled and Cat leaned down to tickle them."If you all are cooking, I suppose it's up to me to set the table, then!"

She grabbed four place settings and set to it, the sounds of laughter punctuating their deep focus. Her life had changed so much in the last twenty-four hours, but already she could see a future like this, with her kids and Torsten, a quiet, happy life, wherever they ended up.

Once they'd finished breakfast they broached the subject of the move with the children.

"Of course we want to go," Halsten started.

"It was our idea in the first place," finished Ursule.

They sat at the table, their twin features blinking and frowning back at Catrin as if she were daft.

Out of the corner of her eye, she could see Torsten suppressing a smile."It could be a big change..."

"Isn't that the point?" Halsten asked. Next to him, Ursule nodded.

"No one will expect Halsten to be different. It's an even better reason to go now." Ursule smiled at her brother and squeezed his hand.

"That is a very good point."

While the twins cleared their plates, Torsten turned to Cat, rubbing his hands up and down her arms."If it doesn't feel like a good fit, kitten, we'll just come home."

Giddiness rose up inside of her. Halsten wasn't the only one who'd be free from expectations. No one in Berggeheimnis knew about Annika or expected Catrin to be anything but herself. Not to mention, Torsten's reassurances made her feel better about going. She didn't *intend* for things to go badly, but if they did, they could just come home. Increasingly though, "home" was feeling less and less like a place, and more and more like Torsten.

Chapter Twenty
Torsten

IN WHICH THERE ARE ENDINGS AND BEGINNINGS

B EING OUT IN SANCTUARY with Catrin and the kids was distinctly better than being alone. When Torsten had wandered the village over the last week or so, he'd been keenly aware of how he didn't fit in any longer. He'd worried if it would ever feel like home again. Out with what he hoped was his new family, everything fit into place.

"Tor, can we go see your dragon friend today?" Halsten asked, his huge eyes hopeful.

"Of course, mate! But we have several errands that are pretty important, first. What's on our list, kitten?"

"Why do you call mama 'Kitten?'" Ursule interjected.

"Well, when she was little, it was because her name was Catrin, and baby cats are kittens. She was always following your uncle Berne and I around like a little lost kitten. Now, it's just who she is to me, and it's a reminder of how even though things are new between us now, I know who she really is: my kitten."

Catrin squeezed his hand and cleared her throat."Yes, so it's a special 'Torsten only' nickname. You can continue calling me Mama, if you please. First on our list is the barber, since I thought Halsten might like the opportunity to get a trim?"

Hal nodded shyly, and so Torsten steered them in that direction. They crossed over several canals, waving toward people they knew. Torsten's chest puffed each time they received knowing looks or chuckles. He loved that Cat proudly held his hand, smiled when people congratulated them, and rolled her eyes when Gunna, the lead councilor told them it was "about damn time" Torsten came to his senses.

"Oh I quite agree," Catrin replied."Fifteen years is a long time to wait for someone to come up to scratch, but he made his way here eventually."

"Sometimes folk are so pig-headed that they can't see what is right in front of their noses."

"Well I see it now," he said."I spent years trying to figure out what I was looking for, but it turns out, it was what I'd left behind."

"Yes, well, that's very sweet, dear. I imagine in light of everything, you'll not be taking that post then..."

"Actually," Catrin chimed in."He will, we'll all be going. We'll come home for visits of course, but we think it would be a nice adventure."

"Well who will make my pottery?" Gunna sputtered.

"One of the other potters, I imagine," she said, squeezing Torsten's hand."Or you could always keep ordering from me via mail."

"Well I suppose I'll have to, can't have things cracking at high temperatures you know. That will suffice, I suppose."[1]

Gunna toddled off, nodding her head in satisfaction.

They continued on, eventually arriving at the barber. As they neared, Halsten slowed his walking, glancing nervously to the side.

"You know," Torsten said."Why don't I pop in really fast, let Edard know what's what?"

---

1. Gunna is, in my opinion, being overdramatic here. None of the pottery I have from other potters in town have cracked at high temperatures. She just doesn't like change.

Catrin smiled at the suggestion."Thank you, good idea."

Gods, I could work forever to earn those smiles. "I'll be just a minute then!"

Torsten opened the door to the barber shop, and Edard, a moose shifter, waved for him to take a seat. He was a tall man, a few years older than Torsten, that kept miniature versions of his antlers even in his human form.

"I'm nearly finished here," he said, indicating the hairy dwarf in the seat."It's a good thing you didn't show up earlier. We've been here a while!" he said, laughing good-naturedly.

"Grand," Torsten said, sitting."I actually came in because I'm here to talk to you about your next customer. You know Cat Broderson, and her kids?"

"Oh of course, though I don't see much of 'em in my shop, as you can imagine."

"Well, sure, that's what I'm here about, one of her kids, the shy one, who you might know as Ingrid, has recently shared that they'd feel much more themselves as a boy. He's trying on the name Halsten for now, and he needs a haircut so he can look a bit more dapper."

"Of course! How exciting! I remember when I transitioned, it was an exciting time. Should we make a good show of it for the little gent?"

"Actually, he's quite shy, so if you please, just the most generic interaction you could muster? I think not fussing over him would make him feel the most accepted."

"Glad to." Edard squinted at the head in front of him, made a final cut, and declared his customer finished. Torsten opened the door and motioned that they should all come inside.

Catrin led them in, Halsten clutching her hand like it was his last lifeline. They sat down in the row of seats with Torsten, Ursule kicking her feet as she sat. Edard rang up his customer, who donned a hat and tipped it to them.

Edard waved Halsten over and Torsten took his hand, helping him hop up into the seat.

"All right, young master," Edard said."What did you have in mind for today?"

"Um... shorter?" Halsten whispered."Less girl-ish?"

"I think we can manage that. Now, I will say, a gent's haircut comes a bit closer to the head than you've probably had so far, but I promise I won't cut you, and we won't have to shave your head like Torsten there has, though if that's something you want at some point, we can easily manage it. If you don't mind, we'll go with a classic boy's style and then you can say if you'd like any changes as we go."

Halsten nodded and released Torsten's hand as he settled in. Taking the chair next to them, Torsten smiled reassuringly as Edard draped the cape around the boy's shoulders.

Edard took a big snip off the side of Hal's head, holding the chunk out to his wee customer. "There we are, first one done, five thousand to go!"

"Five thousand? Really?" Halsten asked.

"No, not really lad, though it might feel like it I'll warrant."

Wide blue eyes took in every movement of Edard's shears in the mirror. Edard's antlers bobbed behind Halsten, a small smile growing on the boy's face.

Catrin came over to stand next to them, placing a hand on Torsten's shoulder where he was seated and spoke to Halsten. "You know, if you don't mind," she said. "The town registry portion of our errands might be quite boring. I need to let them know about the move. If you'd like and you're sure of your name, Ursule and I could pop over and get all of the paperwork taken care of—leave you boys to it."

"I'm sure, mama." Halsten said, his voice barely audible. "That sounds like a good plan."

"Right then, I suppose we'll be off. Whoever gets done first finds the other group?" Cat asked, shifting her attention to Torsten.

"That sounds like a plan, love." Catrin leaned down and placed a soft kiss on Torsten's lips, a sweet reminder of many more to come. She blew Halsten a kiss and the girls swept out of the building.

The cut progressed quickly, tension draining out of Halsten's shoulders as they went along. Once he seemed fairly relaxed, Edard began chatting with him.

"I've noticed you keep wiggling that tooth," he said."Do you think it will pop out soon?"

Halsten wiggled it again, smiling around it."My mama and Torsten say it will fall out soon, and then I'll have tusks, like Tor."

"Well that will look right smart, won't it?" Edard observed.

"Speaking of that, I think we need to talk to your mama about what orcs normally do when they lose a tooth," Torsten mused.

"What do they do?" Hal asked.

"Usually that's when an orc gets their first piercing. But, considering you two didn't know to expect that, I imagine it doesn't sound very appealing," he said.

"Well, I like yours..." Halsten said.

"If you'd like, you could get one that matches my first," Torsten offered.[2] He flicked a simple hoop on his right earlobe and Halsten's eyes lit up. The boy nodded and Edard had to steady his head with a chuckle.

---

2. While it obviously hurt, Halsten wore that first piercing, and all of his others, with pride. Torsten forged their earrings himself and Berne and I flew in for the piercing.

The rest of the cut, Halsten rubbed his earlobe silently, a sweet look of determination setting his brow. In short order, Edard was wrapping up, doing small touch-ups, and Halsten looked more confident by the moment.

They paid, and found the girls just leaving the town registry building. Catrin swept Halsten up in her arms, giving him a tight squeeze and a kiss on the cheek.

"You look very handsome, darling," she whispered to him, earning her a wee smile.

"You dooooooo!" Ursule crooned when Cat had returned him to the floor.

Torsten reached out to grab Catrin's hand and was surprised to find several coins being tucked into his vest pocket.

"I forgot to leave you with money, sorry about that."

Torsten frowned. Things were still early days, of course, but there were obviously some issues they needed to work out between them.

"Cat, you don't need to pay me back for his haircut, in fact, I mean to buy his clothes, too."

"Oh but I can—"

"I didn't say I thought you couldn't afford it. I *want* to."

The kids were running around the large green in the center of town, laughing and playing, so he pulled her over to sit on a bench near the statue of the Lady.

"The only way I have to combat your fear that I'll leave is by showing up and showing my commitment. Spending my money on you all shows that I don't just have an emotional stake in this family, I have a financial one. When I spend money on you, or the kids, I'm trying to show you that you three are the most important priorities in my life. Until now, I've only had myself to worry about, and I've either been on the road or living with my parents, I haven't had much to spend my money on. Honestly, I'm excited to be able to do so. So, when we get to the clothier, I'd like it if you'd let me buy his clothes. And probably some for Suley too. I know how she likes to match and if he has a new wardrobe, they won't be able to match anymore."

Catrin's lower lip trembled and tears gathered in her eyes.

"You really put some thought into that, didn't you?" she asked, burying her face in his chest.

"I did," he chuckled."Are we in agreement?"

"Very well, but you don't get to pay for everything all the time..." she said.

"Well of course. I'm not going to pay for my own gifts!" He kissed her on the head and tickled her side.

"That's not what I meant and you well know it. You've got to let me—"

He caught her in a kiss, and when he released her she was breathless."Please?"

Rolling her eyes at him, she nodded, and he savored how *right* she felt in his arms.

"When we were out, Ursule and I had a chat." Catrin looked up at him.

"Oh?"

"She's a little... confused. She said she's happy to have a brother now, but also sad that she doesn't have a sister anymore. She's always been the one more excited about them being 'the same' all the time."

Torsten nodded, settling his chin on Catrin's head. He and Cat were used to the idea, they'd both known people whose gender had been assigned incorrectly. Once it was remedied, it tended to be such a non-issue that a child wouldn't even realize it had happened or was possible."Understandable. What did you say?"

"I just reminded her that he's the same person, and really, she never *really* had a sister at all," Catrin said."That seemed to help, but I think I should keep an eye on them both, and their interactions."

"Agreed." Torsten pulled back and tipped her chin up to him."*We* should keep an eye on that."

Chest buzzing, he waited for her to answer. They'd committed to each other, they were moving, but was she going to let him in? *Could* she partner with him in this way? This early?

"Right," she said, tears glistening in her eyes. "We should."

Relief flooded through him, and he was overwhelmed with the trust she showed him. "Thank you."

A WEEK LATER, TORSTEN held Catrin's hand as the children skipped ahead of them on their way to Sirin and Berne's. On his shoulder, he carried a bag stuffed full of presents. They were leaving for Berggeheimnis in the morning, and so while it was solstice, they were also having a bit of a goodbye party. They'd still see each other frequently, being best friends with a dragon did have its perks, but it was still going to be a significant change.

On the solstice, the Lady removed her fabricated day night cycle. While the constant darkness didn't bother him for one day a year, Torsten could see why most of the time she simulated something more temperate. To add to the magic, a thick layer of snow coated the ground, and fell around them as they walked. Sirin and Berne had volunteered to come to them for solstice instead, but many of their belongings were already packed away.

As the blue green glow of lunula in the canals faded behind them, the warm glow of Berne's isolated cabin peeked through the trees. Within seconds of entering, they were inundated with hugs, and enveloped by the savory scents of Sirin's cooking. An obligatory visit with Catrin's parents in the morning meant that they'd been able to spend the rest of the day at Sirin and Berne's house.

Sirin had decorated their house with star shaped lanterns, and handed them each steamed rice cakes the second they were in the door.[3]

"Eat them while they're hot!" she urged, waving to an array of accompaniments. Catrin took their contributions to the heavily laden table, a stack of orcish waffles kept warm in a thick iron pot, and a roast chicken she'd spent hours on. Thankfully, Sirin had reserved a small space on the table for them.

They'd only just arrived when more guests came in behind them, a young guard he thought might have been named Abi and a Shade he didn't know.

---

3. My connection to my heritage has strengthened over my time in Sanctuary, and I'll be forever grateful for how my family embraces it. Bibinka are a food I remember fondly from my childhood.

"Look at you!" Sirin squealed when they entered, wrapping them both in a hug.

Holding his hand, Catrin pulled him down to whisper in his ear."Abi Ospak, and her partner, Senka.4 They're guards for the Lady. They've been helping Sirin with her research."

Torsten kissed Catrin's forehead, mumbling to her."Thank you, kitten."

She winked up at him and tugged him to the table. He started dishing up a plate and Catrin giggled at him.

"What? I'm hungry..." he said. It wasn't *that* much food.

"No, I forget you're new to this," she shook her head and clasped his hand."I usually get the kids settled first. It means we have a better chance of eating our own before being interrupted."

"Oh! Oh of course!" he said, immediately wondering if he should put some back.

"That's alright Tor," Halsten said from his other side, patting his shoulder and nodding confidently."That can be my plate. I'm a growing boy, I need lots and lotsa food."

"That you are, good point," Torsten said, piling on more of Sirin's famous noodles.5

---

4. Their story is told in "The Curious Incident of the Great Cookie Snackcident of 979"

5. For interested parties, these are pancit.

Later, a young fishkin man arrived to more fanfare, and eventually, they were all sprawled around the fire, garbling the words to a holiday tune Sirin was trying to teach them. Cat and Berne were doing fine, they spoke the language, but to Torsten and the rest, it was just a jumble of sounds.

Eventually, the children collapsed, drained from the day, and Berne bent next to them.

"Let us have one more night with them?" he asked, the big bear's eyes going glassy.

"Of course," Cat whispered. Torsten helped Berne carry the children upstairs. They tucked them into their small double beds and stood, watching them dream innocently, the light of the Lady's moon shining in through the window.

"You know how important they are to me..." Berne said. "All three of them."

"I do," Torsten said, reaching an arm around to squeeze his friend's shoulder. "I hope you know how important they are to me..."

Berne nodded, his lips in a hard line. "When I suggested you sweep her off her feet, I didn't mean across the damn planet."

"I can't say I'm sorry."

Downstairs, Senka was regaling the group with a tale, using their shadows to depict visuals on the cabin wall. Cat sat, rapt, next to Sirin on the floor.

"They make a pretty pair, don't they?" Berne said from behind them.

"That they do," Torsten replied."We're two lucky bastards."

"I prefer 'favored by the Lady,' if you don't mind." Berne pushed passed him to settle on the ground behind Sirin. Catrin turned, her face spreading into a wide smile when she saw Torsten. She pushed herself and scurried over to him, tugging him toward the door.

"Come here, I have one final present for you..." she whispered, pulling him out into the chill night air.

She steered him under a tree and pulled him down for a sweet kiss. Her big, searching blue eyes met his and he was overwhelmed with gratitude. Just when he'd been the most lost, she'd given his life direction.

"I got you another gift, but I wanted to give it to you privately," she said, clutching something in her hand. She bit her lips and opened it, revealing a small, white rabbit on a leather string. Torsten's heart beat fast in his chest.

"I did some research, and by 'I did some research,' I mean, I spoke with Inigo about mating customs." Her cheeks were bright red.

"So," he asked."You know what this means ?"

Catrin nodded and held out the end of the leather ties to him. With the presentation of a necklace, an orcish woman signaled to a partner that she was ready to commit to a mating. If he bent down and allowed her to tie it around his neck, he was confirming his intention to ask.

"I just want you to be sure, because the last time you kind of botched this..." He smiled down at her, overcome with emotion.

Catrin gasped and smacked his chest."Oh, shut up, you! I know exactly what this means. I wasn't about to mess it up again." She lowered her voice."Not when it matters so much more."

Nodding and unable to keep a dopey smile from his face, Torsten bent to kiss her. The chill of the air made her lips a delight of temperatures, the heat of her mouth startling against his own.

When he stood, the weight of the necklace settled a frenetic feeling in his chest. It was silly that a simple necklace would reassure him more than Catrin's willingness to pick up her life and move with him across the world, but it did.

"Wherever you go, I go," she said, reciting the beginning of the Orcish mating ritual. They likely wouldn't complete it for months yet. It was just the beginning, but it was a start.

"Wherever you go, I go," he answered.

To his people, who spent most of the year away from their partners, it was a symbol that they intended to remain true to each other when they were apart. That she'd sealed a part of her in the necklace for him to carry with on his travels.[6]

When Catrin said it, he knew she meant it literally. Wherever he went, she would go, just as he would follow her to the ends of the world, forever.

---

6. Occasionally, necklaces held locks of hair, but more often, the "part of oneself" was more symbolic. Usually, the giver sleeps with it and focusing on it for a few days.

Epilogue

IN WHICH PREPARATION REAPS REWARDS, HIS CUP FLOWETH OVER, AND A BRIGHT FUTURE IS IN SIGHT

"I THINK WE DID it," Catrin said, flopping back onto the bed. "All three, asleep at the same time, and Bjorn in his own bed nonetheless."

"Aye, we did." Torsten sat onto the bed next to her, toying with her hair. "You're a marvel, love. I didn't realize how little I'd be able to help with him, I suppose. I'm glad now that he's growing I can be of help more."

Their son, Bjorn was six months and since he'd slept through the night for the last week, they'd decided it was time to move him into his own room.

"Agreed. Sadly, you can't nurse him. Still, it's been so much easier this time. Who knew a single child with two parents and two doting older siblings would be so simple compared to twins all by myself," she said, lips curling up in a wry smile.

"Honestly, I was really worried after how Sirin struggled with Tilly."

"It's a humbling experience for anyone, to be sure," she said. "Though, I don't really want to talk about anyone else right now, kids included."

"Oh?" Torsten's eyes hooded as he rolled onto his stomach, propping his head on his hand. His other ran along the neckline of her nightgown. "And what do you want to talk about? Getting a good night's rest?"

"That is a good idea, though admittedly I was thinking more about the plug I've been wearing in my ass for the last few hours."

"Have you?" Torsten's voice rose in excitement. He slipped his hands under her and rolled Catrin onto her stomach. Once she'd started, his mate hadn't been able to stop making herself accessories for the bedroom. Lifting her onto her knees and flipping her nightgown up, he inspected her handiwork.

"Fuck, kitten, you've been wearing that for hours?" He whined.

Against the sheets, Catrin nodded. "I want to see if I can take you and your doppelgänger at the same time, though I think I'd be best if you took my ass..."

"Precious, you don't need to tell me twice," he said, running his fingers up the backs of her thighs to her apex."Though if I know anything, it's that I want you good and languid before then, so show me those beauties, sweet tits."

Catrin's laugh bubbled out of her, and she rolled over. Torsten flipped her nightgown up over her head, exposing her breasts to his gaze and the chill of the air.

"There they are," Torsten whispered, reverent."Bjorn monopolizes them so much these days. Is it alright if I play with them love? They aren't sore or anything?"

"Please," she said, arching up into his large hands."They aren't sore, but they *are* begging for your attention."

"Perfect," he crooned, caging a nipple between his tusks. He began toying gently, running his tongue around her areola, his hand snaking up her thigh to run through her slick cunt.

The sensations of him shot through her, sparking through her nerves from her nipple to her pussy and back again, building and augmenting each other. Torsten chuckled as she felt her other breast begin to leak. He grabbed a towel from the bedside table and pressed it against where she leaked. On the other side, he happily lapped at her weeping nipple.

"Sorry," Catrin mumbled, embarrassed. "You don't have to play with them if they are going to do that."

"Are you kidding me, kitten? When you leak for me like this, it's like when I reach down and feel you soaked for me. You will never, ever hear me complain about physical signs of your desire."

Instead of lapping, he wrapped his lips around her again, sucking hard with deep pulls.

"Especially not when they taste like milk and honey. I'd better keep it even."

He switched to the other breast, his strong tugs timed perfectly with each rub of her clit. He switched to his thumb so he could slip two fingers inside and pump into her, curling his fingers to press into her g–spot. Torsten apparently decided to show her pity, because he left her breasts to kiss her, her sweetness lingering on his tongue. He slid into her mouth, invading in the gentlest way, slow and seductive. He kissed her senseless, each slide of his tongue stealing a bit of her sanity.

Breaking the kiss, Torsten moved to suck on her neck, growling in her ear. "Give me your pleasure kitten, you've earned it, I've earned it. I want to feel you squeeze my fingers. I want to feel that pussy clamped down on me, just the way I like."

Like he was truly in control of her body, she clenched, her muscles contracting and the euphoric ripple of her orgasm overtaking her. He caressed her g-spot, massaging it through her orgasm.

"There's my good girl. You come so sweetly." His words sounded far away as Catrin recovered. The telltale slide of a drawer and the sound of a jar opening told her he was readying her toy. Seconds later, she felt the cool slide of it as her husband slipped the toy inside, gently fucking it into her. With just the two toys, she felt stuffed. She'd made the model of Torsten's cock shockingly accurately sized and the plug she was wearing was significant.

Once it was fully sheathed. Torsten twisted her plug, drawing her attention to where it tugged.

"I'm going to play with you, precious, but I want you to ride me so you can control how much of me you take and how quickly" he whispered. With one hand, he massaged around where the handle stuck out, coaxing the tension from her hole. With the other, he returned to giving her clit attention. The hand near her arse grasped the plug and Torsten pulled back just enough to apply some tension.

"Time to push for me, kitten," he said, circling her clit. He didn't tug, instead he allowed her to work it out herself. As it slipped free into his hand, Torsten lowered to suckle on her clit for a moment."Perfect, love. You're doing so well."

A moment later, his slicked fingers massaged her arse again, the plug making it so that two slipped inside easily. The warmth and give of his fingers was delicious after the unforgiving texture of the plug. She was stretched, but not uncomfortably so, and she knew she'd need more before she took him.

"Another," she said. "I can do another."

"So soon, precious? Are you sure?"

At her nod, she felt a third finger slip in with the other two. The stretch was significant, but not unwelcome. She loved the feeling of fullness and couldn't wait until he filled her completely.

"Are you ready, kitten?" he asked when his fingers were slipping in and out easily.

"Yes," she gasped. She was beyond ready. They moved so she sat atop him, hovering over him. He coated himself, and added more lube to her ass. She lowered, the blunt head of his cock pressing against her tight hole, the metal balls of his piercing a stark contrast to his flesh. She pressed harder, and Catrin hissed at the stretch as he breached her. It burned, and as if it was the first time he'd entered her, she wondered if he'd fit.

"Breathe, precious," he coaxed. "We can stop at any time, but I think you can do this. I know you can take this thick cock because there isn't anything your gorgeous body can't do."

Catrin nodded her head, relaxing, so she sank further. She was so full. The facsimile of his cock filled her pussy and only halfway, he was already filling her ass. Torsten cleaned his fingers as she descended, careful to use that hand only for gripping her hips. The other, he used to roam from her breasts to her clit, teasing and stimulating her until pleasure outweighed the pain. After a few moments, he filled her completely, and Catrin admired the look of pure, tortured pleasure on his face. His eyes rolled back and he grit his mouth in a grimace, blowing thick huffs out of his mouth.

"Are you having trouble restraining yourself, dear?" she teased.

Torsten snapped his eyes open, her taunts giving him something else to focus on.

Swirling her hips, Catrin ground down on him. The pain was gone, and her pleasure was twisting inside her, writhing with need. With agonizing slowness, she raised and lowered herself, whimpering at how exquisite he felt as his cock dragged along his copy through the thin membrane inside her.

He worked her clit, his face set in determination. "I want one more, kitten. I want to feel you squeeze down on me. I want to feel you come on both of my cocks. I want to feel how your arse flutters when you're so full it can barely move."

Moaning, Catrin increased her riding. Orgasm building inside, she felt the tell-tale tingling that heralded let down. Her breasts weren't even heavy with milk, she'd just nursed Bjorn to sleep, but she couldn't control when it happened. She blushed, embarrassed, but Torsten knew her body too well, and she couldn't stop coming if she wanted to.

As her orgasm triggered, she slapped her hands over her breasts so she wouldn't drench Torsten.

Grasping her wrists to pull them away, Torsten admonished her. "Don't you dare keep that from me. I earned that." His thick tongue circled her nipple, latching on and gulping her down. "This is a liquid reminder of my seed that quickened in you. Of how you grew round and full with our son. Of how fucking sexy it is that you are squirting liquid pleasure all over me."

He bucked into her, latched tightly onto her nipple as she felt his hot seed fill her ass. He shook, shivering his aftershocks as he came down, pulling her atop him.

Catrin giggled. "Well, that was new. Guess that's something you're into, love?"

"I suppose so. It's not a forever type of thing, so I'm going to enjoy it while it's here. Now let's get cleaned up... I'm fairly sure we'll want dry sheets," he said, winking and lifting her off him to lay her gently on the bed.

Once they were cleaned up, she stood wrapped in a robe on their balcony, the city of Berggeheimnis spread before her. Torsten's status as ambassador granted them a lofty position in the great cavern. Their home overlooked the bustling dwarven city beneath while giving them a modicum of privacy.[1] Even at night, the city was lit with glowing crystals and mushrooms, their arrays of orange and purple light not quite reminiscent of lunula back home.

They still visited several times a year, and Sirin, Tilly and Berne, came just as often. While she didn't often need to, Catrin could make some small modifications to appear at home in the Empire, which she'd taught Sirin and Berne to emulate. The children, who were only a head shorter than Cat, had gradually gained color in their hair, though little Bjorn's head of black hair at birth had shocked her. Her own remained white, though she'd learned she could force her genetic hair color, a deep honey blonde, if she concentrated.

Two years away, and while she missed home at times, she loved the vibrancy of Berggeheimnis. The streets boasted thriving marketplaces, housing types of pottery she'd never seen. She was learning new techniques and sent plenty of innovative new recipes home.

The rustle of curtains alerted her to Torsten's presence and his arms slipped around her waist. He rested his head atop hers and hummed happily.

---

1. Cat and Torsten's home is carved into the wall of the great cavern, and to say I am supremely jealous of their home is an understatement.

"So, big day tomorrow," she said, squeezing his arms."Are you ready?"

"I think so," he said, his voice rumbling at her back."As ready as I'll ever be."

In the morning, a great summit of the peoples of the Empire would convene. For the first time, elves, dwarves, orcs, humans, and all of the other peoples of the world would meet to negotiate a treaty. If all went well, they'd form a coalition government in secret, the official beginnings of reclaiming their freedom from the high elves. Years of war would likely follow, the Empire wouldn't give up their control without fighting for every plot of land, but after, there was a real chance for peace.[2]

"You are ready." Catrin turned in his arms to look up at the handsome orc she loved."You embody the world we all dream of, you bridge the gaps between peoples and show them a better future. Just by being you. You'll do wonderfully."

"No," he said, rubbing his chin on the top of her head."*We* embody that future, kitten, you and me."

---

2. I imagine most everyone knows of the results of this conference, but should you like to read of it from a more intimate perspective, I will be writing about it, and a few of its attendees in the future.

IF YOU'D LIKE TO see some spicy art of Cat and Torsten and be the first to know about bonus epilogues, you can join Kass's Newsletter!

Reviews are extremely important for authors, especially indie authors. If you enjoyed this book, please leave a review on Amazon and/or your favorite review platform. Even short, 20 word reviews that are rambling (the only variety the author is capable of) are so, so helpful, so never be shy!

The Rake Pre-Order

It only takes a taste...

Lost in strange waters after a narrow escape from captivity, Elspeth the selkie is determined to find and free her brother. When she runs into an orca-shifter who mistakes her for lunch, one drop of his blood on her pelt binds her to him... forever.

Aegir is a notoriously talented shifter, playing pirates and playboys wherever his covert operations--or many lovers--take him. But when the selkie he rescued vanishes, he's plagued by memories of her... and a letter that spells out her doom. As they come together to rescue Elspeth's brother, both must navigate their traumas, a bond neither wanted, and growing feelings for each other. Can Elspeth learn to trust someone who wears a different face every day?

Kass O'Shire returns with more of your favorite

cozy, spicy, monster romantasy and this time its a swashbuckling adventure that flips the traditional selkie tale on its head. As an interconnected standalone, it's the perfect place to dip your toes into the word of the Shades of Sanctuary, where the vibes are cozy, the heat is high, and the mates are monstrous. Grab your favorite drink, a cozy blanket, and preorder The Rake, Or The Orca Who Met His Match in a Selkie Desiring Revenge today!

Pre-order now on Amazon!

https://www.amazon.com/dp/BoCSPRDRRH

Also by Kass O'Shire

Available Now on Kindle Unlimited!

She has everything she needs for a solo trek through the Arctic: a sledge heaped with supplies, a little magic, and evidently, the eye of a polar bear shifter–who shouldn't even *exist*.

Sirin is determined to find the source of magic, and nothing is going to stop her. Not expulsion from her guild, not their warnings about her "certain death," and certainly not the damned polar bear stalking her through the taiga.

Berne is a simple bear. He likes spending time shifted, a good meal, and apparently, round little scientists. When his duty to protect a thousand-year-old secret is tested against the strange pull he feels toward her, Berne can't help but sink his teeth into the one solution that might let him keep his adorable prey.

For fans of determined plus-sized heroines and cinnamon-roll bear shifters, *A Polar Expedition: and Other Stimulating Research Opportunities* is the first standalone novella in The Shades of Sanctuary, where the vibes are cozy, the heat is high and the mates are monstrous. Grab a cup of tea and snuggle in, because while the burn might be slow, the HEA is only a few hours away!

Read the book that started it all, now! A Polar Expedition

Acknowledgements

IN WHICH KASS TRIES NOT TO CRY

A sophmore book is *hard* when you are an anxious bean, and a great many people helped me and got this book over the finish line.

My alpha readers Erin, Melissa E, Kaitlyn and Brittnee: I am so grateful for your enormously helpful feedback and for helping figure out where this book needed to stretch a little harder. I hope you are proud of the changes you influenced here, because I am.

My beta readers, Melissa H, Zoe, Dru, BC and Brittnee: I was nervous as HELL when I sent this to you. I didn't know if I'd *actually* fixed the problems, and didn't know if it was even any good anymore. Thank you for your extremely helpful feedback, but perhaps most importantly, your encouragement.

My sensitivity readers James, and Dani: Halsten was always going to come out, but he surprised me by insisting it would be this book. Thank you for your feedback, I am forever grateful,

and any missteps I have made are wholly on me.
You were wonderful.

My amazing artists PhantomDame, FantasySpriteStudio, Aliiwa, and Bowlish: You inspire me every day, and I am so grateful for the stunning art you produced for this book. My characters look SMOKIN' and that's all your fault, in the best way!

My ARC readers: As I write this, you are actively pointing out typos to save my butt, tagging me in good reviews, letting me ignore some not so good ones, screaming at me in my dms and helping me hold it together. A post or message from on of you raises my spirits for hours or days and is more motivating than a post from me might be for a potential reader. Thank you for all you have done and will do for me and other authors.

My critique partners Lyonne Riley, Sara Ivy Hill, Emily Antoinette and Jenifer Wood: Thank you for not pulling your punches when I needed to hear it and bullying me into being nice to myself. Your feedback is invaluable, but nothing is worth your friendship. I love you all so much and I am the luckiest girl in the world to have found you!

Brittnee: This one's for you, babe.

Meg: You do ridiculous amounts for our community at large and have for me personally. Your tireless support of indie authors is astounding and I can't imagine how many books are purchased because of your hard work. Thank you for editing this book and the myriad other things you to to help me get shit done. To top it off, you are a stellar friend M'fires.

Torri: You are the reason I will always tell people to meet their internet friends. There is something so powerful about being friends with someone based on shared interests instead of proximity. Thanks for listening to me blather for hours about this book and all of the lore, can't wait to do it some more! Thank you for laughter and tears, silly boardgames and letting me steal your babies.

Chris: Thanks for all you do. 12/10 husband. Thanks for jumping feet first into the world of monsterfuckery with me. I love you more than I can possibly express and I'm literally so obsessed with you it's unreal. My biggest wish is that everyone could have a partner as loving, supportive and understanding as you. You taught me that real men can be just as good as book boyfriends.

Finally, you, my reader: Thank you for spending time with me, Cat and Torsten. I cannot express how magical it is to know that people might be enjoying my silly little world. If I provided you with a little bit of joy, comfort or coziness, I am incredibly grateful for the opportunity.

Kass is a reluctant human living in America's own little Shire. Kass uses she/her pronouns and is both is demi and bi. Her writing focuses on body, sex, and equality positive stories with high heat levels and cozy vibes. She loves monster romance/paranormal romance, gas-lamp fantasy romance, historical romance, sci-fi romance (ok, all things romance), epic fantasy and space opera. In her free time, she reads a lot, bakes her pants off, and plays and DMs DnD and other tabletop and board games. She's married to a pretty great guy who is convinced he is Berne (he's not), has one awesome 13 year old son and has done two surrogacies for the most amazing couple.

To pay the bills, Kass is a data analyst in mental and behavioral health. As a result, she's extremely passionate about access to care for all folks. As you could probably guess from the footnotes, she's a HUGE nerd ;)

The best place to hear things before ANYONE is Kass's Patreon! There, even free members find out juicy bits before the public, and she's better at updating it than her newsletter. Paid patrons get free ARCS, access to spicy art, the enire backlog of her extras and epilogues, sneak peeks as to what is coming next, bi-annual mailings of goodies and even book boxes and merch! Sign up now to stay in touch! patreon.com/kassoshire

You can find Kass ALL THE PLACES via her Carrdhttps://kassoshire.carrd.co/(Generally patreon, discord and insta will get you the most up to date info!)